Lavender Tears

a novel

Sondra Cunningham

Edited by Kelly Reed of Red Adept Editing.
Cover and Formatting by Streetlight Graphics.
Author photo by Katie Cassara Photography. Photo copyright © 2020. All rights reserved.
Published by Sondra Cunningham.

ISBN Print: 978-1-7361878-0-7
ISBN eBook: 978-1-7361878-1-4

All scripture quotations and references, unless otherwise indicated, are taken from the New King James Version: Copyright © 1979, 1980, 1982 Thomas Nelson, Inc. Publishers. Used by permission.

Scripture indicated with KJV is from the Authorized King James Version.

Scripture indicated with NKJV is from the New King James Version®. Copyright © 1982 by Thomas Nelson. Used by permission. All rights reserved.

Scripture indicated with NLT is taken from the Holy Bible: New Living Translation. Copyright © 1973, 1978, 1984 by International Bible Society. Used by permission.

Scripture indicated with AMP is from the Amplified® Bible. Copyright © 1954, 1958, 1962, 1964, 1965, 1987 by The Lockman Foundation. Used by permission. www.Lockman.org

Scripture quotations marked TPT are from The Passion Translation®. Copyright © 2017, 2018, by Passion & Fire Ministries, Inc. Used by permission. All rights reserved. The PassionTranslation.com.

Lavender Tears is a work of fiction. Where real people, events, establishments, organizations, or locales appear, they are used fictitiously. All elements of the novel are drawn from the author's imagination.

Check out the latest from Sondra Cunningham on her Facebook page,
www.facebook.com/SongBirdMinistries, and on Instagram,
https://www.instagram.com/sondracunninghambooks/.

Praise for Lavender Tears

"Sondra Cunningham has accomplished something profound in writing *Lavender Tears*. Jesus was a child like every other human being, but we know few details about his childhood. Sondra creatively imagines and masterfully writes a story about what it may have been like to grow up as Mary of Bethany and possibly to have grown up with Jesus. What makes this novel so unique is that Sondra writes in such a genuine and accessible way that we not only relate with Mary, but also see ourselves in her experiences. In many ways, her journey is our journey and her healing, our healing. Sondra has also done something courageous in writing this book. She has tuned in to her own story to capture what it feels like to be afraid, to be loved, to be shamed, to grieve, to be forgiven, and to heal."

–Dr. Shelli L. Haynes, LCSW-R, DMin

Acknowledgments

I wholeheartedly acknowledge and give all praise and glory for this novel, *Lavender Tears,* to the Lord Jesus Christ. He gave me every word as a great and wonderful gift.

I would also like to thank the following people:

My darling husband, Kirk Cunningham, who dreams beside me on this beautiful new adventure of authorship. Thank you for all your countless contributions in the editing and storyline process and for your beautiful patience, love, and passion-filled spirit that lifts me up every step of the way. You are my treasure, and I love you with all of my heart.

Pastor Gary Fishman, thank you for all the hours of spiritual mentoring, life coaching, restoration, and training in dreams and their interpretation. Your ministry ushered in the healing and hope I needed to follow the dreams and gifts God placed within me.

Our dearest friend, David FitzMaurice, thank you for your beautiful lavender drawings throughout *Lavender Tears*. Thank you for your constant unconditional love, support, wisdom, and time spent reading during my writing months. You have always stood by my side, speaking life into my dreams and believing in the best of me.

To all my family and friends who helped with reading and encouragement throughout the writing process, thank you. I speak blessings on you all.

I dedicate this novel to all the beautiful people who have lovingly nurtured the garden of my heart.

To those who loved and love me…

To those who believed in me…

To those who sheltered me…

To those who mentored me…

To those who helped me rise…

Thank you.

Note from the Author

Dear Reader,

For generations, the story of the woman with the alabaster jar has spoken to many. It teaches us the priceless value of surrendering all that we are and all that we have to our merciful and loving Jesus.

When I was inspired to write this novel, I couldn't exactly see the primary message God wanted me to convey. He gave me the inspiration suddenly, and I wrote faithfully, as the Holy Spirit continued to share with me, in my mind's eye. As the pages blossomed and the story changed from a dream to a reality, my spirit was illuminated by the tender message woven through every word.

Lavender Tears is a poetic journey of one woman's life as she not only sought to find her purpose but earnestly hungered for an indescribably real encounter with God.

No matter what paths we find ourselves on, no matter our gender or stage of life, we have all faced tragedy, heartache, and misfortune in some measure. The lying, false voice of the adversary tries to lead us toward defeat through these painful experiences. He wants us to succumb to his lies and his condemning labels that we call "our failures."

When we relate to the sacrifices of the women pouring out their valuable oils unto the Lord, it is because we can relate to the desperate need for a Savior.

Mary of Bethany's life, though unknown through scripture, was quite significant. No matter what her story really looked like, we know she came to the feet of Jesus. We know she was one of, if not the first of, the women to sit publicly at Jesus's feet and learn.

But how did she get there?

The same way we all do...

For me personally, I journeyed through life with many ups and downs. I was trying to seek Jesus, trying to please God, and trying to please man. The mistakes I made in difficult times tainted me and labeled me. Not until everything and nearly everyone in my life turned from me did I truly fall at the feet of Jesus.

I had to see that my life was not solely about accomplishing all of my dreams perfectly. That it's value was and is not determined by a perfect marriage, church, reputation, or position. I had to see that I could never earn His love... yet it was still *mine*.

That's when I was truly listening...

The voice of truth, of our Heavenly Father God, comes up through our spirits and warms our hearts with peace and love. That voice, the only true voice, has called me into flawless love and acceptance.

And He is calling you.

If the one who *is* perfect love calls us to receive it freely, why do we so often find ourselves running from it? It must be that we have listened to the wrong voice for far too long.

Stop running and come out of hiding because you are safe and loved with Jesus.

He sees you; He sees me; He sees it all, and He still wants us. God still longs to draw us all close individually and bathe us in His perfect love. Only then can He reveal his perfect will and path for our future.

We cannot outrun His love. We cannot sin or fail or stumble our way out of His love. It is never ceasing, never ending, and perfectly unconditional. It is a pure, perfect, and permanent gift to all who will receive it.

Then we can passionately run out into the world and find our own Miryam, the one who is waiting for you to be brave. We can lovingly find the other lost ones hiding in fear, shame, and guilt and drowning in lies. Reach out your hand and snatch them from the flood water! You can!

May this story of what Mary's life might have looked like lead you into a new season of strength for overcoming. May we all get back up time and time again, if need be, to keep running the race. May we find our perfect love at the feet of Jesus and be cleansed, redeemed, and restored to our true value.

He purchased you because He wants you, cracks and all. His love is the Pure Gold that mends our flaws and only increases our value. Do not be ashamed; do not hide; just come to His feet and pour out all that you are!

"The Lord is my best friend and my shepherd. I always have more than enough.

He offers a resting place for me in his luxurious love. His tracks take me to an oasis of peace, the quiet brook of bliss.

That's where he restores and revives my life. He opens before me pathways to God's pleasure and leads me along in his footsteps of righteousness so that I can bring honor to his name.

Lord, even when your path takes me through the valley of deepest darkness, fear will never conquer me, for you already have! You remain close to me and lead me through it all the way. Your authority is my strength and my peace. The comfort of your love takes away my fear. I'll never be lonely, for you are near.

You become my delicious feast even when my enemies dare to fight. You anoint me with the fragrance of your Holy Spirit; you give me all I can drink of you until my heart overflows.

So why would I fear the future? For your goodness and love pursue me all the days of my life. Then afterward, when my life is through, I'll return to your glorious presence to be forever with you!"

Psalm 23:1-6, TPT

"Each and every sunrise…"
Psalm 5:3, TPT

A PALE-YELLOW SUN IS STREAMING THROUGH the dusty blue morning. I am always in awe of the ever-changing watercolor skies painted by God, every design unique yet equally stunning in beauty.

Sunrises speak to me… I can feel them…

With wide eyes, I watch the colors and rays of light growing and fading across the horizon. They mark each new day with wondrous potential. Ever since I was young, I have found my escape in the quiet mornings as the world is awakened by indescribable light. I feel as if no boundaries exist between me and the heavens in those dawning hours.

Sitting here, I remember the words of the psalmist, King David: *"At each and every sunrise you will hear my voice."* I lift my hands toward heaven and lay the broken pieces of my life at the altar of my God.

A cool, gentle breeze blows across my face this morning, tossing and twirling my long dark hair in waves around me. The chill is refreshing on my skin after a night of endless weeping. This day, beautiful sunrise or no, holds the hope of my future no longer. For me, it is bleak, still, and empty. My whole world, my whole heart, my life, my dreams, and my plans have completely disintegrated. For the first time in all my days, I have nothing to dream of nor hope for apart from a burning desire to run. I want to run and never look back, to run until my soul shatters free from my skin, tightening around me. *How can I survive when my own body is suffocating the light that once illuminated my ways?* I cannot escape. I have no hope. I am a useless decoration, a piece of pottery found to be untrue, one whose outward beauty is fading and which is unable to hold the precious oils of love and life.

Chapter One

"Power to tread..."
Luke 10:19, KJV

I STOOD FROZEN, PANIC AND FEAR pulsing through my body like lightning strikes. One wrong move, and I would be facing death's poison. I had wandered too far from Lazarus and his group and was lost. That's the price one pays, I guess, for deserting chores for a secret adventure with the boys.

I was not exactly "with" the boys but was following with burning curiosity. Lazarus would often gather a few friends and hike through the valley behind our property. They would use that time to explore nature and to discuss the sections of the Torah they were currently reading and studying. My heart was and has always been hungry for God, so I would trail behind them to listen and capture what I could from their discussions.

This time, however, my shadowing them did not turn out so well. I was lost and alone when a viper rose right in front of me, poised and ready to strike. I had stumbled into its den, and the snake was not about to relent. Its scales were brown and tan, spotted like a leopard. Its body was thick and long. The viper was the one snake I recognized. We were all taught from a young age to identify it because of its track record of death. Hissing at me, the snake darted its head back and forth, daring me to make the first move. I stared into its cold black eyes, looking for a glimmer of mercy but found none. Without warning, the snake lowered to the ground and slithered closer. I stood completely still as pure panic consumed me. The cool, smooth scales wrapped around my ankle and up my left leg as I watched helplessly.

This is it, I thought, *I am going to die.*

Thankfully, I'd shrieked loudly when the viper first lunged at me, just as Lazarus and his friends were passing through the nearby thickets. I could hear them.

"Lord, let them find me," I prayed aloud.

Moments passed, then Eli suddenly called out my name. "Mary! Mary! Was that you? Where are you, Mary?"

I was too afraid to make a sound since I was trapped in the viper's striking range. Mumbling and whimpering, I tried to lead the small group of boys toward me. Before long, they found me and came running through the thickets that separated us.

Lazarus reached me first. Seeing the viper, he immediately called out, "Stop!"

The group came to a halt.

"It's a snake! No one move!" he said.

I closed my eyes the moment I saw my brother. I knew even if I were bitten, Lazarus would somehow find a way to save me. My brother was tall, strong, and brave, a God-fearing young man who knew what to do in almost every situation. He naturally found a way to make my family proud every day... unlike me.

"Lazarus," I whispered, "what do I do?" My legs were trembling from standing still in fear for what seemed like hours. Nervous sweat was dripping down the sides of my neck and frightened tears down my cheeks. The air was damp and heavy from the cool of the morning, chilling me even more.

"Stay perfectly still, Mary. Do not move," he said sternly.

I could hear him slowly climbing up a rock face just behind me. His breathing was intense but controlled.

The snake lowered itself to the ground once more and slithered a short distance from me. It poised up toward the new threatening group of intruders but kept its tail possessively wrapped around me.

Eli stood a few feet behind the viper but still directly in front of me. He was watching with terror in his eyes. After all, this could be the death of his future bride.

Lazarus's newest friend, Jesus, was also there. His family was passing through the popular trade markets in Bethany before heading to Jerusalem. Jesus wasn't just watching, though. He was looking right into my eyes, and the strangest feeling came over me. It was… peace. As long as my eyes were locked with his, I felt safe.

Before anything was said, before I could even shout "No!" Lazarus leapt into the air off the giant boulder behind me and came down directly on top of the snake's head, crushing it completely. Without hesitation, he thrust me up over his shoulder and ran toward home. The crowd of boys scattered, leaving a trail of fading cheers and victorious chants for their newest hero, "Lazarus! Lazarus!" as they headed toward the village.

Eli followed Lazarus and me but couldn't keep up with my brother's long strides and was quickly left behind. Eli was a good friend of ours, but even he knew that was no time for friendly conversation. I was in big trouble, and I was also certain everyone in the village would soon hear of Lazarus's heroic victory.

When I looked back over my brother's shoulder, I caught the eyes of Jesus once more. He stood there staring at the crushed snake then glanced back at me then toward the sky. He was quickly out of my sight, but I could tell he wasn't leaving that spot anytime soon. *Was he praying?* I wondered.

Something was very different about that boy. From the moment Lazarus met Jesus, my brother couldn't stop talking about him. He went on and on, saying Jesus wasn't like any of the other boys. He said Jesus had a deeper understanding of the ancient scriptures, impressive at such a young age. He would often find unique ways of connecting everyday life to the spiritual and his parables wonderfully challenged Lazarus's amazing passion and wealth of spiritual knowledge.

As I flashed back to the incident, I recalled how Jesus's eyes were locked with mine the whole time I was in death's snake-like grip. The more I thought about it, the more I realized I had also felt something.

What had just happened to me was more than what the naked eye could see, but I couldn't explain it. As I replayed the scene in my mind, I could see that Jesus never once flinched or shook like the others. He simply kept my focus. Then, for a split second, he watched as his new friend leapt selflessly into action, crushing one of the deadliest vipers known from here to Galilee. *What was that about?* I thought.

Lazarus was fast. We were nearly home when I came to the realization that I needed him to put me down. I was okay for the moment, but I needed time to think before facing mother.

"Lazarus! Please put me down!" I yelled, in tears.

Just as quickly as he'd scooped me up from the snake's territory, he stopped. Gently, he slid me off his shoulder and looked at me. I was stunned as I noticed tears in his eyes.

"Lazarus, I'm okay. You… you saved me." All I could think to do was wrap my arms around my heroic brother and squeeze him with all the life still left in me.

"You saved me, Lazarus. Oh, thank you!" I cried out.

Lazarus grabbed me by an arm and led me behind a dense group of bushes and cypress trees, probably to avoid causing further shame by airing our conversation to the local families' listening ears. Lazarus was fourteen years old, making him accountable for his actions. I was only twelve at the time.

"Mary, what were you thinking? How long have you been following us?" Lazarus paced back and forth, running his hands through his hair. "It's too dangerous out in the valley! Mother and Father will be so angry when they find out! And… you could have… You would have…"

"I know!" I shouted before he could finish the thought. "I could have died, but I didn't."

After releasing him from my hug, I nudged him in the arm. "And what were *you* thinking, Lazarus? What if you missed? Surely, it would have bitten *you*!"

Lazarus nodded in agreement then paced in a circle around me with his hands toward Heaven, shouting, "God, you have granted me favor today! I give you all the glory! Thank you, oh Lord, for rescuing my sister and me from the den of the serpent." He paused a moment then looked back toward me with tear-filled eyes. "Mary, I would give my life for you, for all of our family. But it is God alone who is worthy of the praise—God alone."

"Yes," I said. "Yes, thanks be to God."

I rested on my knees and began to pray. After a few minutes, the reality of what had happened really hit me.

I stood to adjust my tunic, dusted myself off, and untangled my veil from a bush. My hair was a knotted mess of long, loose dark curls. I tried to braid it quickly and restore my veil before anyone else saw me.

"Oh, the shame this will bring upon Father and Mother," I said while sinking my face into the palms of my shaking hands. "They have told me time and time again to remain at home and focus on my chores! I don't know what my problem is! Rather than staying inside all day, cooking meals and making things, I need to be outside, seeing the world." I paused to collect my thoughts.

"Lazarus, you know I want to learn more about God and the Holy Scriptures. How am I to do that if I'm trapped inside all day?"

"No, Mary!" He said. "Your place is at home, where it is safe. You are to be married soon. Think of Eli. He could have lost you too. Why can't you be more like Martha and stop putting yourself in harm's way?"

I looked him in the eyes with my hands on my hips, and he looked away, knowing the answer.

Lazarus and I have both had difficulty following the traditional expectations of Judaism. We sensed change was coming. We both loved and respected our Jewish faith, but we wanted more—more of God, to be closer to Him. Accepting such a distant and regimented relationship with our Lord was hard for me, when it felt like He should live inside me. I desired a closeness that I couldn't find a way to get. Women in my culture were limited to accessing and studying the Torah, which was why I was always venturing out to hear and learn more.

Lazarus wasn't telling me anything I hadn't heard already, over and over. Just the last month, I'd woken up early to watch another sunrise. I ventured across the tops of two neighboring houses to get a better view. Apparently, while I was climbing, a stone broke loose and dropped down onto one of our neighbor's goats, sending it into a screaming and galloping frenzy. The goat made it up the stairs into the main house, waking their newborn baby, breaking valuable pots and ruining a day's worth of newly set goat cheese. I was in a lot of trouble.

The glaring eyes of my father never faded from my memory. I had to do all my chores *and* help remake the lost goat cheese for our neighbors. I even had to help Martha do extra kitchen work to get her off my back about it. Sometimes, I would worry about her more than about Father.

Mother would give me the You Are the Pearl of the Family talk, then Martha would start teaching me all over again about what it means to be a woman. She informed me repeatedly that I am a priest's wife in training.

I wanted to be what I was supposed to be, but I could never contain my desire for more, no matter how hard I tried.

"I'll go home alone, Lazarus. You know I want to do what is right. I will sit Mother down and tell her I wandered off again, against her wishes, and apologize." Quickly, I headed toward the back of our house, hoping that was enough, but it wasn't.

He shouted after me, "You have to tell her about the snake, Mary! The whole village is going to be talking about it, and you will not lie!"

He was right. I had no way of leaving that out. I had to tell mother everything.

Chapter Two

"Those who seek…"

Proverbs 8:17, NKJV

MY MOTHER, SARAH, SPENT HER mornings and afternoons lost in her garden. Flowers of all kinds bloomed in abundance for her. Red poppies, buttercups, irises, lilies, and white roses, to name a few, flooded our land with color and fragrance. The beauty and variety of mother's gardening were well known. Our whole village watched as she worked the land with our family, showing great confidence in every seed. Sure enough, after years of hiking and gathering, planting and watering, she had built a garden full of wonder. Walking through the rows of vibrant flowers often inspired me to dance and twirl, stirring all my childhood dreams and imaginations. They surrounded me with blooming drops of heavenly colors and luscious scents. The experience was sweetly enchanting.

As I grew older, helping in the garden became one of my favorite chores. I had developed a love for herbs, which Mother nurtured with grace and wisdom. Before long, she had dedicated an entire section to growing the things I loved. Lavender was my favorite. She would pluck small pieces of the pretty purple flowers and use them to decorate my braided hair. My mother, seeing the peace and serenity that lavender brought to me, adopted its name for me. "My little Lavender," she would call me. It became a sweet little bond between us, something she would whisper over me only, maybe before bed or when we were alone working in the soil.

She was gentle, incredibly kind, and ever an expression of loveliness and peace. I would tend to the plants and herbs, staying right by her side, watching her graceful hands at work, and learning. Mother was also a radiant gift of love to all those she helped. At Father's side, she would care for orphans, widows, and the sickly. "God can do wonders through our love," she would often say.

I wanted to be just like her. But at the same time, I was so different.

Both Father and Mother believed I was a gift from God, the "pearl of the family," to be exact. I was told that I was a "rare beauty" and that I was to marry a priest and live in a Levitical estate, furthering our God-ordained purpose. Those words and memories are what shaped me. They founded my plans, my hopes, and my dreams throughout my childhood and even now.

Heading into the village market, I followed Mother closely. My basket was filled to the top with bundles of aromatic herbs to sell. The sweet and calming scents of lavender and mint swept around us in a breeze as we walked. These scents would become a reminder of my mother, bringing me back to the garden time and time again.

Martha and I were to help sell all the herbs we gathered from Mother's garden that spring then prepare for another crop throughout the coming summer. They brought in a nice profit that Father often saved toward the dowries for Martha and me.

Our family was sustained mostly by my father, who was a rabbi here in Bethany. We were originally from Galilee but relocated here years ago for his position. We inherited our home through family, and my father has spent his free time building it up into something grand.

My parents also arranged marriages for Martha and me. Martha was to wed a Pharisee named Simon, and I would be married to Eli, who was a Levite descendant. He was leaving for Jerusalem that day with his whole family. Being thirteen, he'd been asked to follow a Levitical rabbi and begin his formal training.

Lazarus was showing great promise, following in our father's footsteps to one day become a synagogue rabbi. He also helped our uncle Mathias, who owns a large portion of the fishing trade from the Sea of Galilee. A great deal of our family's wealth was earned there, which continues to this day. Lazarus sold fish in many local markets from Galilee to Jerusalem, bringing in more wages. He often traveled with our uncle to provide him extra working hands and learn more about the trade. Uncle Mathias had no living son of his own, so the trade would go on through his son-in-law and his nephews. Lazarus especially loved the traveling because it gave him more time to see and glean wisdom from the many rabbis all over Israel.

On that particular day, Martha and I sold our baskets quickly and had the afternoon free to ourselves before we needed to return home to prepare dinner.

"Do you want to go listen at the synagogue, Martha?" I asked my sister. "It's a lovely day, and I'm sure Rabbi Carmi will be teaching outside near the fountain!"

"Mary, I would rather go back home with Mother and work on a new bread starter. I have been learning new recipes, and *practice makes perfect*! Why don't you come with me, and I can show you this new bread, sourdough, which I'm learning. You cannot live on pancakes and flatbread alone, Mary!" Martha poked my dimpled cheek and hung onto my arm, pulling me toward home.

"I know, I know," I replied, stopping her attempt to lead me home. "I will come, but first, I'd really like to wander down to the synagogue and see what's going on. Then I will come home, and we can practice, okay?"

"Fine, Mary. Go have your adventure, but don't be late! I am not doing your portion of the work, and you know Father and Lazarus will come home hungry!"

I squeezed Martha in return, to assure her I got the message.

Although we were different as little girls, I could always tell Martha loved me. Sometimes, she would surprise me and wake up early to prepare a morning bread, sneaking us a portion to eat while watching the sunrise. Martha always found my hiding spots. No matter how often I explored new locations, she would find me and call me when the time came for the day's work to begin. But on rare occasions, she would join me, and we would sit together in silence, nibbling our bread and watching God paint the sky.

"Okay, Mary! Let go!" Martha gasped as she unwrapped my arms from her waist. "Just go already, and don't be late!"

Smiling and waving goodbye, I turned and skipped toward the fountain. Where the synagogue stood was the most beautiful spot in all of Bethany. All the trees had been cleared in that area of our village, and the sun just set the building aglow. Each adornment, whether glass, copper, bronze, or gold, sparkled brilliantly against the white stone walls.

I was disappointed because Rabbi Carmi was not outside and more crowds of people were in town than usual. Travelers were coming in droves for the famous Bethany spring markets. All along our walled city, wagons and carts were spilling over with trade goods and belongings. Some had journeyed from the east of Galilee or far north of Nazareth, and even from the west, Jerusalem.

That didn't make for a great day of adventuring, and I thought about heading home to help Martha make her fancy bread.

Just then, I heard Lazarus's voice. He was behind the synagogue, calling Eli's name. I hunched over, low and slow, making my way down an alley toward him. I hid behind some large barrels lined up against the synagogue wall to find out what was going on.

Lazarus was with Jesus and two other boys.

I didn't know Jesus and his family were here, I thought. *They must really like the Bethany spring market.*

Lazarus was calling out, "Come on over, Eli. The synagogue is empty, and Jesus is going to share with us about bread!"

Bread? I thought. *What in all Israel would Jesus have to say about bread? Aside from eating it?* I laughed to myself.

Eli ran up to the group but paused a distance away. I knew what he was about to say.

"I cannot join today, Lazarus. We are all packed and ready to leave."

"Already?" Lazarus asked.

"Yes, Mother wants to have the spring and summer to settle back in Jerusalem before I begin my training with the Levitical high priests. I haven't been there since I was a small child, and Mother says there is much to see."

"Right," Lazarus replied. "I knew the time was coming. I heard Mother and Mary talking about it in the kitchen yesterday morning."

Eli nodded and kicked some dirt with the side of his sandal. "I will miss you all throughout the next few years. When I return, I will be a man, ready to wed your sister and serve in the holy priesthood in Jerusalem!"

He tried to muster up strength during his little speech. I knew that was to impress Lazarus and show he was already well on his way to accountability.

"Run along then, Eli. May God be with you on your journey and bring you home safely to us all!" Lazarus walked over to my friend, embraced him with a full smile, and tapped him on the shoulder in encouragement.

At that point, I wanted to jump out and surprise them. Maybe I could even get an extra hug from Eli, but I didn't. We had already said our goodbyes and needed to accept how things were. I was blessed to know Eli and enjoy a simple friendship. Most girls were arranged in marriages to men they had never met. Martha knew of her future husband, Simon the Pharisee, but he was at least ten years older than her. I was just glad she would be married first and I could learn from her experience.

I watched as the rest of the boys said their goodbyes to Eli then regathered in a small circle so that Lazarus could introduce them to Jesus. Seeing him again was great, even if it was from a distance. I'll never forget the moment we shared when I was entangled with that viper. He witnessed a life-and-death situation with us—my life, to be exact. How many people can you say that about?

After a few minutes of chatting, Lazarus led the boys in my direction.

They must be going inside the synagogue, I thought. So I sat down in the dirt behind the barrels, pretty sure I would not be noticed. *Maybe I should just go home and leave them to their business.*

But it's not just any group of boys. Jesus is with them! I replied to myself.

All my brother can talk about are the revelations Jesus's teachings have been giving him. I would love to glean one for myself.

I was going to win this debate, as I so often did.

Okay, I will listen... but only for a few minutes.

Chapter Three

"To feed the world."
John 6:33, TPT

FTER ALL THE BOYS ENTERED the synagogue, I quickly ran to the closing door and cautiously slipped a piece of my tunic between the door and the clasp, stopping it from latching. After waiting a few minutes for them to settle down, I entered unseen.

Sitting against an ancient spiritual stone wall in the cool, dark entryway, I listened. The voices of amazement, debate, and inspiration echoed throughout the synagogue. I loved to hear the stories of old, about how God was faithful to provide and save His chosen people. Even if God was as far away as the heavens and limited to the Holy of Holies here on Earth, the stories of Moses made me feel hope, the hope that God could appear to us, there and then, however He chose. After all, if God could appear in a flaming bush, why couldn't He appear to me? I wanted to meet God, to sit on His lap and ask Him questions, and to show my love and devotion to Him. My thoughts about being a great high priest's wife made me smile. God would be so proud of me one day! Joy filled my heart.

Then Jesus began to speak.

His voice was strong and sure. He spoke about the manna sent down from God Almighty to feed and sustain the Hebrew people during the great Exodus. But when he spoke of it, he sounded different from Rabbi Carmi and my father. His main focus wasn't on the miracle of old but on a new miracle, one that was coming.

"This manna," Jesus declared with such passion, "though our fathers ate of it, was still not enough. They all perished. I speak to you today of new manna, a bread, the Word made flesh, the Messiah, One who will give His flesh for all mankind. If you eat of this bread, accepting Him and believing in Him, you will live forever."

Jesus was painting a clear picture of what God was doing, and it was something I could understand. I knew a way had to exist for God to be closer to His people. It was the Messiah. He was coming. As I sat listening to Jesus, a longing for that love bloomed in my heart.

Jesus further stated, "Isaiah the prophet told us that a virgin will give birth, and she will call His name Immanuel, which means 'God with us.' He is the manna. Isaiah also prophesied that He would give himself as a guilt offering, the atonement for sin, who bears all responsibility by pouring out His very life in death."

I was unable to keep myself from inching closer to the entry door. I was hanging on his every word and wanted to have a look. Peering through a wide crack in the wood, I could see him. Jesus was standing in front of my brother and the boys, teaching with his hands raised high. Suddenly, he caught my eye through the crack in the door. I froze, fearing I would be called out and asked to leave. But he kept on teaching and almost… smiled at me.

Jesus went on to say, "Unlike the manna in the wilderness, the Son of Man will not end in death! Remember, Jonah was in the belly of the great fish for three days and nights then was released upon the shore. I tell you the Son of Man will be three days and nights in the heart of the earth. Then He will rise up in life and victory, redeeming and reuniting with all who accept and believe in Him. Not only has he done this to forever remove our iniquity, but also to make us joint heirs with him.

"God's purpose in sending the manna and giving us Immanuel was to demonstrate His love toward us. His love is not condemning but gracious and abounding in mercy and grace. Now, we are called to love the Lord our God with everything we have then pour that love out on others."

Never had I ever heard anyone, even a rabbi, teach with such wisdom and passion about the coming Messiah. I'd heard about the one who would come, mostly from my father and brother at home, but never from a teacher. I sat there absorbing everything that I could: bread, manna, sacrifice, Messiah, and a poured-out love. The wonder of it all was almost too much to contain, but a brilliant bundle of wisdom to meditate on. It gave me many questions to ask my father and brother later at dinner.

Creeeak!

The outside door slowly opened, and I jumped to my feet and dashed into a dark corner of the hallway like a startled mouse. It was Rabbi Carmi. As soon as he passed me, entering the main sanctuary, I bolted for the exit. Once outside the door, I intended to run straight down the synagogue's alley, but I crashed instead, plowing right into the two barrels against the outer wall, which were full of rainwater. I went tumbling head over heels in a tangled mess of chaos, right into the dirt.

"Ah! Ouch!" someone screamed.

I sat straight up in an instant, adrenalin still pumping. "What?" I shouted in reply. *Whose voice was that?* Then I saw her. "Oh, no! I am so sorry!" I replied instinctively. "I was just... running... I wasn't looking where I was going. Please, let me help you up."

"No, thank you, I'm all right... ugh, just thoroughly drenched in water," she said to me.

I laughed at the awareness that I, too, had gotten covered in water and mud. "My name is Mary. What's yours?" I reached out for her hand anyway.

"Deborah," she replied with a smile, allowing me to help her up.

"Nice to meet you, Deborah. If it's all right to ask, what were you doing there, hiding behind the barrels?"

"Oh..." Deborah hesitated. "I was... uh... watching through this window."

"You were? Were you watching that group of boys?" I asked her.

Her cheeks flushed, and she looked like she was about to turn and run, so I added, "because I was too! Well, not from out here. I was inside the doorway." I giggled."You see that tall, gangly fellow in there?" I pointed.

She nodded.

"That's my brother, Lazarus!"

"Your brother is Lazarus? So you're the one he saved from the viper last year?" She exclaimed.

"Yep, that was me, unfortunately," I said, amazed at her sudden boldness.

All the children in Bethany had definitely heard the epic story of "Lazarus and the Viper."

"Why? Do you know him?" I asked her.

"No, I don't know your brother—just… of him." She blushed again and looked away.

"Do you see that other boy, the one standing talking to Rabbi Carmi? His name is Jesus. He was the one doing most of the teaching today. That was why I snuck inside to listen," I explained.

"But he's just a boy. He looks younger than your brother! Was he really teaching?" Deborah asked.

"He is! He's my age, and yes, he was teaching. My brother says that Jesus has wonderful things to say about many scriptures. The wisdom and knowledge that boy has is beyond most, if not all, people I've ever heard. Or so Lazarus says, anyway." I went on to explain everything Lazarus had been telling me about him, and I noticed Deborah was really interested. *Maybe her interest is in my brother?*

"My brother knows a great deal more than I. Would you like to come for dinner? I can introduce you to him and my father. We have great conversations about the things of God in our house."

"That would be wonderful!" She said, blushing a rosy pink once again.

I was right. She likes him. "Let's find your mother," I suggested. "You can introduce me to her! She will most likely know my father and mother, Samuel and Sarah of Galilee. My father is one of the priests here in Bethany, and my mother is the one with the well-known garden! Have you heard?" I was so happy to have found another young girl like myself that I didn't waste any time starting a friendship.

"I'm pretty sure we've seen your father many times at the synagogue, yes. He's a very kind man. Both your parents are kind. Your mother and father are the ones who often go through the village checking on the sickly. Is that right?" Deborah asked.

"Yes, that's right. More than teaching, my father believes the true call of God is love and looking out for those in need. Though sometimes my mother worries that they could get sick, nonetheless, they go." I felt great pride for my parents at that moment. They truly were such amazing people. Not only did my father provide for us and care for us, but he and my mother touched the lives of many people who were hurting and in need.

"My sister, Martha, is an amazing cook. She prepares a large pot of soup for the sick every week, the day after Sabbath. Mother and Father bring their love along with the soup."

"That is so beautiful, Mary. My family doesn't do as much for others as we should. You see, my mother is very ill, and I believe it's your parents who have come to check on her for some time now," Deborah said gratefully.

"I didn't know. I'm so sorry, Deborah."

"Thank you. We don't know how much longer she will live. It could be months or even years. These days are very somber for us right now. Today is a good day, though. She's here with me in the market, somewhere. My mother is a spinner, and she makes clothing with her beautiful threads. I have been learning from her this past year. Father says I need to be prepared to earn before he can think about finding me a husband." Deborah's eyes drifted from mine back to the synagogue in a daydream.

"Deborah, may I ask how old you are?"

"I'm thirteen now. How about you?"

"Thirteen! Same as you! Thank you for sharing with me about your family. I'm very sorry for the pain you all must be feeling. If there is anything I can ever do, please let me know," I said with a warm smile.

She smiled back and nodded appreciatively.

"My sister Martha is expecting me home soon so she can help me with some bread making. Would you enjoy that?" I asked her.

"Oh, yes! I love to cook and bake! My mother has taught me how.

I'll ask her if I can come along with you today. I'm sure she will say yes because Father is here with us today, selling some of his crops from a wagon!"

Together we made our way through the crowds of busy travelers, arm in arm, in search of Deborah's mother.

What an unexpected day. Mother was so wise, taking Martha and me out this morning to pick and sell herbs. I knew she was trying to distract me from Eli's move. But then, hearing Jesus talk about this coming new bread, the new Messiah and His love... How could my heart be downcast? So much change was coming, good change... I was excited for what was ahead and incredibly blessed that God had sent me a friend for the journey.

Best day ever!

Chapter Four

"It will be poured out soon..."
Luke 22:20, TPT

DEBORAH AND I RACED AROUND the property, chasing each other through the back fields, around the garden fence, and back to the front of the house. She was fast! For two years, time and time again, I'd attempted to beat her in races of all kinds and failed.

"It's just not fair!" I yelled, defeated once again. "How am I supposed to beat a farmer's daughter in a race? I bet you were raised chasing after chickens for dinner!" Sticking my tongue out at Deborah, I noticed my mother peering out at me with disappointment from the front window.

She came outside with her arms crossed. "Now, girls, is this any way for two young ladies to be carrying on?" she scolded dryly, pointing at us.

"After all, if you're going to race, you cannot brag unless you beat the fastest competition!"

Suddenly, my mother sprang into a sprint, laughing as she passed us in a cloud of swirling dust. She quickly turned the corner, heading straight for the back fields.

"Oh no you don't, Mother!" I yelled after her, urging Deborah to catch her first as I knew she could.

The three of us ran well past our property line and into the wild fields of flowers. Butterflies and bees took sudden flight as we pushed past them in our jovial race. Mother ran so far and fast that even Deborah couldn't catch her until she came to rest up ahead in a lush green plain. There, we all collapsed, out of breath, giggling and bantering back and forth about the unfair head start Mother had gotten.

"Look, Mary." Mother rose to her knees and pointed at a huge patch of purple just over a stream.

It was lavender, growing wildly through the plain.

"I bet we can uproot some of those and plant them in our garden, Mary! Won't you help us, Deborah?"

"Well, uh…" Deborah hesitated. "I think I'd better go instead, Sarah. I… I… need to get cleaned up." Deborah stood, pulling her tunic up higher and retying her shawl around her waist.

"Oh? Is everything all right, Deborah?" Mother stood to meet her.

"It's just… I think I've started my flow…" she said in a whisper.

"Oh, I see," said Mother. "You go on ahead then, sweet one, and be sure to tell your mother."

I sprang up and wrapped my friend in my arms. "I'm happy for you, Deborah! Do you know? This means you are a woman now! Fifteen is bringing you a bounty of blessings! I love you, Deborah!" I let her go and offered to walk her home.

"Thank you! It is good news, isn't it?" Relief shone in her eyes, erasing the embarrassment. "You stay and help your mother gather more lavender for your garden. It will increase your harvest greatly. It's probably best that I head home alone. My mother hasn't been well for the last few days, and she may not be up for unexpected company," she explained.

"I'm sorry to hear about your mother's decline, Deborah. She has been battling this for many years, and you have been so strong through it all. Samuel and I will come by this evening and pray with her if you think it may be time," Mother offered.

"Yes, I think that would be for the best, Sarah."

Deborah looked out over the wild lavender patch, closed her eyes, and took a long, deep breath.

My mother and I waited patiently while Deborah had her moment, and my heart swelled with compassion for my dear friend. She was so strong...

"Please know we are here for you and your father," my mother said quietly.

She had been visiting with Deborah's mother for years. Ever since Deborah and I met at the synagogue and became friends, we realized our parents knew each other through sick visits. What began as chronic fatigue, dizziness, and horrible headaches was determined by doctors to be a tumor growing in Deborah's mother's head. The understanding that she would one day pass away because of it brought only a minor amount of emotional preparation. My whole family had joined Deborah and her father in support ever since, bringing meals and comfort through prayer.

"It will be great news... for your mother," I said gently, trying to lighten the mood ever so slightly. "She will be at peace to know you're on your way to becoming a mother yourself one day." I spoke softly and reached for her hand. "If it's all right, I will come with my parents this evening," I offered with a smile.

"Sure, Mary. Please do. Thank you both for a fun afternoon, and I'll see that Mother and Father are prepared for your visit this evening." Deborah squeezed our hands then headed through the back fields toward her home.

We worked together, uprooting and dividing the wild lavender plants while we continued to talk.

"You were very kind to Deborah, celebrating her moment. I know you must be thinking about your own body, Mary."

My mother was right. Sometimes I had thoughts that caused me worry. The moment Deborah shared what had happened to her, a jealous feeling rose in the pit of my stomach. I couldn't help but think about myself.

"Do you think something is wrong, Mother? With me? Because Martha started hers at fourteen, and now I'm fifteen like Deborah, but my flow has yet to begin."

"It will be all right, Mary. There is no set time for any young woman's body to begin its courses. No two are alike, and most likely by your sixteenth birthday, you will be right along with Deborah." My mother explained.

"I sure hope so. What would I do... Who would I be if I could not be a mother?" I asked desperately.

"Mary, many women of the ancient days were faced with these issues. Take your hope from their stories. Know that God is faithful to hear and answer the prayers and cries of women. Think of Leah, Rachel, and Hannah. Do not let doubt win, my sweet Lavender. No matter what happens, God will take care of you." Mother held my cheek in her hand, sweeping her thumb down my dimple.

She was right. Doubt would only cause me to carry troubles that didn't exist.

"Now," my mother said suddenly and with excitement, "I have a great idea! You know that small patch of herbs you and I planted two years ago? I think it's time for expansion. You have done a wonderful job tending to your portion of the garden. So I've been thinking. If we open up the back fence, we could put in a whole new row of just lavender!" Her eyes glimmered with creativity and vision, the same glow Father said I had in my eyes whenever I had a new idea. "Here, give me your shawl."

Mother slipped it off my shoulders and spread it out on the ground. I followed her lead, and we placed several uprooted plants onto it. Then we each took a side and carried it together, back to the house.

"We will have to work quickly, Mary. Simon will be coming in three days to ask for your sister's hand in marriage. With so much to do, we can't have the garden looking like a mess. Are you ready for the challenge?" she asked with an adventurous smile.

"I sure am, Mother! And don't you worry—I will work hard in the kitchen with you. I want everything to be perfect for Martha. Maybe, if Deborah is well enough, she will join us."

We laid the shawl just inside the garden walkway.

"I'll get Lazarus to take down the fence and move it farther out, Mary." Mother went into the house in search of my brother.

As I stood there, alone in the garden, I took a moment to walk amongst the flowers, smelling them as I passed through each section. I noticed how mother's bushes of white roses were so large that they reached up to the kitchen windowsill. I'm sure that was one of the reasons she put them there. With roses being her favorite, she could enjoy their aroma and beauty when the kitchen window was open.

The other more colorful roses lined the left side of the garden fence and were showered in perfect sunlight for at least six hours a day. That was her secret to such opulent blooms. Harsh winds would occasionally blow through our land, so mother secured her roses with sturdy posts placed inside each bush.

Martha's favorite was the iris, of which we had an entire row of blue, yellow, and pink. Mother spent a great deal of time planning where everything was planted. She knew how to get the most out of each type of flower, causing them to thrive. She was very gifted.

Maybe I will have a garden like Mother's one day, I thought as I dreamt about the wondrous possibilities of my future, married to Eli and living in Jerusalem.

Chapter Five

"Never leave… nor forsake…"
Hebrews 13:5, KJV

I WOKE UP EXTRA EARLY ONE wonderful day. I did not want to miss that sunrise. After dressing quickly and wrapping myself in a thick blanket, I hurried out through Mother's garden, past the rosebushes, around the gate, up the stone pile, and onto the roof. As I reached up for the smooth white tree limbs that grew along side our home, my smile burst wide. Expectation was in the air. Love was bubbling from every chamber of my heart. Three years had gone by since Eli left for Jerusalem, and at the perfect age of sixteen, He was ready to take a wife. He'd sent word that he was journeying across the land from Jerusalem… to come and declare his love for me. *I am to be betrothed!*

Once I reached the top of the roofline, I sat on the smooth tiles and waited. The sun was peeking above the horizon, and light was spilling over the hills, down into the valleys, and across each home in our village in Bethany. The sky started as a deep ruby red. Slowly, as the sun rose through wisps of streaming clouds, it shifted to the color of luscious raspberries.

After a moment, I heard the rustling of leaves and turned to find Martha struggling up the side of the roofline, clinging to the branches.

Her eyes were wide with worry, so I took off my shawl and slid down to help her up.

"Good morning, Mary," Martha said quietly. "I brought us some fresh bread and butter for the sunrise. I heard you get up this morning. I was in the kitchen, waiting for you."

"Aw, Martha. You were? Thank you!"

"I know today is a special day for you. Eli should arrive this afternoon! You were so kind when Simon came to ask for my hand in marriage, with all the cooking and cleaning you did that day." She giggled. "Even if the food wasn't that good..."

We both laughed.

"Of course, Martha! You are my beloved sister. Thankfully, Mother never left my side in the kitchen, so nothing was too bad." I poked my tongue out at her.

"I won't have to do much cooking where Eli and I will be living. Thank God for that!"

Martha and I sat together on an old stone slab safely tucked behind the low cement wall father had built for protection. He'd designed that area for emergencies, but I took it over years ago for the view.

"It's perfect up here, isn't it?" I asked Martha.

"Well, it's a beautiful view—that's for sure. How did you get this old slab up here? I don't remember this."

"Oh, Lazarus, Eli, and I tied it with rope last autumn, when he was visiting. They lifted it up for me, but I helped a little too!" I said with a smile. "We tossed the ropes over that large branch over there"—I pointed at the biggest one—"and hoisted it up."

"So much work," Martha said.

"I guess, but look, Martha. See why?" I pointed at the wondrous view.

"Mother says you're like a 'sweet songbird' out here 'on your own little perch,'" she said with a soft giggle.

"My own little perch? Huh, I like that."

The sun was rising farther and farther into the air, and the once-raspberry sky was shifting into a reddish orange. With wide eyes, Martha and I sat in silence, nibbling our bread and soaking in the memory.

"Your year is almost up, Martha. Soon, you will be moving in with Simon of Bethany! How have you been feeling about that? I mean being married to a Pharisee."

"Oh, it's fine," Martha said quietly. "Mother and Father picked a good match for me. I trust in that. Besides, I hear he likes to eat, and well… we know I am becoming the best cook in our village." She sat up straight and wiggled her fingers over her adorable round tummy.

"That you are, Martha!" I exclaimed.

"You know, I think it's great that you will be here in Bethany. I'm almost sad to leave. I know Jerusalem is lovely, and the Levitical priests do live in such luxury. But I'm going to miss having our own land to work and helping in the garden. I will miss Mother and Father so much! And how will I ever manage not having you close by or Lazarus… Oh, and Deborah!"

"You will adjust," Martha said. "You will find your place and your way. You always do, Mary. A year goes by fast, but it's enough time to prepare your heart to say goodbye. Most of your time will be spent bathing and oiling your skin!" Martha laughed, but she sounded exasperated. "Plus, Mother is going to love shopping for your new wardrobe. You're going to look like a princess every day, compared to us!"

"I don't know about all that, Martha. We shall see. I'm just glad Eli and I are friends, you know? We actually know each other, and our love started as a little friendship! How sweet is that?"

"You are blessed, Mary. I think I'll head back down now and leave you to the sky."

"All right, dear sister. Thank you for sitting with me. It means a lot."

Eli arrived at almost exactly noon. Our doors burst open, sending maidens and workers flying in all directions, setting everything into place. Eli and his family came inside the house, and we all shared a joyous greeting. The time had come.

Mother rejoined Grandmother and me in my chambers with the news though I was watching from my window. I'd come down from the roof earlier that morning and found Grandmother waiting for me, ready to help me bathe.

We used freshly pressed olive oil on my skin, and Mother braided long stems of lavender into my hair. I wore a medium-sapphire-blue dress with a light lavender shawl embroidered with sapphire thread at the edges. A few precious stones and gems hung from silver threads on the ends of the shawl. Deborah had made that for me with the help of my mother. Each stone was a piece of my dowry on display.

Grandmother pulled a few curls from my braid to frame my face and laid a matching veil over my head. I noticed she left the front of my hair showing just a little. I suppose that's because Eli was to be my husband, and we were familiar with him and his family. Either way, I thought I looked my absolute best in the mirror.

"Don't be nervous, Mary. Be yourself and smile. Your father will do most of the talking. You must hold your excitement in until the celebration begins. Eli will declare his love for you." Mother and I squealed… just a little. "Then he will offer your father the mohar, your bridal price. After that, he will ask you for your hand in marriage, asking you to leave here and join him in Jerusalem. Then, once you say yes, the mohar will be given, and you two will be pledged to each other!"

"Yes, you will make a lovely *kalah*, young Mary," Grandmother said softly. "A bride."

"How exciting, Mother!" I placed one hand upon my beating heart and closed my eyes.

"Your father has a special vessel of wine for you two to drink from, and then the celebration will begin! Don't worry, I already sent word for Deborah to join us for the evening feast. She will be here." Mother had thought of everything.

"Sometime this day or the next, we will sit down and sign the *ketubah*, your wedding contract, and the covenant will be sealed! That is when Eli and his family will return to Jerusalem. Mother twirled me around in a circle, kissed my hands, and stood back looking at me.

"My beauty, my pearl! You will make us so proud on this day. Surely, God will shine his light upon you, my little Lavender."

"May I have a moment alone with Mary, dearest Sarah?" grandmother asked.

"Sure, Mother. I will leave you to your words. I'll go check on Martha. Don't be long. I'm sure we will be heading outside to join Samuel in just a moment."

Mother smiled at me with sparkling eyes then turned and left the room.

Grandmother Lillian and I spent those final moments quietly seated on my bed. She was a woman of few words, strong and graceful, a woman of unwavering faith who knew her God deeply. Mother often proclaimed, within our house, that Grandmother Lillian was a prophetess.

She slid to the floor on her knees and reached into a faded white satchel she'd hidden under my bed. After pulling out the most beautiful white alabaster jar, she sat back upon my bed and handed it to me.

"This is for you, Mary. The Lord spoke to me in a dream many years ago, to purchase this for you. I searched many markets in many towns and villages until I found this piece. I knew as soon as I saw it that it matched the one in my dream." She spoke with such satisfaction that I couldn't help but smile and share her passion.

"Grandmother, this is beautiful. I've never seen one so tall and intricate. Look at the curves around the top, sculpted so seamlessly. And the lid fits so securely. What's inside, Grandmother?" I asked as I lifted the lid and peered down with curiosity.

"Oh, just a small portion of freshly pressed olive oil, right from the Mount of Olives—such a spiritual place, Mary." As I sat upon the edge of my bed, admiring this beautiful gift, Grandmother prayed, "May the God of our ancestors be with you, and may His grace be lavished upon you. May His favor and mercy sweep over you each day like a fresh morning breeze. May He open your womb and prepare you for children. And may your heart be as this jar, ready to contain a valuable love reserved only for the bridegroom."

Suddenly, I realized something. I'd still shown no blood. Grandmother's words shook me from thinking about the jar and reminded me of bearing children. I was sixteen years old, with still no flow of blood. *I need to talk to Mother.*

Mother had spoken very little about that for the past year except to check with me and see if it had begun. *I wonder if I should tell Eli?* Surely, he would understand that not every woman begins at the same time. Mine was just late—two or three years late, but still... It would come. *Won't it?* I thought heavily. My eyebrows crinkled together, and my worry spoke to Grandmother.

"Mary." She spoke softly. "Are you listening? God has an important plan for your life. You will hold a great and valuable story of unending love. You, my dear one, will come to be loved by the greatest love ever known. One who will never leave nor forsake you. And your story will be told throughout the ages."

Closing my eyes and forgetting my fears, I saw Eli. Flashing forward to a year from then, I imagined the details. I pictured Eli waiting at the altar with Mother's flowers lining my path toward him. Becoming his wife, his forever love, had been my dream.

Grandmother's words flooded me with so much happiness that I felt like a flower blossomed and bloomed within me. Her words surely spoke of my future, one with children and a lasting love.

I shook my head. *Everything will be just fine! My life is beginning,* I assured myself.

"Thank you, Grandmother. This is beautiful! Your words and your prayer have brought me so much peace. Thank you. Thank you so much." I wrapped my arms around her, thanking her over and over for such a touching wedding gift.

She then placed the jar upon my windowsill and kissed my forehead, saying, "Do not worry, Mary, do not lose hope. God has a good plan for your life." Then she slowly left the room, heading out to find my mother.

In a few moments, my mother returned to inspect my hair and veil, adjusting this and that with excitement.

"Mother?" I asked.

"Yes, my sweet Lavender? What is it?"

"Well… It's just… We haven't talked about my issue of blood, Mother," I said shyly while looking at the floor. "Grandmother is so sure that everything will be fine and that I will bear children. But what if she's wrong, Mother? Should I tell Eli? After all, he's coming all this way to declare his love for me. Is this something he should know, that I'm still waiting?" I asked with slight panic in my voice.

"I see. Come sit down with me, Mary." She led me back to the bed where grandmother and I just sat.

"All your questions are important, but what most concerns me is the fear in your voice. You have to trust God, Mary. As for telling Eli, most women would feel it was inappropriate to disclose such private information to a man who was not yet her husband. You are not the only woman to be behind on her flow, and like many, it will come, and you will walk further into your purpose. Since you and Eli have known each other for so long, along with our families, I can understand your desire to share. That is completely up to you, and both your father and I are here for you no matter what you decide. If you were older, your father would most likely sit Eli down and explain everything, but you're only sixteen, and there is still so much time for things to occur."

I took a deep breath, walked over to my window, and lifted the jar from grandmother. Turning toward my mother, I shared it with her, along with every word Grandmother had spoken to me. She sat there quietly listening while admiring the beautiful alabaster gift.

After I told her everything, my mother simply smiled and said, "How wonderful, Mary."

"I'm not sure what I will do, but I will pray and ask God for guidance. I do have faith that all will be well, no matter what I decide." I stood and placed the jar back on the windowsill.

Mother nodded, embraced me, kissed my hands, then led me out into the kitchen.

Chapter Six

"Within your heart…"
Proverbs 16:9, TPT

ELI STOOD IN OUR HOME, dressed in a fine linen tunic and turban. They were dark sapphire, lined with gold and silver embroidery. My father, Samuel, stood in front of my mother and me and began the ritual.

"Eli, young priest from Jerusalem, you have traveled from your home to the house of Samuel and Sarah of Galilee, to claim my younger daughter, Mary, as your bride." He motioned for me to come stand by his side. Mother let go of my hand and whispered in my ear. "Go, my little Lavender."

Eli began to speak. "Yes, on behalf of myself and my mother's house, I offer the house of Samuel my mohar. I bring four hundred *zuzim*, a fine pair of young healthy donkeys, barrels of fresh fruit, nuts, and wine for a celebration, and for you, my dear Mary, a rare glass jar of jasmine spikenard."

"We humbly accept your highly valued price for our daughter," My father said.

"Mary," Eli continued, "I have great love for you, my dearest friend, O woman of God. Will you accept me as your husband and join me in Jerusalem, where we will continue in the Levitical priesthood together, as *khatan* and *kalah*? Husband and wife."

"I accept, Eli. Yes, I will marry you." The words left my lips in one simple, sweet breath.

A roar of laughter, shouting, and praise erupted from both our families.

Eli reached for my hand and drew me in for an embrace, whispering in my ear, "I love you."

My father tilted his head back and cheered from deep within as he held my brother's shoulder.

Lazarus pulled Eli in for an embrace and thanked him for all the wonderful gifts of food and wine. "You have come with such generosity, Eli! Such an honorable husband for my dear sister!" he exclaimed.

Martha appeared from the kitchen. She was clean and dressed in a fine tunic, not her usual kitchen attire.

"We are so happy for you, Mary. May you be most useful to your husband and have a blessed future!" she said respectfully.

My father asked for quiet in the room and brought Eli and me back together. "Today, my daughter and my future son-in-law will be joined in their ketubah! Bring out the scroll, Sarah, and we will sit together and prepare everything."

"Oh, let us wait, dearest Samuel." My mother smiled warmly. "The papers can wait! Let us begin the celebration!" she suggested with bubbling enthusiasm.

"Oh, all right!" my father replied. "As long as that is okay with Eli and his mother!"

My mother opened the back door to the garden, where Lazarus and my father had prepared the most beautiful sanctuary for our celebration. I was wonderfully surprised. Tables spilled over with fine treats and flowers. Torches lined the outer fence, waiting to be lit for the evening, and a few musicians gathered on the open grass. It was wonderful.

Mother whispered in Martha's ear as she prepared to lead me outside, "Martha, see to the servants now, and remember—no service or cooking for you! Just make sure our guests have everything they need. Let the feast begin!"

As the sun faded, the torch fires lit Mother's garden with a warm amber glow. The musicians were playing their last ballad, and beautiful tones of harp and flute floated through the air. Each table was filled with laughter and jovial conversation as our family and friends enjoyed the fine wine Eli and his mother had brought. Deborah and Mary were talking about wedding dresses, and Lazarus and Eli shared in what looked like a deep debate.

I sensed a moment of stillness as I stood looking at all my beloved ones. Mother and Father caught my eye and smiled with deep love and pride. I felt incredible peace, ready to begin the next adventure God had in store for me. I took a piece of date bread, wrapped it in linen, and disappeared from the crowd.

It was my moment alone with the sunset.

Up I climbed, feeling more appreciative with every step I took.

One more year… One more year of this climb, of this spot, of these hidden treasures. I etched every sensation on my heart: the wind on my face, the smell of mother's blooming lilac, father's bountiful laughter, the housetops lining my view, and of course, my people.

"Thank you, God. Thank you for helping throughout my life. May I bless you in faithfulness all my days. May I make a good wife to Eli, may I raise strong, godly children for the priesthood, and may I always wait to see each and every sunrise, knowing You are God." I whispered my prayer into the evening wind and watched the night appear.

"Still sitting up here, huh, Mary?" Eli teased as he popped up over the roofline.

"Do you need some help? We both know who really lifted this stone." I slapped the cold empty space next to me, teasing him right back.

"Oh, you keep telling yourself that, young lady," he replied as he stepped over the small ledge into *my* little perch.

"Mmm, a beautiful sunset on a beautiful day. Thank you, Mary, for being a nice friend, for accepting me today," Eli continued as I sat, quietly absorbing every word. "It's hard to believe we're here, ready to be betrothed… and married thereafter. You will love it in Jerusalem. It's not here, where you have the land to work and Deborah to get into trouble with. But you will like it, and I will do whatever I can to see to that, Mary." He smiled at me as he fidgeted with his hands. He was so sweet and sincere. "When my father died, Mother brought us back here to Bethany to live with her relatives until I was of age to join the priesthood. You know all that. Since I have been back, I'm amazed at how little I miss this place. I hope you will feel the same one day." Eli was stumbling over his words as he tried to express all the promise our new life would hold.

"Thank you, Eli. It is a lot to prepare for, I can say that much! Please be sure to anticipate visits back home, though. Lazarus will marry eventually, and Deborah… Who knows? Maybe they will… Well, anyway." I turned back toward the fading light and decided to just listen.

"Of course we will, Mary! Your parents will want to see their grandchildren as often as possible. And yes, weddings!" He placed a hand on my shoulder and looked at me with joy and intention.

Right away, at the mention of grandchildren, I thought again about my concerns. *If I'm going to tell him, now would be the best time. Breathe, Mary, and just speak slowly. It will all be all right.* I prepared myself to share, knowing it was my decision and being confident in the outcome.

"So, Eli, may I speak with you about something? It's very personal, and my parents have given me their blessing to share with you since we have entered into our betrothal today." I waited.

"Okay. Sure, Mary." He shifted his body from the sunset, facing toward me, leaving a larger separation between us.

"It's probably nothing. Mother says it's quite normal for a young woman my age." I cleared my throat and went on. "It's simply that I have had no showing of age yet, that is… no flow of blood." I stared straight at the ground and closed my eyes, for just a moment, to regain my strength. "Mother said women are all different and that my delay is not uncommon. Within the next year or so, we should know for sure," I added.

"Know what?" Eli asked dryly.

Startled by his direct question, I answered, "If I can bear children. Mother says at that time we could consult a physician to be sure everything is all right."

"Oh…" Eli let out a long breath and turned back toward the sun's final light.

"It will be okay, Eli. We will pray and seek God for a miracle. I'm sure everything will take its natural course soon enough," I replied.

"You're sure? Then why do you speak of miracles, Mary?"

"I suppose it's not needed, I just… I don't know," I muttered.

"I don't know"? Is that the best response you can give, Mary? I beat myself up about it internally.

We sat there in still silence, neither one of us moving or attempting any further conversation.

He just needs time to think and understand, I told myself. However, the choice to share with Eli suddenly seemed inappropriate and hasty. Maybe I should have kept it in and allowed Mother and Father to share with him the following year. *What have I done?* My hands trembled.

"Eli, we have known each other since we were young. I thought it was right to tell you of my concerns."

"Your concerns?" he whipped back at me.

"We have a year, a year to be betrothed, as you prepare a place for me… In that time—"

"Please excuse me, Mary. I need to find my mother. It's getting dark, and I should probably get you down from here before you cannot see." With that, Eli stood, took my hand, and led us down the roofline to the tree. Not another word was said.

Deborah was in the kitchen with Martha, guiding the serving maidens in their cleaning while Grandmother sat at the kitchen table. I sneaked in behind them and nudged Deborah quietly, trying to get her attention. Sure enough, she turned and immediately exclaimed, "Oh, it's the bride!"

"Shhh!" I responded, covering my ears to encourage her quietness.

"Hi, Martha." I waved. "Can I please talk to Deborah for a moment? If you can spare her, that is." I waited, staring insistently at my sister.

"Sure, sister! This is your day today. I can talk about my wedding dress with Deborah another time." Martha made sure we all heard her, and they all laughed, including the kitchen maidens.

"Why don't you go outside and find Mother, Martha, so you don't end up working in here," I whispered in her ear. "You know you're not permitted right now. And would you please tell mother that *I did*."

"You did?" Martha repeated quietly, with curiosity.

"Yes, tell Mother that *I did*. She will understand." I took Martha's hand and pulled her toward the back entry and motioned for her to go.

"Go on, Martha," Grandmother added with a smile. "Please find your mother for me. I think I need to lie down for the night, and I'd like her to assist me. I'm feeling quite tired."

Martha nodded, having two good reasons to find Mother, and went out the door. Once she was outside, I kissed Grandmother on the cheek then took Deborah by the hand and led her up to my room and told her everything. I sobbed like a little child.

Deborah didn't say much that evening. She just sat there with me and tried to reassure me that everything would be all right. But I knew it wouldn't.

Eli had turned white as soon as the words "if I can bear children" exited my mouth. I scared him, and next, the only miracle I required was for him to understand.

Not long after Deborah left me, I removed my veil and shawl and laid them across the small chair next to my table.

What have I done? I asked myself again one last time before crawling into bed.

About an hour later, I heard Mother enter the room. She came and sat on the edge of my bed and touched my hair. As she sat there unbraiding it, she spoke.

"Mary? Are you awake, my little Lavender?"

I didn't respond.

"Martha told me. Eli's mother pulled me aside tonight, not long after you came down from the roof. She wanted to discuss everything

with me… Oh Mary, my sweet, darling little girl. Please talk with me."
She waited for me to respond.

I just couldn't. I waited for her to go on.

"Eli chose to depart this evening, Mary. He told your father and me
he would send word when he arrived in Jerusalem, and he left this."

I knew she was holding something for me, but I didn't look.

"Please, Mother… Please go." I whimpered.

"Mary? It will be all right. Give him time to think. Maybe in
time—"

"No, Mother, you weren't there. Please, just go."

I felt her rise from my bed and listened as she placed some things
on my table then left the room. Turning abruptly toward the oil lamp
burning at my bedside, I inhaled a deep breath and blew it out. In an
instant, my room went dark, like the flame within my heart.

Chapter Seven

"All are of the dust..."
Ecclesiastes 3:20, KJV

S LIDING DOWN ALONG THE WHITE limbs of our sycamore
tree, with King David's words still on my lips, I touched my
bare foot to the smooth clay shingles of the lower roof. Slowly,
I walked down along the slanted roofline until I reached the pile of
stone leaning against the house. I couldn't bring myself to see anyone
that morning, but I knew if I was going to breathe again, I needed to
watch the sunrise.

The colors were fading, and soon the sky would be its normal dusty
blue. The day would go on, leaving me and my broken pieces behind
to lament. I lifted my tunic above my ankles and tied it tightly in place
with my sash. Each step into the cold, tilled soil of my mother's garden
awakened me. The earth seemed to seep into my tightening skin, nour-
ishing my desolate spirit. The ground was sensitive enough to know
not to speak but real enough to simply be there with me.

Maybe I wouldn't run...

"Hide me, Lord," I sang to the God of my life, still wondering if
He could hear me. "Let me hide."

I walked from the front of the garden, through the gate, and out into
the field where Mother's flowers gradually blended into wild wheat
and tall grass. Mother could never close in the back of the garden after
the lavender began to spread. I was glad. As I walked slowly, brushing

the tips of purple, I could no longer see a line where her plants ended and the wild ones began...

When I felt like I'd faded far enough into the wild, I sank to my knees and wept.

Violently grasping onto grass and weeds, I tore through the dirt, frantically ripping whatever life I could right out of the ground, desperately trying to make something else suffer like I was suffering.

I couldn't process what had happened. My thoughts were a tangled web. Grandmother's words swirled in and out of the cloud of pain in my head, making me more confused and angry. Understanding tried to knock at the door of my heart, but I would not answer. *This is unfair. This is wrong.* I was to be Eli's wife. He was to be my love. *What future can I possibly have now? Who will want me now?*

Ripping and pulling. Ripping and pulling.

On and on I went until my body trembled with exhaustion. Winded and fainting with fatigue, I finally collapsed. I lay there for a while, panting and gasping for air between bouts of tears, screams, and pitiful cries.

"Why would you do this to me, O God?

"How am I ever to live?"

"How am I ever to be worthy?"

"I am nothing! I am no vessel for love. I am worthless!"

I rolled onto my back and gazed into the endless sky, watching for a sign that God might be listening.

There was nothing.

Silently, I waited for the ground to open and swallow me back into the dirt where I felt I belonged.

———————

"God did not do this to you, my little Lavender. You are not worthless, and you will live on." Mother quietly consoled me from across the grass.

She had followed me out into the wild field and sat down a little way behind me.

"Oh, Mother, how long have you been here?"

"Long enough to watch how well you can clear a field." She sighed.

"You know… I have always wanted to clear this area of weeds and wildness. It would make such a lovely addition to our garden, Mary." She paused with a smile. "Your lavender plants are really taking off… Remember that day when we found the wild patch growing out by the stream?"

"Oh…" I sat up and tried to clean the dirt from my hands and fingernails. "Yes, I remember. That was a good day. A big day for Deborah as well." I sighed at the memory, which reminded me of my broken body then threw myself back into a pile of weeds.

"I told him, Mother. I told him last night."

She waited patiently for me to open up, just sitting and listening.

"I told him that though it was unusual, I was still only sixteen and it could be that I'm just… late. He looked terrified, Mother! I couldn't understand it! We practically grew up together. I told him that it didn't feel right to keep this potential issue from him. I thought he loved me enough to understand. I never thought he would leave me, Mother. Never…"

Mother crawled over to me and sat near. She wrapped an arm around me and pulled me closer. "For what it's worth, I think what you did took great courage. I told your father during the celebration that you may try to explain these concerns to Eli. He offered to step in and speak on your behalf, but I told him it was your decision. And I believe Eli does have love for you, Mary. He left your bride price behind: the donkeys, the money, the jasmine oil… and a note… for you. I haven't read it… I left it in your room, for when you're ready."

"What does any of that matter now?" I asked desperately.

"Well, for one thing, it shows he wanted you. If you were just some 'purchase,' he would have taken his mohar with him. I believe the pressure of his family and position are what influenced his decision. I think you will come to understand that in time, but we don't have to discuss all of that now."

Mother briefly went silent, as if she was collecting another thought.

"Unfortunately, I have something else to tell you." She turned her face toward the earth, and tears fell down her cheeks.

"What is it, Mother? What's wrong?" I turned toward her, reaching out to hold her hand.

Taking a deep slow breath, she looked at me. "Grandmother passed away in the night, my little Lavender. I found her early this morning at rest in her bed. She is in her eternal home now."

"No... No! Why is this happening?" I searched her face for answers but found none. "She just needed rest. She was tired. Wasn't she just tired, Mother?"

More and more tears spilled from our eyes, but we had no answers. My grandmother's time had come, and I mourned no longer for myself but for her.

"Oh, my sweet girl," my mother said. "Come here. Sit with me in the soil. Today, we weep together."

Chapter Eight

"Arise and go down to the potter's house…"
Jeremiah 18:2, AMP

T HE SOUND OF KNOCKING WOKE me from a dreary night's sleep, and Mother's sweet voice followed.

"Good morning, Mary. It's time to get up and ready. We are going into the village today, to Jehoshaphat and Elizabeth's pottery workshop. They sent word to your father and me last evening, that they are happy to have you. You will begin a trial apprenticeship today, and by Sabbath, Jehoshaphat agreed to evaluate your potential future there."

Sighing and yawning, I stumbled out of bed and over to Mother at my water basin.

"All right, Mother, I will do my best. But you know I have never made anything with these hands… that has turned out well. Not even bread," I said doubtfully.

"But I will go, and I understand this opportunity is a gift from God."

As I finished cleaning my face, Mother dropped a new white cotton shift down over my shoulders. It felt like a soft cloud had descended upon my skin, something nice and light for a warm summer day.

"Deborah's?" I asked.

"Yes, she dropped it off early this morning." Smiling, Mother continued, "She came looking for you at sunrise, you know. She wanted to see you and pray a blessing over your day. When she saw you hadn't ventured up to your usual morning spot, she came in and found me."

"Deborah makes the finest things, doesn't she, Mother?"

"She sure does. God has blessed her! And she is such a good friend to you, Mary. It warms my heart."

Mother held out a pale-blue tunic for me, also made by Deborah, and I put it on. When I wrapped its sash around my waist, my hands could not help but drift toward my belly. I looked downward and lost myself in an eerie thought:

"You will never be worthy. No skill will make you worthy. You can bear no children."

Mother lifted my chin, regaining my attention, and spoke softly into my heart. "You, Mary, are also blessed by God. You will succeed today, and you will find God's good purpose through all of this. And I believe you will be healed. If not by a miracle, then God will touch you through one of our physicians. Your father and I will do everything we can."

She lifted my hands into hers and kissed them.

"God has never failed us, and He will not now. Have faith, my little Lavender, and be brave."

Mother tucked three sprigs of small purple buds into my braid and covered my hair with a white veil.

"I wish Grandmother was here." I sighed. "Maybe God took her to spare her from my shame," I said cynically.

"Mary!" Mother replied sharply then paused in thought. "Your grandmother lived a long and wonderful life, and not one moment of it was spent fearing or worrying about your future. She knew, more than anyone, what God was saying. And her joyous expectations for you were not made from imaginations. She could see something in you Mary, something rare and beautiful. We all can. You may not know what that 'something' is just yet, but I have faith… that God will be faithful. You, my sweet and gentle daughter, are a gift to us all."

Along our walk down through Bethany village, I meditated on Mother's loving words of hope. I knew she was trying to prepare me the best she could, and she was right. God had always been faithful to our people. Many women thought to be barren ended up birthing many sons and daughters, to the glory of God. I was not going to be a woman of doubt. I was going to be a woman of faith, like my grandmother and my mother.

Bravery and confidence began to fill my spirit as we approached the potter's workshop.

Starting this new adventure, I thought, *one of clay and fire, will be my Exodus!* I cheered myself on. My journey had once been planned for a priestly heritage, but I was being led into uncharted territory, one still chosen and directed by God.

You will have faith! I said to my soul. *Just like King David, just like Ruth, and just like Hannah.*

Sometimes the pain and memories of Eli tried to overwhelm me, but they had faded somewhat over the last two years. However, being a young, unmarried woman of eighteen had its moments of discomfort. People asked questions.

I was thankful to have Deborah, who was also waiting for the one God had for her. The more I embraced my true reality, possibly never having children of my own, the more I was able to accept that Eli had to walk away. After all, no Levitical priest could marry a woman he knew could not bear children. Even the possibility that they might not would be reason enough. That would defeat the whole purpose of carrying the important Levitical lineage on to the next generation.

The reality of gradual acceptance was hard to believe. I was growing into a place of understanding, despite how painful and unbearable Eli's rejection was. But life did—and does—go on.

"Now, Mary, you remember that Elizabeth and Jehoshaphat lost their only daughter, Asa, right?"

I nodded silently.

"Taking you on to become their potential apprentice is a big deal. With no child of their own, understand, they are placing their hopes and their faith in you to carry on their business. Elizabeth, I'm sure, will be very emotional about this. So please be extra sensitive to her needs. Work hard to follow all of their instructions and give it your very best. They are investing in you, Mary, where they would have relied on their daughter."

"Yes, Mother, I will do my best and try to bring honor to their family."

"I consider it a great blessing that you have this opportunity, Mary. Jehoshaphat's work is known all throughout Israel, especially in Jerusalem. And with your natural eye for color, I think you will discover a talent hidden within."

I smiled at her words. She took so much time to notice me, the real me. No matter how many times I ditched my chores and went off exploring, my mother understood why. She could see that my eyes were full of wonder, ready and always searching for something new. I never disliked being home or helping out—I enjoyed our family very much—but the more I learned about God, the more I saw him in everything around me.

That's why I'm still drawn to every sunrise and why I still find my peace while lost in gardens and overgrown valleys.

"We are all praying for you," Mother said, "that God would bless the work of your hands. You never know what life may bring, and it gives me and your father peace to know you have a trade to sustain you. Just don't ever give up, not on yourself or on God."

Mother took hold of my arm and pulled me close to her side. I switched my basket to my other hand. It was full of the garden gifts I'd selected for Jehoshaphat and Elizabeth. Then I wrapped my arm tightly around Mother's waist.

"Thank you, Mother, I'm sorry it has taken me so long to pull myself out of despair. I'm trying. I thank God for you. Thank you for understanding me, loving me, and believing in me. I don't know what I would do without you."

"You would go on, my little Lavender. At each and every sunrise, you would regain your strength from God. And my love for you would echo on through the birds and the butterflies."

"Shalom!" Jehoshaphat chuckled. He had a big, round belly that jiggled when he laughed. Pushing through the door to his pottery shop, he came eagerly toward me, to pick me up in a big hug.

My mother laughed and winked at me while she covered her blushing cheeks.

"You are welcome here, young Mary!" Jehoshaphat exclaimed.

Elizabeth appeared from behind her husband, quiet and timid. "Hello, Mary. Yes, we are very pleased to have you join us today. Please, come inside. Sarah? You will stay as well?"

My mother nodded and said, "Yes, I would love to have a look around and see what Mary will be learning!"

Once inside, I had little to say but just looked at the shelves upon shelves of pots, vases, jugs, and jars. Some were painted, some were plain, and some were even glazed. *My favorite!*

"May I look closer?" I asked Jehoshaphat.

"Absolutely! Which ones are you drawn to, Mary?"

"Oh, the glazed ones! And these with the painted designs! I would love to learn how to make something like this!"

"Wonderful." He chuckled again. There was that jiggle.

I laughed inside at his contagious excitement. Elizabeth was laughing as well. They both seemed to be bursting with heavenly joy that was hard to miss.

"Those pieces have been fired in what we call the 'permanent kiln.' I'll show you after we finish the tour!" he explained.

I walked from the front of the shop, which was a small storefront, through a wide beamed doorway into the back work area. A small kitchen sat to the right, just under a window, with a table and three chairs. To the left was a large water barrel with lines of drying rags. A long slender table stood against the wall with all kinds of interesting things neatly laid on it. *I guess those are tools.*

Two doors led to the outside area, one straight out the back of the shop, another off to the back left. The back of the shop was divided by another beam and wall. Outside was a working area to the right with two turning tables, benches, and some other tools on a table. Behind that were large stacks of hay bales and different kinds of wood towering up to the ceiling. I could smell fires burning just outside the back door, and Elizabeth took my hand and led me to get a closer look.

"These two fire pits here are for firing smaller pots and things." Elizabeth looked toward mother, who was behind me. "She won't be doing any of her own work for quite some time, Sarah, so don't worry about the fires. Jehoshaphat and I will teach her how to be an assistant first. When she is ready to move on from there, she will use these!" Elizabeth picked up a large pair of thick leather gloves that seemed long enough to reach my elbows and waved them at me. We all giggled at their enormity, and I commented that they could fit a bear.

"It's all wonderful," Mother said. "Samuel and I are thrilled for Mary. This will be a wonderful adventure for our young girl. We are praying she blesses you with her help and, one day, her work."

"Elizabeth!" Jehoshaphat called from inside. "See Mary's mother out, if you please. I have a piece ready to be turned, and I'd like Mary to watch!"

My mother and I hugged one more time, and with her beautiful face full of hope, love, and joy, she kissed my cheek.

"I love you, my little Lavender. Enjoy this new day, and I will see you at home!"

"Thank you, Mother, for everything," I said with both my words and eyes.

"I love you."

Elizabeth and my mother talked outside the front of the shop as I watched for a few minutes. They laughed at something, then mother embraced Elizabeth. They clearly shared a bond. My mother was so tender toward her. It brought me comfort to know that my parents didn't pick just anyone to train me. They'd obviously thought long and hard about what I could learn and from whom.

Jehoshaphat led me out the back left door, where I could see a deep water structure. It was dug into the ground and lined with stone and cement.

"This is the system I had built for storing water, young Mary. There is a trough underground that leads to a small river beyond the walls of Bethany. Everything you will see here has a function. We built the shop just inside the outer wall of the village to make water access easy."

I was amazed at all the work and planning that went into running a successful pottery shop.

"Back here, along the back end of the property, is the permanent kiln I was telling you about." Jehoshaphat led me around.

The kiln was made of two large chambers and sat under a shingled roof protruding from the side of the shop.

"This side here"—he pointed to the left—"is the kindling box, or the firebox. You will help me see that it is filled with the proper kindling for each project. There are benefits to different woods, branches, and yes, even hay. It's all about temperature, young Mary. You will learn."

I bent down to the ground and peered into the chamber, where the flames were raging and dancing without restraint. The chamber hissed and popped as the wood splintered and cracked under the intense, consuming fire. My face was getting too hot and the smoke nearly choking me when I felt Elizabeth take my hand and lead me back, away from the opening.

"Don't get too close now, Mary. I can't have you getting burned now that your mother is gone."

Jehoshaphat waved his hands down toward the ground, "Oh, Elizabeth, she's fine! She's just curious to see how it all works. Look here, young Mary. This chamber is for the pottery vessels. It's here that the pieces are fired!"

"It really is amazing! Thank you for showing me," I said with true interest.

Jehoshaphat then slid his large hands into a pair of thick leather gloves, grabbed hold of a long iron rod with a wide flat edge, and maneuvered it inside the vessel chamber. With it, he very carefully lifted a large jug from underneath and turned it to face a new side toward the flames. Then he shifted a large flat stone over the opening of the chamber and turned toward me with satisfaction.

"We will have some fun working together, young Mary! Just be patient, and you will do fine. Elizabeth is quite skilled in her ceramic work, and you will work alongside her indoors for a while. I will call you to assist me from time to time and teach you about setting the fires. There is much to learn from both watching and doing."

"There are many types of clay and tools to use," Elizabeth added.

"Then there are the moisture techniques to learn, wrapping and storing your vessels as you shape them. You can also learn to design, paint, and glaze your pieces, like the ones you saw at the front of the shop!"Jehoshaphat chuckled and rolled his eyes. "They are becoming the most popular in style and functionality. Women love the colors and patterns. Let us go back inside for now. Elizabeth, I suggest you show young Mary where you store the clay and start there."

Chapter Nine

"In Thee is my trust…"
Psalm 141:2,8, KJV

"WHAT A DAY," I SAID aloud.

The cool of the evening had come, and I'd officially survived my first day in the potter's workshop. I was walking home, filled with pride and hope after a successful day, and I decided to stop by Deborah's house to thank her for the new shift. Another song of King David rose in my spirit, and I began to sing: "*Let my prayer be set before Thee as incense and the lifting up of my hands as the evening sacrifice. My eyes are unto Thee, O God the Lord. In Thee is my trust.*"

The songs of the birds were fading with the coming dusk as I rounded a corner and approached Deborah's home. I was startled to hear the cries of a woman echoing in the street. Pausing with the sudden realization that the cries were coming from Deborah's home, I stood still on the cool cobblestone path. A loud smashing sound came from inside, followed by deep shouts from her father.

"I will not plow the field this season! You will commit more time to your sewing, Deborah!" he demanded violently.

I heard Deborah reply, "But Father, I have no more time. I'm working as hard as I can. If you would only prepare the fields, maybe we could hire workers to tend to the crops for you. Please, Father, I want to marry."

"You have no time for such foolish things! Marriage is fleeting, and your job is to serve me!" he replied.

The sounds of crashing continued, and my dear friend's cries echoed in the street. I watched as the neighbors hurried their children inside, and my cheeks flushed with sorrow and embarrassment for my dear friend. Just then, her front door flew open, and she emerged in sudden flight.

I quickly ran to catch her, looking back over my shoulder to see if he was following. He was not. Once I saw we were far enough away, I shouted after her.

"Deborah! Deborah!"

She stopped running and turned toward me in surprise. Her right cheek was swelling with a deep red imprint of her father's hand.

"Oh, Deborah," I said as I wrapped my arms around her, pulling her close.

She wept in my arms. After those first few moments of consolation, we continued down the street close together, away from prying eyes.

"Let's take the back way to your house," Deborah suggested desperately.

I nodded, understanding her desire to be unseen. She lived with constant shame, knowing her neighbors could hear everything that went on in her home.

"Are you all right? Are you hurt?" I asked.

"I'm all right." She held her cheek gently, confirming what I'd assumed. "He's just awfully drunk, Mary, pushing me harder and harder to work. He's refusing to plow the fields now that we are coming to the end of summer. He doesn't want to prepare them for an autumn harvest. Instead, he is demanding I take on more orders from Jerusalem. I'm too young, Mary. I'm too tired. I'm only one person. And my dreams to be married, Mary... He won't even consider them. I'm so trapped!" She buried her face in her hands and sobbed uncontrollably. Desperation and pain poured from her weary heart, and all I could do was pray.

"Dearest Lord, come. Come and comfort your precious one. We

put our trust in you. Lead Deborah into your safe pastures." I embraced her tightly as we stood there in the tall grass. Wiping her tears with my hands, I hummed the song of trust I was just singing on my way to her home.

"Thank you, Mary. I love it when you pray. No one prays like you. I thank God you came. You are the only one who understands. Oh, I am just so grateful for you." She cried.

"Come, my friend. Come stay with us tonight. Mother and Father won't be home until early morning tomorrow or maybe even the next. They traveled out suddenly, late this afternoon, to Galilee. A very sick couple called on them. My brother sent word to me at the potter's shop that the people were struck with a severe fever and needed my parents' prayers and support. I'm sure Lazarus will understand your situation and allow you to stay the night with me."

I knew there would be no trouble from my brother. Over the years, he had enjoyed her friendship as well, hurting for her when trouble arose from her father's drinking. Mother had always welcomed her at any time to come and find refuge with us, and my father had visited with her father every time things became too unbearable.

"Thank you. I would like that very much. And Mary, I never asked you about your day. Did it go well?" Deborah managed sweetly.

"Yes, it was a good day. Thank you for the clothes, by the way. I am sorry I missed you this morning." I hugged her once again. "I think Mother found the right opportunity for me. She knows me well. And Jehoshaphat and Elizabeth are the sweetest, most jovial people you will ever meet. You will have to come down to the shop sometime soon and meet them officially. But for now, let's just get home and rest. I can put together a stew for the three of us, and I made another batch of lavender oil. We will put some on your face before bed. I'm sure it will be fine by morning.

After dinner, Deborah and I sat quietly in my room, sharing the lavender oil. She applied some to her face and arms, as did I. The calming scent filled the room, and we reminisced in the memories it brought.

As she sat before my back window, gazing out into the night, the moonlight glistened upon the glass jar on the windowsill.

"You know, Mary, maybe it's time you did something with this jar from Eli. It seems like a somber reminder of what you lost—of what was, rather." She lifted it from the sill, opened the jar, and sampled the unique fragrance of jasmine.

"I know. I have given it thought as well. The value is so significant I couldn't possibly just pour it out. And the idea of gifting it to someone else wouldn't be right... In some way, it still holds a monetary value toward my dowry. I don't know what to do with it."

"Hmm." Deborah thought for a moment while holding it. "Why not store the oil in something that is less of a reminder? Then sell or trade the jar for something else your house could use," she suggested kindly.

"That might work. I'm sure I could get something nice from the jar. It is a beautiful piece of blown glass, and it shines with multiple colors when you hold it up into the sunlight. But where would I store the oil?" I paused to consider.

"What about in here?" Deborah lifted my grandmother's alabaster jar from my table. "What's inside, Mary?"

"Oh, that's the olive oil from the Mount of Olives Grandmother gave me, also for my wedding," I said sadly.

Her words rose within my heart: *"May your heart be as this jar, ready to contain a valuable love."*

"Well... the more I think about it, this jar wasn't exactly a wedding present. It was for me. Grandmother said it was to be a symbol of my heart that would one day contain a valuable love."

"That is so beautiful, Mary. Of course it was for you! It's almost as if she knew... After all, she never said 'Eli's' love," Deborah added.

"True. I never thought of it that way. I believe you're right. Mother has always said Grandmother heard from God. She told me God gave her a dream of this alabaster jar. Grandmother searched far and wide to find the right one. I think you are right, Deborah. It is perfect." I took both jars to my bed and slowly poured the jasmine oil into the alabaster. As the precious perfumed oils mixed together, I felt the past give way to the future.

"Wonderful, Mary. Simply wonderful," Deborah declared. "This evening, we lay our past at the throne of our God and move forward in trust, together. If you would like, Mary, I'll take the glass jar with me to Jerusalem next week. I'm sure I can sell it for you and bring home the value." Deborah offered.

"Yes. I think that would be for the best. I will let Lazarus know so he can expect to collect it from you when you return. I don't want to know any more about it." Standing, I took the glass jar and put it in Deborah's open hands then placed my alabaster jar back upon my windowsill to glow in the moonlight.

"Let's get some rest, Deborah. It's been a long and tiresome day with another sunrise to come by morning."

We rolled out some of our traveling mats on the floor, dressed them with many blankets, and settled for a restful sleep.

Lord, I prayed from my heart, *please keep Deborah safe on her journey. Prepare a place for us. Lead us to the right path and shine your favor upon us. Kiss grandmother for me—let her know I'm listening.*

Chapter Ten

"To every thing there is a season…"
Ecclesiastes 3:1, KJV

T HE MORNING CAME, SURE AND strong, bringing a radiant
sunrise for Deborah and me to enjoy. We ate together then prepared for the tasks of that new day. I had to see to the garden
early in the morning and make preparations for Lazarus's and my parents' afternoon meals. Lazarus anticipated their arrival before I left for
the potter's workshop, so he journeyed out to meet them just outside
town.

Deborah and I were out in the garden, picking tomatoes and raspberries, when Lazarus quickly and loudly returned. He was searching
the house and property frantically for us.

"Here, Lazarus!" I stood, waving him in our direction.

He ran to meet us.

"What is all the fuss about, brother? We're just here in the garden!"
I said with a chuckle.

Deborah came over, and we walked to the gate to meet him.

"It's Father and Mother, Mary! They've arrived just outside town,
and Father says Mother has taken ill!" Lazarus explained.

"What? How? What's wrong with her?" I questioned him rapidly,
thrusting my basket into Deborah's arms.

"Fever," he said desperately. "You and Deborah must go down to

Jehoshaphat's house. Father insists that the two of you are not to enter the home until she is well again," he informed us with haste.

"What! I'm not going anywhere! Mother will need me to care for her!" I replied as I left the garden, heading toward the road.

"No, Mary! Father and I will care for her. You are to go into town and find Martha. She will know what food to prepare. Then head to the house of Jehoshaphat and let them know Father requests their assistance in taking you two girls in, temporarily." Lazarus showed no sign of allowing a discussion, staring into my eyes with great authority.

"All right, brother, I will do as you say. Please send word to me once they are home." But then I realized something. "Lazarus, please go into my room and get the small pot of lavender oil that I made. Have Mother apply it to her neck and keep it near. Please… tell her I will be praying." Tears flooded down my cheeks, and I felt Deborah's hand grasp mine.

"Go now, Mary. Gather your things for a few days. Why don't you leave the oil by mother's bedside and take what portions you have gathered from the garden as a gift to Jehoshaphat." He then turned and ran back down the road out of sight.

"Mary, I'll go to your room and put our clothes and things into a satchel. Then I'll prepare a basket from the garden for Jehoshaphat and Elizabeth." Deborah disappeared into the house without another word.

I stood outside the garden in utter shock. "Mother!" I cried desperately. "O God, if you can hear me, please bring healing to her body. O God, O God." I prayed aloud.

Then I picked up the gardening blade and quickly severed two large white roses and a cluster of lavender. I ran up the stairs to Mother and Father's room and set the flowers in a small vase of water next to her bedside. Next to them I set the tiny clay pot I'd made, poorly, during my first lesson—with the lavender oil in it. I cried bitterly with worry as I left their room, grasping Mother's gardening shawl as I closed the door.

"Come, Mary. I have everything just as your brother said. We will head to the house of Simon the Pharisee and inform your sister." Deborah led the way out the door with the strength I needed yet so greatly lacked.

Martha went to work quickly, preparing a chicken broth with matzo and a dish of roasted onions and garlic. She sent Deborah into town to gather a couple new jars of raw honey. Before long, we had a large basket prepared for Mother and headed back to my house to drop it off.

Lazarus didn't have much to say. He sternly reminded us to be on our way to Jehoshaphat's. We needed to explain why I was late for my apprenticeship training and relay father's request. Father called down from the window that everything would be fine and we should take courage and pray. After exchanging a few brief words of love and faith with him, Deborah and I left.

Elizabeth came to her front door with a warm smile and greeted Deborah and me with slight curiosity.

"Hello, Mary, and who is your friend?" she asked kindly.

"Hello, Elizabeth. This is my dearest friend, Deborah. She is going to be staying with me for a few days. May we come in?" I asked politely.

"Certainly." She opened her door wide and welcomed us into the kitchen.

"Mary, is everything all right? We expected you at the workshop about two hours ago. Jehoshaphat sent me home just in case you stopped by." Elizabeth waited.

"No, actually. My father has asked for your husband to approve…" I drifted into tears before I could finish.

Deborah took over for me while reaching over to hold my hand. "Sarah has returned ill from their trip to Galilee, Elizabeth. Rabbi Samuel asks if we can stay at your house until he sends word she is recovered."

"Lazarus says it's fever, Elizabeth," I managed to mutter.

"Oh, dear Lord, have mercy!" Elizabeth responded. She got up at once and took our things. After setting them down upon her chair, she returned with her shawl. "I will be quick. Please allow me to go gather Jehoshaphat." She bent down to catch my gaze and held my chin in her tiny hand, just like Mother.

"It will be all right, dearest girl. You and your friend will stay here until she is well again." With that, she stood, nodded at Deborah, and turned to leave.

A few minutes later, both Jehoshaphat and Elizabeth returned.

"Young Mary," Jehoshaphat said as he walked up to me. "You are welcome with us, both of you. Please, take our spare bedroom down the hall and settle in. Our home is your home. I shall head down to your father's house right away and give him my blessing to keep you here. Is there anything your mother needs that I can bring?" he asked with immense kindness and concern.

"I don't believe so. Thank you," I managed.

"Take the fresh ginger root, Jehoshaphat, it can be steeped in water with lemon and garlic to help with fever," Elizabeth added.

She grew quiet immediately after speaking, not wanting to draw attention to the word *fever* any longer. Asa, their only daughter, had passed away from a severe fever at just under two years old. Elizabeth's experience was quickly turned into useful advice. My heart began to ache for her hidden pain, then I realized my mother could share the same fate as Asa.

"All right, my dear, I will go now. I will also make sure that word has been brought to the synagogue for prayer and check with the town physician. I'm sure your brother has already made arrangements, but I will make sure." With that, Jehoshaphat took the small sack Elizabeth had filled with the fresh ginger and left again.

As I spilled into sobs, Deborah and Elizabeth led me down the hall into the bedroom, and I didn't leave until morning.

Nobody slept much in the house of Jehoshaphat that night. Our prayers filled the house from one hour to the next. No matter how often Elizabeth and Deborah encouraged me to eat, I could not. I spent the evening and morning pacing, crying, and praying for my mother. Jehoshaphat had returned the day before with the news that the physician was with my mother and the synagogue had in fact received word.

No one came with the sunrise. That was good news. It meant mother had made it through the night—I hoped. Noon came and went with still no word.

"Elizabeth?" I found her sitting at the kitchen table, sewing one of Jehoshaphat's torn tunics.

"Yes, Mary, she replied quickly. "What is it, dear one?"

"May Deborah and I visit my sister, Martha, to see if there is any bit of news?" I asked.

"Of course, Mary! That is a good idea. Try not to stay out too long, and please bring word to us. If there is anything we can do, we will. Jehoshaphat went down to the spring today. He decided to work on his new work shop. Would you stop down there if you return near evening?" Elizabeth put her work down and came to walk us out the door.

"Yes, we will, Elizabeth," Deborah answered on our behalf, warmly receiving Elizabeth's goodbye embrace.

For the first time, Deborah and I didn't speak during our walk to Martha's house. The tension of worry and sickness saturated the air. Every passing glance from our neighbors felt like sorrow and pity. Word must have spread quickly through the night because everyone clearly knew.

We arrived at Martha's and knocked. At first, nobody answered. Then, shortly after, a man came to the door, Simon, Martha's husband.

"Hello, Mary, Deborah," Simon said with little emotion. "Your sister isn't here. She left not long ago with another pot of broth for your mother and father."

"Oh, thank you, Simon. What do you mean, Mother and Father?" I asked with greater concern.

"You haven't heard?" He paused then realized I obviously had not. "Lazarus came at dawn, looking for more broth. He said your father had collapsed at your mother's bedside in the late-night hours. The fever has spread to him as well, Mary."

He opened the door wider to welcome us inside, but I took off running. Sand and stones shifted under my sandals as I raced through town on the cobblestone path leading to my house. My heart pulsed in my ears, and all I could see was my mother's face as I kissed her goodbye just the day prior at the workshop. I could hear my father's contagious laughter replaying in my mind.

My house was coming into view when I saw Lazarus sitting on the front step with his head between his hands. As I got closer, I cried out his name.

"Lazarus!"

No answer.

"Lazarus!"

He lifted his head, and I stopped. His tunic was torn, and his eyes were dark and sunken. He rose and walked toward me.

"Lazarus!" I cried out, eyes welling with tears. My throat knotted, and my lungs burned. He reached out both hands and pulled me against his chest, and we both collapsed to the ground. His cries were louder than mine, and he trembled as he spoke.

"I'm sorry, Mary. I am so sorry…" His voice faded into weeping, and he held me more tightly than ever before.

"Where is Father?" I asked, pushing him backward.

I looked into his bloodshot eyes and saw the truth before he could utter a word. At that same moment, Deborah arrived behind me, falling to the ground next to us.

Lazarus looked toward the ground and said the four words I was dreading with all my being.

"They are both gone."

Chapter Eleven

"His song shall be with me…"
Psalm 42:8, KJV

T HE RAIN POURED DOWN FROM dark billowy clouds onto Mother's garden for days after my parents passed. They were so beloved that even the earth mourned their departure. *Tishrei*, the rainy season, came quickly that year. The rain would lead us out of harvest season and into the cooler month of *Tevet*.

As I stood under the overhanging roofline, I watched the flowers getting trampled by great drops of rain without the slightest desire to touch them. I was still numb to the reality that Mother and Father would not be coming home. I mourned for the land, thinking about how it would never feel Mother's touch again, nor would I.

On that day, most of the final visitors had gone, leaving Lazarus, Deborah, Martha, her husband, and me to ourselves. I was having trouble accepting that the time of traditional mourning was coming to an end and that Lazarus would soon depart. Jehoshaphat and Elizabeth spoke with the physician and the rabbis just outside the house. They were discussing the cleansing ritual for our home while Lazarus and I spent our time away.

The grief was almost too much to bear.

Through it all, Deborah never left my side. She was the one who helped me keep myself together during *shiva*. But the time had come for life to, somehow, carry on. I would be moving into the house of Jehoshaphat for three months while Lazarus traveled to Nazareth.

Deborah would return home to her father. He'd been struck with such unexpected sorrow at the death of my parents that he made every attempt to cleanse himself and return to his farming. That lifted the burden on Deborah and allowed her the peace she needed to return home.

Gifts brought during our time in shiva were sent out and dispersed, by Martha's husband, to the leprosy camps outside Jerusalem and Bethany. Father and Mother had managed to write their final wishes before passing, and they asked for the needs of the sick and helpless to be considered, in their sweet memory. Many times, Lazarus, Martha, Deborah, and I wept at the generosity of our little village of Bethany. Lines of people stood silently outside our home to show respect and sympathy to our family. Smooth stones were placed upon the stoop of their sepulcher as villagers partook in their *levayah*, their funeral. Despite the magnitude of grief our family and village felt, love was showering all around us.

After the first seven days of mourning passed, Deborah, Martha, and I took a large section of mother's beloved white rosebushes and planted them near the front entrance of their tomb. It brought the three of us girls comfort to know her beautiful roses would remain near her resting place.

Though the time of grieving was over, I knew I would never be the same. All I had were the beautiful memories of my father and mother. They were gone and never coming back. I prayed desperately for strength nearly every hour of every day.

Elizabeth's gentle voice called from outside the garden gate. "Mary, dearest. Come, my dear one. The rain isn't slowing down, and Jehoshaphat wants to head home before we catch a chill." She waved at me to come.

I took a deep breath and tried to imprint Mother's garden, just as she'd left it, into my memory. I stepped into the rain and met Elizabeth's open arms with mine.

"It will be all right, my dear one. It will be all right." Elizabeth took my arm, and we scurried out of the yard over to Jehoshaphat, who was waiting with a large cover for the two of us.

When we arrived back at Jehoshaphat's house, Elizabeth encouraged us to dry quickly and ready ourselves for the evening meal. At least ten days had passed since I ate even the smallest morsel, and my stomach turned violently at the thought of food. As I changed, I could smell the delicious scents of fish stew filling the house. Sure enough, when I entered the eating area, Deborah, Martha, and Lazarus were sitting with Elizabeth and Jehoshaphat, at the table.

"Deborah, Martha, brother, you came," I said with the faintest smile.

"It's time we break our fast together, Mary, together, as a family," Lazarus declared as he stood with open arms. He welcomed us all to stand as he prayed and broke the bread over our meal.

With one sip of the rich fish broth, my body warmed and relaxed, finally getting the nourishment it so desperately needed.

"What a fine meal, Deborah!" Jehoshaphat said with his unwavering joy.

"Oh, most excellent, Deborah!" Martha said as well.

I added to the praise she so wonderfully deserved. "Yes, it is delicious and my personal favorite, dear friend."

"And Elizabeth, the bread is wonderful! Did you make it?" I asked her.

"That would be the very talented Martha." She lifted a hand toward my sister, who smiled proudly.

We all chuckled at her glowing pride and nodded with recognition.

"I did, however, put together a nice sweet *pai*. For that, I will take full credit!" Elizabeth blushed and pointed at the steaming dessert cooling on the windowsill in the kitchen.

"I hope you made two, my love, because we all know that one is enough for me!" Jehoshaphat patted his large round belly and grinned into her warm brown eyes.

"Not to worry," Martha chimed in, "I also have a dozen *teiglach*, dosed in sweet honey syrup, tucked away in my basket!"

"Oh!" I said with a sudden and unexpected burst of joy. "Those were Mother's favorite." I quieted down subtly.

Were…

Everyone was getting a little nervous at the mention of my mother, so I added, "What a thoughtful touch, dear sister."

Everyone sighed and nodded.

We sat and fellowshipped over our meal, taking turns sharing about the end of the harvest and discussing our intentions for the coming cold season. Lazarus would depart the next morning, at dawn, with another friend of his, who was also training for a rabbi position in Bethany. He decided that during that difficult time, he would spend the cooler months in Nazareth, visiting Jesus and his family. From there, he would travel southeast to the Sea of Galilee and join Uncle Mathias at the shore to do some fishing. Three months was a long time for him to travel, but he would earn decent wages from our uncle. He was sure I would be safe with Jehoshaphat and Elizabeth, not to mention Martha and Deborah only being a short walk away.

I could understand his desire to go. The house needed to be empty for an extended cleansing period, and the memories it held were just too painful to handle. Martha was the strongest of the three of us. She and her husband volunteered to do the cleaning, selling, and donating some of Father and Mother's things before Lazarus and I returned home.

Not everything would go. Mother's gardening shawl, which I'd worn every day since the moment she returned home ill, was mine, and we would keep all the kitchenware and Father's scroll collection.

When Lazarus returned, he would take over as head of the house. He stated that he would move into Father and Mother's bedroom, leaving me with the choice of my old room or his. I decided to stay in my room.

I felt no pressure to recommence my training with Jehoshaphat and Elizabeth, but I decided that was best. After Sabbath, I would return to work with my guardians and give it my all.

Mother's final words and moments with me echoed through my heart. *"You would go on, my little Lavender."*

I must go on… for Mother, I thought.

She had believed in me. I would pray to find my strength and start each day afresh with every rising sun, looking for her love in the birds and the butterflies.

Later that evening, after everyone had said their goodbyes, I sat on my new bed, feeling the contentment of a day well spent. A knock sounded at the doorway, and Elizabeth entered.

"May I join you for just a moment, Mary?" she asked.

"Of course, come in. I was just reflecting on the day. What a blessing it has been to see all the love and appreciation for my parents. I just feel so proud and yet so terribly sad all at once," I said.

She nodded and sat next to me on the corner of the bed.

"I have something for you, dearest Mary." Elizabeth handed me a square folded letter-size package. It was wrapped in twine and stamped with white candle wax, in which a small sprig of lavender was embedded.

"It's a note from your mother to you," she said simply.

I knew the moment I saw the lavender sealed within the wax that it was from her.

"It was left with a copy of their final wishes. Your brother gave it to me and asked me to give it to you when everyone had gone." And with that, Elizabeth rose from the bed, kissed my forehead, and left the room.

I sat staring at the small paper package, and a tiny glimmer of hope crept into my weary heart.

Something else. Mother left me something else to hold onto. Do I tear it open and read it now?

I sat pondering. The more I waited, the more I desired to wait. I curled up into my bed, wrapped myself in Mother's shawl, and tucked the package safely under my pillow. I drifted into sleep through clouded tears, remembering another comforting psalm of King David that my father had taught me:

"My deep need calls out to the deep kindness of your love.
Your waterfall of weeping sent waves of sorrow over my

soul, carrying me away, cascading over me like a thundering cataract. Yet all day long, God's promises of love pour over me. Through the night, I sing his songs, for my prayer to God has become my life."

Chapter Twelve

"My song of joy will return."
Psalm 51:8, TPT

MOTHER'S NOTE STAYED WITH ME everywhere I went for the first few months after her death. I tucked it safely in my tunic pocket, patting it every so often to ensure it was still there. Months passed slowly, and the time did eventually come for my brother and me to return home. My time with Jehoshaphat and Elizabeth had been exactly what I needed. After they suffered such a great loss in the early years of their marriage, God gifted them with such tender, understanding hearts. And the joy they exuded was miraculous. Elizabeth tended to me sweetly during the initial loss and never once forced me beyond what I was ready for.

The move home was somber. The house was dark and unlit, with a faint layer of dust settled on every surface. True to her word, Martha came after the cleansing period and collected the donations and the sellable items. All the money we raised went right back into the estate, to ensure it would remain within our family for generations. Martha selected a journal of my father's, a few special cooking vessels, and a blanket or two Grandmother Lillian had made. Lazarus was left with my father's entire collection of scrolls and books, along with his rabbinical clothing.

I entered my room slowly, anticipating some kind of encounter with the afterlife, but I had none. My room was just as I had left it, with the additions Martha had left for me on my bed. I pulled Mother's shawl closed with one hand and stepped in closer for a look.

On my windowsill remained the alabaster jar from my grandmother. On my table sat my mother's combs and brushes, which Martha knew were precious to me. My mother and I would bond during the brushing of our long, dark hair.

In addition to those items sat a small, white marble box containing a few special pieces of mother's jewelry I'd requested, pieces made with rare precious gemstones.

Across my bed Martha had laid two of my mother's tunics. They were her favorites, made by Deborah. Two of mother's finer dresses were there also. The first was from her own wedding day, and the other was one she'd planned to wear on mine. I let the tips of my fingers trace the embroidery gently before gathering them up to put them away. I spent that morning cleaning and freshening up my room then tucked Mother's letter safely under my pillow before getting to work in the kitchen.

"Will you be tending to the garden today, Mary?" Lazarus asked me quietly, meeting me in the kitchen.

"No. I don't believe so," I replied. The thought of working in the garden was something I wasn't ready for, and my brother didn't seem surprised by my response.

"That's all right, Mary," he said sympathetically.

"There's so much I want to share with you about my travels, Mary. What do you think about inviting Deborah over for our first evening meal? Then we can all share together, and it may help us adjust to being home a little more easily," he suggested with a smile.

"I think that's a nice idea, Lazarus. I'll finish preparing the kitchen for an evening fire, and Father taught me how to write a simple list for the market. Deborah will be making her rounds today as well, so I will ask her when I see her in the village."

"Good," he said simply.

"I'll see to the dead plants and weeds, Mary. I'll clean out whatever needs to go from the garden and check in with Martha. She may have time to help as well until you are ready. I hope that will relieve any pressure. And please, bring some of your pieces home from the workshop today. I am excited to see what you have done. I am sure they are beautiful!"

My brother placed a large, gentle hand on my shoulder and smiled at me, exuding unspoken love and understanding.

Almost a year passed before I entered my mother's garden.

I spent most of that first year assisting Elizabeth at the shop, learning how to store and moisten the different clays. I observed how she threw pots and bowls on the turntable. Then she taught me how to carefully carve simple designs into the flesh of her pieces. I didn't make much at first, besides that small clay pot I'd left at Mother's bedside. I don't know if that was because I had much to learn or if Jehoshaphat and Elizabeth kept my load light because of my grieving. Nonetheless, the more I watched, the more I learned. Jehoshaphat gave me a small piece of clay to practice on at the end of each workday. And only some of the pieces were fired.

He or his wife would stand behind me and give me guidance as they watched me practice. Before long, I was making bowls and plates with great ease. So Jehoshaphat began giving me simple assignments for the shop. I was to make a certain number of plates per week and work on creating new designs and patterns with the paints and glazes. He also taught me how to fire pieces in the sand bonfires on my own. I needed to master that skill before moving on to the permanent kiln. My work was improving daily, and the joy it brought all three of us lifted our spirits.

Deborah was the first one to receive a large stew pot from me. It was my biggest piece that made it through the permanent kiln without cracking or bursting under the intense heat. Jehoshaphat was quite proud. Elizabeth helped me carve stalks of wheat from the bottom up toward the mouth of the pot, and I painted them with a deeper red glaze to make them stand out.

Deborah was always complaining about the difficulty of maneuvering the lids of her stew pots over the cooking flames. So I designed a lid with a hollow curved handle that she could insert a spoon into for easy lifting. No more needless burns or loss of grip—she was thrilled.

That particular cooking vessel became the first item requested by our customers. Pretty soon, Elizabeth, Martha, and many other local women had one. The number of mistakes I made kept diminishing, and Jehoshaphat and Elizabeth sang praises to God for my growing gift. More and more people traveled to our little shop, looking to see what other new pieces we had come up with. We were earning so much profit that Jehoshaphat's second shop was no longer a dream but a nearly finished reality.

My heart was mending slowly but surely. Mother had been incredibly wise to send me here. She saw something in me that I did not. Without pottery, I would have been lost in hopelessness and despair. Instead, I was moving forward with growing confidence and purpose.

The second year after the passing of my parents brought some difficulties and heartache for Martha. Her husband, Simon the Pharisee of Bethany, became sick with leprosy. He was forced, after being examined by the local physician, to move out of his home and into a leprosy camp just past the graveyards of Bethany. Martha was two years older than me, and at twenty-two years, she was hoping to have a home and begin having children. Simon's sickness broke her dreams of being a mother. Little by little, my sister had to sell most of their belongings to help support the camp outside the village. Lazarus offered to let her move back into our father's house, but Martha declared she would do so only if she had no other options.

Whenever Lazarus returned from Nazareth, he had so much more to share with us. He spoke often and with much more certainty about Jesus. He shared with us about Jesus's unique interpretations of the prophetic scrolls time and time again. Martha, Deborah, and I could not ignore what my brother was seeing in him. It was a change, a present and clear change, in the Jewish way of life. However, it was not received by all. Many times, Lazarus said that people would oppose the teaching of Jesus, ridiculing his insight and turning from him. But we were among the few who could feel the power when he spoke, and we knew God was with him.

Deborah and I spent many dinners with my brother asking about and receiving as much as we could from his trips. We were safe learning about the prophets in our own home and kept the knowledge to ourselves, treasuring it greatly.

Eventually, I worked my way back into the garden. Martha had managed to save the irises and poppies, and she tended to Mother's roses with trimming. Sadly, Lazarus had removed several flower beds and plants that were no longer salvageable, leaving great empty gaps toward the back end of the garden. I remember standing there with great guilt over having selfishly neglected Mother's most favorite place. I needed to get to work and restore what had been lost.

I began with what little was left, starting randomly until I found a groove. I split and planted a couple of roots of aloe and mustard, just the way mother had taught me. Then I planted new rows of sage. They took off wonderfully, spreading faster than I anticipated. Later in the year, Elizabeth brought me many new seeds from her trips to Jerusalem: rosemary, thyme, basil, and a favorite of Mother's, mint. I planted them all, and the ground received them with gladness.

Lazarus helped me add an almond tree to the grounds, along with a wild fig tree. Watching them grow was amazing, and they brought us all unexpected peace. The more I worked, the more saw the garden becoming something new. It had the beautiful elements of Mother, yet it was clearly becoming an expression of me.

What used to be a garden of great color and velvet petals was becoming a productive land of harvestable herbs and crops. That pleased Lazarus because it gave us another source of income and this garden was also less demanding. He could travel to the fishing grounds and spend ample time practicing the oral traditions of the rabbi without the pressures of being stuck at home. I was able to garden during most early mornings—after sunrise, of course—then focus the workday on my pottery lessons and creations.

Life was flowing again, and we all found our ways of working together as a family.

Chapter Thirteen

"He will lift you up…"
1 Peter 5:6-7, NLT

THE SPRING ALMOND BLOSSOMS WERE blooming all throughout Israel, bringing a pretty white-and-pink glow to the end of the winter season. Spring was coming, the season called *adar* and the time we celebrate *Tu BiShvat*, The New Year for Trees, otherwise known as Rosh Hashanah.

Jehoshaphat and Elizabeth were heading to Jerusalem soon to enjoy the excellent selection of freshly harvested almonds and nuts. That brought a nice crowd to the markets, and they never wasted any opportunity for profit.

On my way to the potter's workshop, I took the time to hum along with the singing birds, lifting my thoughts toward heaven and sending Father and Mother a smile.

"Mary!" Elizabeth was calling my name from across the street. She was the tiniest woman in all Bethany, and her voice could only be so loud.

"Good morning, Elizabeth!" I replied from across the way, waving my hand through floating blossom petals and sunshine. "What's all the excitement about today?" I quickened my steps to close the gap between us before she felt the need to continue carrying on loudly.

"Oh, Mary! I have such great news for you! Jehoshaphat and I are going to Jerusalem!" she said with a beaming smile.

"But of course you are. We just spoke of this yesterday!" I giggled.

"Oh, but that's not all, my dear one. Jehoshaphat has decided to take a selection of your work with us! He wants to see if there is a similar response to your designs in Jerusalem. He is confident now that your creations will reach far beyond Bethany. If they sell well there, he wants to bring you along during the Festival of Tabernacles this fall. That would mean you can start turning your own profits, dear Mary!" Elizabeth squeezed me with all her might.

Like proud parents, Jehoshaphat and Elizabeth celebrated my discovered talents regularly. Once my pieces began drawing in the local crowds, Jehoshaphat continued expanding his business with the addition of that other workshop. He would tell me often that it would someday be mine and that God had unveiled everyone's eyes to see my gifts.

"Elizabeth, I am so grateful. Thank you for believing in me so much. I'm overjoyed as well. I'm not sure about traveling with you, though. I am quite content being in the background. A woman my age, unmarried, without children… I don't need to be traveling and creating even more rumors everywhere I go." I spoke honestly with Elizabeth about my concerns, for she was the only woman besides my sister and Deborah who knew about my condition.

"Now, Mary, you cannot let the rumors spread by jealous people hold you back from your destiny. Don't you pay any mind to them, for God is on your side, dear child!" Elizabeth wouldn't hear another word about it unless I agreed, of course.

"Good morning to you, young Mary!" chuckled Jehoshaphat as Elizabeth and I entered the shop.

I tipped my head down. "Good morning, Jehoshaphat. Is everything ready for your journey today?"

"Yes, we have everything packed and ready to go. Elizabeth and I were just waiting for you, to discuss a few things." He chuckled again, rumbling his jovial belly. "But I have a feeling that Elizabeth, my love, has already spun the clay!"

"If you are referring to you bringing my work along," I said with a smile, "then yes. Yes, she has. Are you sure that's what you want? I'm quite content with how things are now. I'm not sure I have what it takes to make it in the bigger cities."

"I admire your humility, young Mary, but the time for that is now over. You are our rising star, and it is time for the world to see what your gifted hands can make. Please go gather a decent selection for us to take with us, and prepare your heart for the blessings to come!" Jehoshaphat placed a hand on each of my shoulders and grinned with fatherly pride.

Who was I to crush his spirits? So I did as he so confidently requested. I gathered a basket with all my small honey pots along with their corresponding corks; two large cooking vessels, the ones with the hollow handles; and one tall earthen pitcher. That was my prized piece. It was made from a fine, deep-red clay. The neck was long, thin, and attractive, widening again toward the delicate spout, which I'd designed to resemble the curved edge of a lily petal. Elizabeth took extra care teaching me to achieve the smoothest finish and red glaze on that pitcher, and it was a striking piece of artwork.

"All right, dearest guardians." I bowed my head and held out my tunic as one would do before royalty. "Here are your required offerings." I lifted my head to reveal my coy, teasing smile.

"Well, thank you, young Mary." Jehoshaphat regally replied.

The two of them played along as they packed my basket safely under the burlap covering of their wagon. Jehoshaphat carefully assisted Elizabeth onto the small bench, and I reassured them I would take good care while they were gone. Their trip would last for only two days.

After they began their journey down the village road, Jehoshaphat called back to me, "Be sure to take Deborah down by the stream and check on things at the new shop!" And with his final wink, they were off.

His warm laughter trailed behind them then softly faded as they turned the corner, out of sight.

He was up to something, and I loved it.

Deborah and I were quite pleased to find that Jehoshaphat had completed his project and the new small cottage was no longer a dream. We took a quick tour and made sure everything was locked up before nightfall.

The two days had come and gone, and Jehoshaphat and Elizabeth were due back shortly. We needed as much time as we could get to prepare a welcoming meal for them. Lazarus would join us at Jehoshaphat's house, and we would have everything ready to surprise them. That was Deborah's idea, after their generosity with my pottery work, and Lazarus agreed. He thought the time had come for a celebratory dinner since the last time we'd all broken bread together was for the passing of our parents. Martha was invited, but she chose to stay home. We didn't try to force her to join us, understanding that she was keeping a great deal of hidden pain locked away since that sickness had reached her Simon.

The sun was just starting to dip below the distant mountain ridge when we heard Jehoshaphat and Elizabeth's wagon coming up the road. Lazarus went out to meet them, welcoming them home to a warm cooked meal made by Deborah of course. I still tried to avoid cooking whenever possible. I had, however, selected a beautiful arrangement of herbs and flowers for Elizabeth's table.

Deborah and I waited at the entrance of their home, ready to greet them with extra-long hugs.

"Oh, my girls! It's so good to see your beautiful faces!" Elizabeth exclaimed. "What are you doing here? It's nearly nightfall!"

"We wanted to welcome you home with a special meal and show you both how much we appreciate all you have done for us," I replied.

"What's this about a meal?" Jehoshaphat interrupted with enthusiasm. "I've nearly wasted away on this long, trying journey. I think that is Elizabeth's true intention for these trips, you know," he whispered in my ear with bulging eyes, just loud enough for everyone to hear. "That's right," he continued, walking into his house. "She's trying to make me skinny like you, Lazarus! Long and lean... like a string bean!" We all broke out in laughter as we followed them inside.

After cleaning up after dinner, we all gathered around the table to hear about their trip. Deborah didn't waste any time but came right out and asked Jehoshaphat about my pottery sales.

"So Jehoshaphat, how did Mary's vessels do?"

"Shh! Deborah! I'm sure Jehoshaphat and Elizabeth will share the details after they settle in from their trip."

Nobody could contain Deborah's personality when she was within the safety of our family. And I was slightly embarrassed to find out in front of everyone.

What if they didn't sell? I thought with concern.

"No, no, young Mary, we are happy to share! Don't be silly. There is no need to wait! They sold wonderfully, just as I'd expected!" Jehoshaphat replied.

"That's right, Mary, we sold every one of your pieces!" Elizabeth said. "And your red earthenware pitcher… It sold for five denarii on its own! A very wealthy Roman woman couldn't take her eyes off of it! Once she was allowed to touch it and feel the smooth, delicate design, she made us an offer we couldn't refuse! She then bought all your little honey pots and requested more information about the 'exquisite potter'!" She clapped her hands and shook with delight as she shared the news.

"Wow, five denarii! Mary, that is incredible!" Lazarus sat back in his chair with amazement.

"That's right! I told her it was made by our apprentice, Mary of Bethany, and the woman then insisted we bring more of your vessels on our next trip."

"Ha ha! What joy, young Mary! What joy you bring us all!" Jehoshaphat placed a small coin purse on the table and looked at Lazarus, who nodded as he slid the purse to me.

"For you, my dear girl," Elizabeth added.

"Good for you, Mary. Father and Mother would be so proud. You deserve this!" Lazarus clapped with pride, bringing tears to my eyes.

"Thank you all so much. I wouldn't be in this place if it wasn't for your kind love and guidance. If it's all right with everyone, I'd like you to bring this to Martha, Lazarus. I have more than I need in our house, brother. God has been so good to us, with the wages earned from the garden," I responded politely.

"Ah, dear Mary, I think that's a wonderful idea," Elizabeth responded.

"Lazarus will know what to do with all your earnings. There will be much more to come. Don't you worry about that! Did you happen to make it down to the stream?" Jehoshaphat asked.

"Oh, yes! Deborah and I went down this morning and were so delighted to see everything complete! It's a lovely little cottage, and the two fire pits will be so helpful!"

Deborah and I carried on with enthusiasm, expressing how much we liked this and that.

"I'm glad you like it, young Mary! I would like to give you that place to work from someday, and I plan to build a permanent kiln there as well. Did you see I have already begun digging the ditch?"

"Yes, I did. I would be honored," I replied.

"We would be honored, dearest Mary. What is ours is yours." Elizabeth dabbed little tears from her eyes with the end of her shawl.

"We are just so proud of you, and I know your mother and father gave us the greatest blessing when they asked for you to join us."

More tears flowed, and I rose from my place to embrace her.

Then Lazarus began talking business with Jehoshaphat and Deborah, so Elizabeth and I took that moment to head outside. We walked over to the wagon to unpack all their personal items as well as their newly acquired sacks of almonds and pistachios. Elizabeth pulled out a small wrapped cloth filled with dates and figs.

"I tucked these away from Jehoshaphat during the trip home. I want to make another pai, and I know he would have eaten them all if he had the chance." Elizabeth winked as we giggled.

"Mary?" Elizabeth was about to go on, when Deborah appeared ready to help. She handed her a few things and sent her back inside. Elizabeth spoke quietly to keep our conversation private.

"Yes?" I asked, my head tilted.

"I hope you don't mind that we gave out your name. Jehoshaphat and I were so blessed by the interest in your vessels that we thought some of the people may just travel to Bethany to purchase more. I never stopped to think if that would be okay with you," she said cautiously.

"Oh, I see. Elizabeth, it's fine. I'm honored, really. I understand that my work is becoming desirable, and I am blessed to earn wages for my family"—I took her tiny hand in mine—"my whole family."

Elizabeth lifted my hands together and kissed them, just like Mother used to. "I don't know what is coming around the corner for you, dearest Mary. But I do know God is with you. I feel it every time I hear you speak. Thank you for your love."

She stepped away and selected a few more satchels before going inside. I had a few minutes alone, so I decided to pray.

Most of our prayers were memorized and recited at certain times of day or on special occasions. But I was different. I was always different. Something would rise up inside me, from my belly, and lead me to simply talk to God. Whenever I closed my eyes, I just believed God could hear me.

"God, thank you for my blessings. Thank you for Jehoshaphat and Elizabeth. Thank you for my family. I yield my life to you, like clay in the potter's hands. Please bring me the love Grandmother spoke of. I do not want to be a burden to my family any longer." A few desperate tears dripped down onto my hands, and I lifted my head up toward the twinkling stars.

"You are somewhere up there, God. I don't know where or how, but I believe. I may not understand much, but I know there is more to life… and I am searching."

Chapter Fourteen

"The welfare of your innermost being…"
Proverbs 4:23, TPT

I WAS TWENTY YEARS OLD ON the day he walked in. Elizabeth and I were alone in the workshop while Jehoshaphat was taking some extra pieces down to the small pottery cottage by the stream. I heard the bell chime at the opening of the door but didn't lift my head. The summer season of Tammuz was so hot and dry that I'd removed my hair veil and tied my hair up above my head. I was in the privacy of my family and in the back of the shop, where I was unseen. Or so I thought.

I could hear Elizabeth in conversation with a man up front and continued to work while she conducted business as usual.

"How may I help you, sir?" Elizabeth welcomed the tall stranger into her shop.

"Hello, my name is Lavan. I'm here in search of a potter," he said in a commanding voice.

"Well, you have come to the right place! All potters and pottery here! Do you speak of my husband, Jehoshaphat?" she asked.

"There was a name given on the streets of Jerusalem during the almond blossom market, a Mary of Bethany? Her work is deeply desired, and I have come to inquire if there are any new pieces for sale."

"Oh, how wonderful. Yes, if you would follow me over here to this corner, you'll find everything made by Mary. There are a few earthenware cooking vessels. They are her most popular pieces among the women in the village. And here are a few pitchers and vases. She also makes a variety of our plates in an array of colors and patterns."

The man grunted in reply, seeing the prices posted near the pieces.

"I see you have traveled quite a distance. I can sell you any of the marked vessels here, but if you wish to speak with my husband on the cost, you will have to wait until after the noon hour. He will be back by that time, and I'm sure he can discuss them with you. Please take your time looking around, and I will be right back to assist you."

Elizabeth came through the hinged middle doors to inform me of the customer's lingering presence. When she did, the door swung open, and I was suddenly looking up at a pair of dark brown eyes on a statuesque physique.

"Your hair, Mary!" Elizabeth quickly whispered.

But it was too late. The man leaned his head to the side to catch another glimpse of me, seeing the messy tassel of dark waves spilling down my neck and shoulders.

I quickly pulled down my hair, tossed it into a braid, and wrapped it up, not allowing even the slightest curl to show.

"The man out front is here to see your work, dearest Mary. Go wash up, and I will wrap up your work and go fetch Jehoshaphat," Elizabeth said with excitement.

About twenty minutes later, I emerged through the front door of the shop. I entered from the outside in an attempt to seem composed. The man stood at the counter with a small selection of plates and pitchers waiting to be wrapped.

"Hello, my name is Mary, sister of Lazarus, apprentice of the master potter, Jehoshaphat." I bowed my head to be respectful and continued, "He will be back shortly to see you have found everything you need."

"Oh, but I have!" he said with the brightest smile.

"In that case, I can collect the purchase price and wrap your things for you," I said with a smile, walking behind the counter. "Jehoshaphat is coming back from our other work site. It's been a work in progress, but this additional shop will allow us to produce a greater quantity of vessels per month. I'm glad you have found everything you came for." I wrapped the plates in a thin burlap cloth, placing everything into a thicker leather satchel the man provided.

"I would enjoy meeting the shop owner. The woman who was here before you said he would return by the noon hour. Is that correct?" he asked.

"Yes, or sooner," I replied simply.

Jehoshaphat didn't normally leave Elizabeth and me to ourselves in the shop. I wanted to encourage the man to step outside as quickly as possible.

"If it would be all right with you, I'm very hungry from my trip, and I'm not sure where I can go around here for a meal. Would you show me?" The man placed a generous pile of coins upon the counter-top for the pottery.

"Oh, that's far too much, sir. Please allow me to count out the proper amount for you."

"No, thank you. I have given the correct price. Simply put it away for your teacher," he demanded.

"Yes, sir." I nodded. "Thank you very much. I can lead you down the road toward the village market, if you please. You will find many carts to choose from there." I held open the shop door, encouraging the man outside.

"Does your husband deal in trade, Mary? Might I meet him down in the market to thank him for your pieces?" he asked with surprising interest.

"Thank you, but no. I have no husband. I live with my brother, Lazarus, in our late father's estate. He will most likely be found down at the local synagogue. He's a rabbi who also deals in the fishing trade. I would be happy to lead you to him if you like." I felt relieved to be outside among the locals, walking and talking in public.

"That won't be necessary, thank you. I'm… uh… a tradesman my-self. I travel often from Jerusalem out into the neighboring countries. I purchase and acquire goods for the Roman palace." He spoke openly, slightly hesitant with his words.

I was taken aback by his desire for further conversation.

"How interesting. So you're a Roman?" I asked with respect.

"No! A Roman? What gave you that idea? I am… Jewish, like you. I work as a… liaison between the Roman palace and the Jewish people." He said quickly, almost seeming nervous.

"My, what a prestigious job you have," I said as we continued toward the gathering of tradesmen and into the market square.

"You should find all that you need here, sir. Thank you for your purchase, and please come again." I bowed my head and attempted to turn and leave. But the man took hold of my arm and turned me back toward him firmly.

"Thank you, Mary. May I see you again?" He released my arm almost as quickly as he took it, not wanting to be seen reaching out for an unknown woman.

"If you wish." I nodded politely. "Please, stop by after your meal, and I will introduce you to Jehoshaphat properly. What did you say your name was, again?" I bowed my head again to show him respect.

"My name is Lavan, of… uh… Jerusalem. And yes, I think I will return later this afternoon before I travel home. Thank you for your assistance, Mary. I will be sure to express your helpfulness to your master." He waved a bronzed hand in the air to say goodbye and turned to head toward the market.

I felt butterflies fluttering within me. The man, though more forward than most, was extremely handsome, and not melting at his feet had taken great composure. After a short few steps, I peered back over my shoulder to see him gazing back at me while biting into an apple.

A few hours later, we were all gathered in front of the shop. Elizabeth had returned with her husband, and they were in awe of the stranger's generous payment. I had taken my afternoon meal at Deborah's, telling her all about this man's obvious interest in me while she worked on another sewing project. We giggled at his failed attempts to make conversation. She was convinced he would return and encouraged me to pay attention. After a quick meal, I hurried back to the shop with curiosity.

I sat on a small stool behind the counter, listening to Jehoshaphat's ideas for new inventory and wondering if Deborah was right. *Will he come back?*

Then the door bell chimed, and in walked Lavan.

"Greetings!" said Jehoshaphat.

The man nodded as he turned to close the door.

"Welcome back, sir!" said Elizabeth. "This is my husband, Jehoshaphat, the master potter here. We are so grateful for your generous purchase this afternoon. I trust you found everything you needed?" She placed a hand on her husband's back, smiling and tilting her head in the man's direction.

"Ah! What a blessing it is to meet you, sir." Jehoshaphat reached out his hand for a shake.

The man took a strong grasp of his hand and said, "Lavan. My name is Lavan. I come from Jerusalem. I have purchased all of Mary's vessels that would suit my needs, and I have returned to have a word with the woman if she is able," the man asked boldly.

Jehoshaphat turned toward me with surprise then smiled.

I stood up at once and nodded in agreement. *What does he want now? Surely, he isn't interested in me.*

"Sure! Mary, why don't you speak with Lavan here in the shop? Take down any special orders he may have, and Elizabeth and I will take our discussion into the back room. Call if you need anything else, Lavan." With that, Jehoshaphat shook his hand once more and took his wife behind the swinging middle door.

Once we were alone, I remained behind the counter, and Lavan stepped forward and sat at the counter stool.

"Thank you for leading me to find a meal. I was again able to get everything I needed," Lavan said.

"You are welcome. It's a lovely village market here in Bethany. We have a large number of travelers that pass through, either from Jerusalem to the Sea of Galilee or the reverse," I said factually.

"I frequently pass through as well, in my trade dealings, that is," he replied. "I wondered, Mary. Might I see you again?" He stood and adjusted his clothing, looking deep into my eyes.

"I'm mostly here, at the potter's shop, or occasionally at the new workshop Jehoshaphat is finishing. I'm sure I will have more vessels made by the time of your next visit," I responded in an attempt to filter out his intentions. It worked.

"Thank you. As much as I will have an interest in your work, I'd like to see you again, Mary, if I may be so bold. I would like to share a meal with you and get to know you some more. I have traveled through Bethany many times but somehow missed a beauty such as yourself. When you shared that you are unmarried, I wondered if I might just have a chance!" Again, he spoke boldly.

Something about him was very untraditional. He never truly crossed any lines that any interested man might have to cross to get to know a woman.

I hesitated for a moment, then responded, "I'm sure I could speak to my brother, and we could entertain you for a meal if you would like his blessing to see me again." I could feel my face turning strawberry red, and I stared at the floor, waiting for his response.

"Yes! If that is best…" he nearly shouted in his eagerness. "That is… May I take a few walks with you in the village first so we might get to know one another before something so formal?"

"Well, as you know, it could stir some rumors if we are seen by the villagers sharing in private conversation…" I paused, thinking of a solution. "Why don't you collect some food on your way to the shop on your next trip? Then we can share here with Jehoshaphat and Eliza-beth. I'm sure they won't mind allowing us an afternoon break outside under the tree. We will be in their sight and can continue to share." I rested my hands on the counter, leaning slightly toward this beautiful man, awaiting his response.

"What a great idea. That's what I'll do! I will be passing through again in four days. Look for me just before noon?" he asked again with his bright gleaming smile.

"I will," I replied.

Lavan nodded and slapped one hand on the counter, nearly touching mine.

"Tell your master of our plans, and I will see you again."

He almost stumbled, walking backward toward the door. He was fidgeting with his hands and couldn't take his eyes off me. I couldn't believe what was happening.

After Lavan had gone, I turned quickly in search of Elizabeth. I shared with her everything that had happened with the man and told her about his intentions.

Jehoshaphat and Elizabeth spoke privately about it for a few days after that then gave me their blessing to visit with the man once again if he should return. They asked only that I stay within sight and keep it brief.

Sure enough, in four days, Lavan returned. Then again and again, week by week, he would come during the afternoon meal and share it with me under the back tree. To my surprise, he asked about my life. He asked why I hadn't married and if my brother Lazarus would consent to a new betrothal. I explained my likely condition in the vaguest way possible and spoke of my lack of expectation to be wed. Lavan didn't seem moved a bit by my situation. If anything, he was more eager each time he came to visit.

Meeting Lavan felt like a dream. He'd come so simply into my life, and talking to him was easy. I'd never met a man so interested in me and my daily routines.

As the months passed, I was beginning to imagine a life with Lavan. Deborah couldn't believe that such an attractive Jewish man even existed, and she wanted me to introduce her on his next visit.

Lavan agreed that on his next trip, we would gather for an evening meal and arrange the details when he got into the village. Unfortunately, that would have to wait several months. He and his assistants would be traveling to Egypt in search of a particular load of stone.

Chapter Fifteen

"With the skill of a poet…"
Psalm 71:15-17, TPT

E LIZABETH HAD GONE HOME EARLY for the night, leaving me to finish my work alone. Jehoshaphat had not yet returned from the marketplace, so I had a few more hours until he closed the shop. That was the day before Sabbath, and the crowds were often cumbersome. I was grateful for his delay.

I was working on some new designs for lidded bowls and couldn't seem to get the handles just right—too thin, and they would burst in the kiln; too thick, and they wouldn't have that feminine style I was going for. After all, women were the main source of my elegant pottery sales. Although nothing I was making was ready for firing just yet, I was onto something.

Hours went by in near silence as I worked alone. Only the sounds of my wheel turning, the water splashing through my hands, and the gentle wind on the shutters kept me company.

Just as suddenly as the wind changed, in walked Lavan. He came in through the side entrance of the workshop, avoiding the bell, most likely in an attempt to surprise me. I rose from my work, clay and water dripping from my hands.

"You surprised me! What are you doing here, Lavan?" I asked.

"I came in early to see you, Mary! I know I'll be traveling quite far over the next few months, and I didn't want to go that long without seeing you."

Lavan was very tall and very bronze, and had the silkiest black hair spilling down to his shoulders. His nose was straight and slightly pointed, coming down just over the thick mustache covering his sculpted lips. He stood there smiling with his deep, dark-brown eyes, broad-chested and muscular, with the brightest teeth I'd ever seen.

Knowing that Lavan was a Jewish tradesman working for the head Roman guard made me feel great pride at the sight of him. He was often traveling to and from Jerusalem, out into the smaller towns and villages, in search of whatever was needed at the palace. His size and stature were rare for a Jewish man, which made him perfect for the role of bartering and making demands between two cultures. I could see why he said most people would not dare to challenge him.

"Well, I am delighted to see you! Let me just wrap up my work and clean up. Then we can enjoy the lovely evening together."

My heart racing, I hurried to wrap my newly shaped lid in a sopping wet cloth, then I lifted my largest ceramic wine jug back up onto its shelf to be glazed another day. Once I was finished washing and tidying up the shop, I found Lavan seated on a large bale of hay, waiting for me in a doze.

"All finished," I said like a little girl who'd just completed her chores. "Jehoshaphat should be tied up at the market for a few more hours, and Elizabeth has gone home early this evening. Would you like to head over to my home? Martha, my sister, is staying with us. She will have dinner started, I'm sure. Lazarus is back from his trip to Galilee, and he is eager to meet you!"

"Ah, so you've told your brother about me?" he asked.

"I did. I shared about the pottery you purchased from Jehoshaphat at the market a few months back and how that sent you to his village shop for more. Each trip you made to see me not only blessed me but showed my brother your intentions were serious. I told Lazarus about your job and where you are from, and that, well… like you said, you wanted to come back after your next trip to talk about a betrothal. Even though it's so sudden, I thought it best to share that much with my brother." My face must have turned bright pink, because Lavan cleared his throat in embarrassment. "Don't be worried, though. I assured him of your character and that he would get to meet you well before that." I sat down beside him on the hay and waited for his response. I could hardly contain my excitement, so I bit my lip to keep from going on and on.

"Mary, you are such a delight for weary traveling eyes. I have something for you." Lavan leaned over and reached into his satchel. He pulled out a small golden pot and handed it to me.

Gasping, I shifted my weight to face him. "Lavan, this is... beautiful!"

"Its beauty does not compare with yours, Mary. Please accept this as your bride price, for your hand in marriage. It's pure gold, poured and shaped in Rome. See those crystals? Those are diamonds from a faraway country. And these here? Fresh pearls pulled from the Mediterranean. Open it." He spoke with such dominance and excitement that I was moved to obey. "Smell that? The most expensive spikenard from the markets in India. This gift is worth far too little, compared to you, Mary."

"Oh, Lavan, I don't know what to say! It smells wonderful, like something I have only dreamed about. It's as if I'm there, in India!"

I rose from my seat and pulled Lavan by the hands until we were both standing face to face. "Let's go to my home and share this moment with Lazarus! You can stay as long as you'd like, to get to know everyone. Oh, Deborah and Martha will be thrilled! Then we will make all our arrangements together. Surely, you will want me to come with you, back to Jerusalem?"

"Now, Mary, I did come early to surprise you, but unfortunately, I am headed into Egypt for the next few months. I don't have the time to stay and celebrate with you right now or meet your brother. My group is down at the village fountain, preparing to leave first thing in the morning."

"All right, then... why don't I run home to fetch him? I can have him meet us in the village. I'm sure he will be pleased to thank you for your generous gift, on behalf of my late father."

"You see, Mary? Look, I have more." He pulled from his satchel a large folded cloth, and in it were cheese, olives, figs, and a long, crusty loaf of bread. He also took out a small clay pot. I immediately recognized it. It was one of many starter pots I'd made some time ago.

How did he get that?

He must have purchased one from the spring sale in Jerusalem, I quickly answered myself, brushing off the suspicion entirely.

He then lifted up a large jug. I thought it was full of water, but Lavan went on to tell me it was wine.

"I am going to be gone for such a long time I want to spend these moments here with you, my bride. Celebrate with me, Mary, and we can plan to meet your family and do whatever you wish when I return. I have made no further plans beyond this trip to Egypt. Afterward, I will return to Bethany and stay."

"What can I say, Lavan? Of course we can."

Inside my heart, I had a pang of curiosity, but I gave it no time to bloom into something more. Lavan sat us back down on the large bale of hay and laid out a spread of delicious treats. He walked up to the front of the shop and pulled two fine ceramic chalices from the shelf, leaving two gold coins on the counter in their stead. While pouring the aromatic red wine, he smiled down at me, gazing into my eyes, melting me into a puddle. He was the most handsome man I had ever laid eyes on. I could not believe he was choosing me.

Just then I had a horrifying thought: *You can bear him no children. You are worthless. What man would want you?*

Fear rose up in my heart. I suddenly realized he'd never responded to my explanation about children and not being married.

Lavan handed me a chalice, and I paused.

After taking a deep breath, I asked him, "Do you remember that day you and I spoke about marriage, under the tree? When I told you about... my possible barrenness." I swallowed hard, cringing inside, grasping my chalice to the point of nearly breaking it.

"Yes, Mary, I remember. I have thought about it and decided you are worth it. I come from a large family, and children are of an abundance. If your God—" He cleared his throat. "Our God, wants to grant us a child, I will be overjoyed. And if not, like I said, you are worth it."

He waited patiently for my response, with his hand gently on mine. I turned his palm around and twisted my fingers into his.

Lavan didn't move a muscle except to lift our celebratory wine to his lips.

"Drink with me, Mary! Today is going to be the most wonderful day!"

I drank.

About an hour had gone by, and I was feeling dizzy and giggly. Lavan had his strong secure arms around me, protecting me from anything that might dare to ruin our moment. As I rested against him, full and drowsy, he shifted his weight. He cleaned up all the food and tucked each item, except my golden pot of spikenard, into his satchel. Then he returned to me.

"Mary?" he asked me.

I was too dazed to respond beyond a subtle "hmm?"

"I plan to kiss you just now." He lifted me from the hay bale and laid me back against a sloping pile on the floor. Lavan knelt beside me, and I felt his lips touch mine. The taste of honey was sweet on his tongue, followed by the spice of the fragrant wine. I was in heaven, or so I thought.

All his weight began to bear down on top of me, and I could feel the scruff of his beard against my neck.

"Lavan," I whispered.

But he did not respond. My arms were being lifted above my head. I noticed he had grasped my wrists tightly in one hand.

"Lavan," I said again, clearing my throat with more effort.

But he did not respond. His kisses left my mouth and trailed all over me. In a sudden moment, he pressed down upon me, lifted my tunic, and took me as his wife.

"Lavan, you mustn't!" I cried out desperately.

He continued, ignoring my pleas. My breath was faint, and tears welled up in my eyes. Feeling his strength crushing and holding my body down in the hay, I gave up all hope of freeing myself.

Before I knew what had happened, Lavan was off me, lifting me back onto the bale of hay where we'd shared our wine. Pulling hay from my tunic and his, he quickly looked around the shop, I assumed he wanted to make sure we were still alone.

I wrapped my arms around myself and began to shake. The room was spinning, and I could hardly keep one thought from blurring into another.

Lavan took my shawl and wrapped it around my shoulders.

"Come, Mary, I'll walk you home before it gets too dark." He reached down for my hand.

"I... I... I cannot go home like this. I have had too much to drink. Lazarus will be suspicious. It's not right for a woman to drink, in my circumstances."

"How about the new potter's shed you told me about, down the valley by the stream? Has Jehoshaphat finished it yet?"

"Yes, he has. I suppose I can gather a few things and go. It isn't unbelievable that I would have worked too long on a piece and decided to stay the night."

"Good," Lavan sounded pleased.

"Mary, do not worry. This secret is safe between us. I will be back for you in a few months. Then we will have all the time in the world to share our news with your friends and family."

I nodded, helpless and at his mercy. Wiping the tears from my eyes, I tried to compose myself.

What do I do, Mother? I cried in my heart. *God, forgive me.*

"Show me which vessels you want to bring with you, and I'll gather them. Then I'll walk you down the valley to the shed."

After selecting a few meaningless clay pots, Lavan and I locked up and headed for the new potter's shed. It was just past the outer wall, down a fertile valley lined with cypress trees, wildflowers, and tall grass. Jehoshaphat had been using the new cottage for larger vessels. He was building the permanent kiln twice the size of the one in town. With less concern for intense heat and flames, he could fire larger pieces. I knew that when we got close enough, the dull embers from the stone firepit would be glowing and would light the way.

The night was dark and on the hunt for more helpless victims. The songs of the sweet day birds were replaced by the occasional calling of owls and the barking of dogs. Insects flew wildly through the black sky, chased by hungry bats now impatient for their long-awaited meals.

I was cold and confused. *What just happened?* As the effects of the wine faded, I could think more clearly, and reality began to overwhelm me. Lavan was walking quietly beside me. He grunted and sighed with relief, lost in his own thoughts. I am sure he was reliving the satisfaction of those stolen moments.

Why isn't he saying anything? I wondered as a brand-new battle between fear and confusion was birthed inside my mind.

"Lavan..." I muttered.

He turned and looked down toward me.

"Did we...? Did you—"

"Mary, don't be so naïve. What we did is only normal. We are to be married, and I was only claiming what is now mine. You have the golden pot of Indian spikenard I gave you, right?"

I could feel the pot rubbing against my thigh as I walked, reminding me of his claim.

"Yes," I said.

"Good. When you are ready, give it to your brother. Or you can wait until I return, and we can give it to him together."

"When will you be back for me?"

"Mary, I already told you, in about three to four months. After my trip to Egypt, we will be transporting a great load of white marble stone to the palace in Jerusalem. Then, once everything is finished, I will come to you here in Bethany."

I reached for his big strong hand and held on to it.

"All right, Lavan, I will wait."

After a few more moments, the faint amber light of the dying fires lit up the newly cleared path, and the cottage became visible.

"Is this it, Mary?" Lavan asked.

"We are here. Won't you come in?"

"I'd better be off now. The fellows will be turning in soon, and they'll be looking for me."

He handed me the satchel with the leftover food and clay pots, reached out, and grasped my shoulder. "Mary, your beauty is enchanting. The pleasure of you will stay with me along my journey." Then he turned and walked off into the night.

―――――――

After unlatching the door, I pushed it open into a dark, lightless space. I dropped the satchel to the ground and took off the shawl Lavan had wrapped me in. Reaching up to my head, I felt my veil still in place. I tore it off and threw it to the floor. I stood staring into nothingness and didn't move a muscle. Fear danced around me in the pitch-black room, and I didn't try to stop it. I simply stood there, alone, ready to be taken by whatever might have been lurking there.

I removed my sandals and turned around, reentering the danger of the night. I picked up a large iron fire poker and split open some of the remaining ashen logs. Glowing embers of dust floated up into the sky. I watched them float into the trees and disappear.

I wanted to disappear.

I tossed a new log into the fire, and it began to burn violently. So I sat in the sand and watched the flames consume the flesh of the wood.

Lavan will come back for me. After all, he gave me a highly valuable price. No man would give such expensive spikenard for any other reason.

I repeated that thought again and again in an attempt to drown out fear's stinging voice: ***"It wasn't love, Mary. You are not worthy of love. He took the only thing you have to offer, your beauty. This is your future now, your worthless future."***

"No!"

I screamed into the darkness.

"Nooo! Mother, where are you? Mother, why is this happening to me? Mother, help me!"

I fell facedown in the sand, trembling in fear and holding myself around my knees, crying and sobbing. I continued to call for help.

"God… Please, God, be near to me."

"I am a broken vessel, one unworthy of holding anything precious."

"Oh, God, please cleanse me. Have mercy. Where are you? Where am I?"

"Please bring him back to me, my true love."

"Grandmother prophesied over me. She said a love will come for me, one who will never leave nor forsake me. Let it be as you have said."

Chapter Sixteen

"Out of thee shall he come…"
Micah 5:2, KJV

I LIFTED MY BODY OFF THE hard dewy sand and sat there. The flame that had burned through the night was extinguished, leaving behind the dead, charred remains of wood. I wiped my face with the edge of my wrinkled tunic and swept sand from my ear. My limbs were weak and quaking as I stood exposed to the wilderness around me. Quickly, I straightened my clothes and my belongings in the cottage. At any moment, someone might have come looking for me to account for my absence. I had to make the cottage look like I'd been working throughout the night.

I started a new fire and set up the sand firing pit in preparation for my… already fired clay pot.

Why did I grab something already fired? How convincing, Mary. Way to go, I criticized myself as I hurried.

"The bucket hanging on the edge of the fence should be filled with water!" I shouted.

I grabbed it and took off for the stream. When I reached the water's edge, I dipped my toes into the cool water and, for one minute, began to unwind. The stones were smooth and slippery under my feet, so I moved slowly. Birds were singing again, the sun was rising, and a new day had come. Things did not look as desolate.

I scooped as much water into the bucket as I could carry and set it on the ground next to me. Lifting my tunic and shift above my knees,

I knelt upon the smooth, rocky edge. Untying my braid, I loosed my hair. It fell into dark sweeping waves around my face and spilled down to my waist. I cupped my hands into the water and lifted it up onto my head over and over until I could feel the cold water trickling down my neck. Each splash felt so-cold and refreshing… So cleansing. I rinsed my hair thoroughly then washed my face and arms of the charcoal smears left from sleeping too close to the fire. I sat back into the water and washed the rest of my body as quickly as I could, trying to remove the memory he had left with me. After I was finished, I rebraided my hair, dried myself, and headed back to the shed.

When I returned to the gate, I could see someone had opened the cottage door and propped it with a stone.

Who is here?

"Relax, Mary. No one will know anything. Just explain how tired you were from working far too late."

Where did that thought come from? Am I really going to lie?

"Hello?" I called out. "Anyone there?" I waited outside the gate.

For a split second, I wondered if Lavan was back, coming to say a quick goodbye. But I knew that was foolish.

A familiar voice rang through the air. "Mary!" Out popped Deborah. "Mary! You are here! I stopped by your place this morning to see if you wanted to spend the day together. It's nearly Sabbath, you know. While I was there, Lazarus mentioned you didn't come home last night. He'd gone down to Jehoshaphat's pottery workshop last night, looking for you. When you weren't there, he assumed you were with me. So, obviously, to his surprise, when I showed up without you, he was worried. I told him you might have come here to work last night, and sure enough, here you are!"

"Oh," I managed pathetically.

"You were right. I was here." I came through the gate and set the bucket down near the fire.

"Mary, why didn't you send word to your brother?" Deborah asked. "It's not like you to wander off in the dark of night."

I walked past her into the shed and sat on one of the benches. "Here, come sit with me. I have some figs and bread left from my dinner last night, and I have something to show you."

Deborah came inside and joined me at the small table.

I reached into the deep inner pocket of my shift and pulled out the golden pot Lavan had given to me and set it on the table.

"What is that?" Wide-eyed and excited, Deborah lifted it into the air so the sunlight could shine upon it.

"Wow! Mary, where on earth did you get this!"

"It's from Lavan."

"No…" she said in disbelief. "The man from the market? The one buying up all your fancy jars and vases? Really? Why?"

"Well, I told you he was serious about me, Deborah. He surprised me yesterday evening at Jehoshaphat's shop and gave me this. He asked for my hand in marriage and said this was the finest price he could think to offer Lazarus. He said I could keep it and wait until he returns, and we could give it to him together, or I could give it to him now and tell him we are to be married."

Deborah leaped from her bench, knocking it over and nearly spilling the food to the floor.

"That's amazing, Mary! Congratulations! A little untraditional, but nonetheless amazing! You are betrothed, Mary!"

"I guess I am, aren't I?" I said with a growing smile.

"Uh, yeah you are! I'm so surprised you didn't come running to me or home at least afterward. Where is Lavan now?"

"Well," I repeated, looking out the window, "he couldn't stay. Lavan and his men left early this morning for Egypt. He had only enough time to see me and give me this," I lied.

I stood and walked back outside, trying to compose myself and put on a smile.

"He wants to marry me! He really wants to marry me. I could tell. He was… very passionate about it," I said.

"So let's go home and tell Lazarus everything! When will he be back?" Deborah asked.

"Three or four months from now. Then he plans to stay in Bethany and meet all of you, staying until our plans are finished."

"That's not bad at all, Mary. You have to wait a year anyway, and it gives you plenty of time to consider everything. Like where you will live, what you will do… Wait! What will… I do?" She paused suddenly, bug-eyed at the thought of me leaving.

"Will you move to Jerusalem?"

"I'm not sure. I thought that was what he would want, but he didn't say."

"Well, not if I have a say in it!" she said, laughing. "You're twenty years old now, you old lady! You can't be moving your bones across Israel on a whim." Deborah skipped over to me and embraced me while spilling her joy into the air.

Finding her emotion contagious, I danced with her, twirling in the sand. "Oh, Mother would be so pleased to know I am wanted, that I am going to be married… Aren't I?" *Aren't I?*

"I doubt she ever thought otherwise, Mary. You are one of the most, if not *the* most, beautiful woman in all of Bethany! You are kind, smart, adventurous, and a godly woman! Someone worthy was bound to come along and sweep you off your feet! Now, let me see that *gold* again!" She let me go and went on the hunt for my bounty.

On our way home, Deborah and I talked about her father's current situation. He had never fully returned from the land of mourning, even after a season of working his fields. After the harvest season, her father ended up right back in the bottle. Deborah was been left to pick up the pieces again, just like when she was little.

Her mother had been a well-known seamstress. Even while she battled her sickness, her work was simply wonderful. Without her mother, Deborah had to take on the cleaning, cooking, sewing, selling in the market, and so much more.

She was a true woman of God, despite everything she has gone through. Her joy never once diminished, and she kept moving forward. I was blessed to have her friendship and support. As we walked and I listened to her new idea, about embroidering designs on veils, I felt the pain of guilt. Not once, since we were young girls, had I ever kept a secret from Deborah.

Maybe I should tell her.

She interrupted my private thoughts. "So what do you think, Mary?"

"Great! I think it's a great idea, Deborah!" I grabbed her arm and hugged it. "In fact, Jehoshaphat has been considering inviting me to travel with him and Elizabeth into Jerusalem this October for the Festival of Booths. Maybe I should tell him we both would love to join."

"What? Of course you should! This is more great news! With your pottery and my clothing, we will take over the Jerusalem marketplace! You know my uncle has brought my work with him for the last few years. I have gone a couple of times, but never to have my own booth! That is where I've gotten all my big business from, Mary. Apparently, someone in the high priest's chamber service was wearing one of my garments, and word spread like wildfire. Now I'm designing tunics, veils, turbans, and shawls for all the servants within the temple priest's palace. Hence, the issue with my father's farming. He doesn't want to take to the fields, with all the wages I'm earning. We will lose our fields if he doesn't do the work or if I can't find someone to help. I suppose I could afford to hire help, especially if we take to Jerusalem in October! I can bring more garments than I have in the past, and we will make a fortune!" Deborah spoke with such excitement, her creative mind flowing from one thought to another with ease.

"I still need to mention it to Lazarus. I wouldn't feel comfortable going without him. And then there is Mother's garden. I'll need to be sure I've tended to it for autumn. I suppose I could pack all the extra herbs and plants for sale as well."

"That's a good idea, Mary. Ask your brother to come!"

I got an elbow in the side, and when I turned to look at her face, she was glaring at me, chin raised to the sky.

"Yes, Mary, invite your brother."

This friend of mine could make me laugh with ease. I didn't know if her occasional weirdness or her loyal faithfulness made me love her more. She was definitely the one I would pick for Lazarus. Having her as an official sister would be a dream come true, and I knew Martha would agree. Whenever those two were together, we feasted. She would be thrilled to have a seasoned cook in the kitchen by her side for the festivities.

"Speaking of my brother," I said, "I don't think I'm going to show him the golden pot of nard just yet. I think it would be better if Lazarus meets Lavan first. I appreciate his passion, but Lazarus and Martha will want to see a more traditional proposal. What do you think?"

Deborah thought for a little while then said, "You will know what's right for your family. If you think waiting is better, then go with that. When Lavan comes back into town, you can introduce him to me first. That will make your brother feel more comfortable as well."

"Thanks, Deborah, for everything. You are such a good friend." And I meant it. I really needed her right then.

My eyes flooded with fresh tears as painful flashes of the previous night crowded my mind.

I love Deborah so much. How can I hide this from her? She's been with me since we were young girls. She helped pick me up after Eli, after Grandmother, and after Father and Mother. Where would I be without her?

We walked on, listening to the birds and watching the butterflies and bumblebees, just enjoying the endless possibilities of the new things coming toward us in life.

"Remember when we first met, Mary?" Deborah asked me.

"Of course I do, silly! I clobbered you with a giant barrel of rainwater!"

We laughed.

"Right! But more important was what Jesus was saying that day, in the back of the empty synagogue," she continued. "I know Jesus was talking about fresh manna from heaven and how God would send the Israelites just enough for each day, right?"

I nodded.

"But what he said after, about new bread and new wine coming… He was talking about the coming Messiah, right?"

"Yes, that was what I thought." I added, "Lazarus has gone back to Nazareth twice since then you know, to meet with Jesus and hear him teach. You're not the only one who brings up his teachings. Lazarus says the older Jesus gets, the more passion burns inside him and the more profound his teachings become. Why do you ask?"

"Well, it's just for that reason. Don't tell anyone I said this, but…

what if Jesus is the Messiah? He was born in Bethlehem, right? Well, I was recently reading through some copies of Micah your brother lent me, and it seemed like a prophecy about the coming Messiah. I know I am no student of the ancient scrolls, but it froze me in my tracks when I read 'Bethlehem.' I thought of Jesus right away." Deborah had stopped walking and drifted into the grassy shade off the road.

I followed her and we sat down. "You know, I don't know for sure, Deborah. That is something Lazarus would know, though. You should ask him when we reach home. He talks about the coming Messiah differently from most rabbis. I do know there have been a couple times when Jesus and his words touched my life. That incident with the snake when we were children? I'll never forget that. It was like he locked eyes with me on purpose, and I felt no fear as long as I looked at him, like he already knew I was going to be fine..."

"Wow." Deborah just sat there in thought.

"And when I was in the synagogue, watching through the crack in that old wooden door, he saw me. He never stopped talking, but I know he saw me. I thought for sure I would be in trouble and be asked to leave. Instead, it was like he smiled at me like he was happy I was listening. I turned against the wall and stopped looking after that, though, but his words truly felt like nourishment to my bones..." I paused, trying to recall more.

"You know what? He kept referring to the manna of our forefathers because he was comparing... how the coming Messiah would be the new bread, the bread of life. Now that I'm thinking about it... I felt a warmth blooming in my heart as he spoke of that. For the first time in my life, it felt like God was close to me, almost... inside me."

"That's it. I am going. We are going! The next trip your brother takes to follow the teachings of Jesus, we are going!" Deborah demanded.

I didn't disagree with her. I wanted to go too.

Maybe she's right. Maybe that's what all this has been about. All the inner searching, the waiting and expectations since my youth...

My curiosity was stirring. We got back on the road and allowed our thoughts to rule over any further conversation.

Chapter Seventeen

"The thoughts that I think…"
Jeremiah 29:11, KJV

JEHOSHAPHAT AND ELIZABETH WERE FINISHING up for the day, packing up the last few completed pots and jugs for the upcoming trip to Jerusalem. The Festival of Booths was near, the time during the autumn season for celebrating the Exodus out of Egypt and the end of our agricultural year. Many families in trade would travel to the large market festival inside and outside Jerusalem, setting up booths and tents to sell their goods. Among them were farmers, jewelers, tailors, butchers, fishermen, potters, and so many more.

Deborah and I would be traveling with them that time, opening our own booths for personal profit. I couldn't believe I'd been training under Elizabeth since I was sixteen years old. Ever since my own vessels had been selling out, requested by our customers, Jehoshaphat gave me more time and supplies to build a large collection for the festival.

I was taught to fire the smaller, simpler clay items in the open fires set up outside the shop. Learning this technique was considered only the common knowledge of pottery making. However, every so often, I would create a special bowl or vase that Elizabeth would adore, and she would ask her husband to allow me to help throughout the whole process. I was getting better and better and growing more independent in my capabilities. I thanked God regularly for this enjoyable gift.

"This trip, young Mary, will be very important for you and your pottery!" Jehoshaphat declared. "If your work can sell in Jerusalem, like the samples we brought before, then you will finally see how God has blessed the work of your hands! No more doubting!"

I was still extremely surprised to hear such confidence in me and my work. Full of gratitude, I replied, "Jehoshaphat, Elizabeth, I am so grateful to you both. You have blessed me with your knowledge and kindness through the years. I pray that God increases you both for your generosity."

Smiling, Jehoshaphat reached for Elizabeth's hand. "You have blessed us, Mary! After losing our daughter Asa at such a young age, Elizabeth and I were broken. It took great healing and trust in the Lord to restore our joy. Then God sent us your gifted hands to not only help support our livelihood but to fill the cracks in our hearts. Surely our God will continue to bless you, Mary!"

He surely has blessed me,... with Lavan! Oh, the joy that will come in just a few months when Lavan returns to make our betrothal public! Then I can finally stop worrying about what happened... Father and Mother would have been so proud, knowing their younger daughter, their precious 'pearl,' was to be married to such a man as Lavan. Surely, the news would bless Lazarus, Jehoshaphat, and Elizabeth, seeing how we all have become like one family!

Jehoshaphat startled me from my thoughts. "See to the wagon, Mary."

"Be sure that all of your pottery, and Deborah's things, are securely fastened, and that your donkey is well rested for the journey," Elizabeth added. "Well, I am sure Lazarus will help you with the preparations. Such a fine young man your brother is. We leave at dawn tomorrow!" She nodded as the two headed home to finalize their personal affairs.

As I walked around my wagon, I was amazed by how many pieces I had actually made—pots for cooking, jugs for wine, water bowls, pitchers, vases for flowers, and lidded jars for oils and spices. Each piece I'd made had unique colors and features, showing a visible increase in my skill. I'd discovered a new way to adjust the depth of color and a method of achieving different textures by adding varying amounts of sand during the firing process. Seeing the work of my hands packed up and ready for sale made me feel, just maybe, that I did have some worth left within me.

After all, Lavan had met me in Jehoshaphat's little pottery shop, tucked away in Bethany, Israel. My unique pottery brought him there, looking for more. Despite all the pain of losing Eli, I could see how that must have been God's plan for my life. The work of my hands was different from Martha's but was still very respectable and needed. And Lavan had to be the man Grandmother had always spoken of, the man who would love me and never forsake me. Maybe I wouldn't be a priest's wife, but a successful potter to a fine tradesman like Lavan... That was worthy.

Just then, a familiar, dark, cold thought entered my mind: *"You cannot bear him children. He will leave you. They will all leave you. No man will ever love you because you are worthless."*

I shook my head loose from the thought and from the fears about what had happened... I covered my items in burlap and tied them down tightly then headed to Deborah's.

The time for evening meals was approaching, and the streets were quieting. I could smell Deborah's delicious fish stew as I arrived. The warm scent of herbs and spices, which she used in her fried sourdough pancakes, filled the air. My stomach was hoping for an invitation. Sure enough, Deborah burst through her doorway, embracing me with a joyous squeeze.

"Mary! Dinner is finished, and Father has already eaten. He just left. He is going down to his brother Simeon's house for evening wine. Please come in and share it with me!"

"I'd love to, Deborah! I am so hungry, and your cooking is always a treat! But first, let's make sure you have all you'll need packed into the wagon for our trip tomorrow. Jehoshaphat wants to leave at dawn, and there will be no time to return if we forget something."

"All right," Deborah replied. "I have one more veil I finished embroidering this morning. I'll go wrap it up and grab the extra thread I bought today for any repairs that might be requested in Jerusalem. How exciting, Mary—our own booths!"

I followed her inside, listening as she went on talking while gathering her things.

"Lazarus is still coming, right? Father will not allow me to go unless he is there, not to mention that I enjoy his company." She winked at me. "We always have the most intriguing conversations about the scriptures, you know? I have been memorizing a passage from Jeremiah to impress him!"

Rolling my eyes, I replied, "Oh, Deborah, nothing pleases me more than to hear how much you adore my older brother." I giggled. "You know he is focused on being a rabbi, traveling from town to town all over Israel, learning the oral traditions. You may be waiting for quite some time before he is ready to take a wife."

Deborah carried on, quoting beautifully from Jeremiah, *"For I know the thoughts that I think toward you, says the Lord, thoughts of peace and not of evil, to give you a future and a hope."*

"Wow, that was great, Deborah! We are blessed women to have learned from my brother and father, aren't we?" I took a moment to appreciate how uncommon it was for women to be taught anything from the Torah, let alone to memorize pieces of it.

She agreed then continued, "I know most women are already married by now, and I know I may not be his first choice. But Mary, I know God thinks of me, and I trust Him to be faithful, just as He was to Ruth. Just like this scripture says, God has a future for us, one full of hope. I will honor my father, work hard to please him, and provide since his... sickness. And when God sees fit, He will lead me to my husband."

"To Lazarus, you mean."

We both broke out in laughter as Deborah blushed a rosy pink.

"There. All set," she said.

"This is the last satchel I have to pack, Mary. Oh, and by the way, did you tell your brother yet?"

Deborah handed her things to me, and I shook my head.

"No. I'm still sure I want to wait until Lavan is here with me."

"Hmm, all right. But I want to have another look at that golden pot, Mary!" Deborah teased with laughter.

I turned and headed out to secure her items in the wagon and tie off the donkey in the small common stable. The smells of dinner were making me eager to get back inside, and I skipped with anticipation.

I still wasn't the best cook, no matter how many lessons Martha gave me, so I really appreciated Deborah's cooking.

I'd better bring some home for Lazarus.

That night was a rare quiet one for Deborah and me, and we ate, laughed, and fellowshipped without anyone else needing our attention. It was a perfect night for me to come clean and share everything with her.

I chose not to.

Ever since her mother had passed away the year before, her father continued to lose himself in drinking and mourning. He still had sudden bouts of rage, often getting violent and belligerent toward her. And because he neglected the land, Deborah's once delicate hobby had become a full trade for her in just a matter of weeks. Fortunately, her spinning, weaving, and tailoring skills supplied her and her father with more than enough money to upkeep their home and basic needs. Once again, Deborah's strength amazed me.

God had blessed her work and given her favor above many other seamstresses in the region. Oftentimes, she would receive special orders from the Roman palace and even the high priest in Jerusalem. Deborah's tunics and garments had dressed the maids and servants in those palaces, spreading the desire for her work throughout the wealthy in Jerusalem. She earned a substantial profit, which allowed her the ability to purchase rare and luxurious fabrics to work with, often setting her clothing far above the competition. Deborah wasn't changed by the demand or adoration, though. She took on the orders that she could while the rest simply waited for her. She was pleased to take care of our hometown first, giving the local women priority. Bethany was already known for its trade markets, and her high demand only helped to draw more people.

Lazarus, training for ministry, still did not commit to a full-time trade. Our uncle, Mathias, continued to employ Lazarus whenever he needed the work. That was why he'd agreed to join us on our journey to Jerusalem that season. He was bringing baskets of salted fish to sell once we arrived.

After two hours of good fellowship over a good meal, I said my goodbyes to Deborah and set off for home, hardly able to wait for the sunrise.

Chapter Eighteen

"The partial will fade away."
1 Corinthians 13:9-10, TPT

IT WAS NEARLY NOON, THE Festival of Booths was upon us, and the sales didn't stop coming. I was amazed to see how busy all the potter's booths were, including mine and Jehoshaphat's. Even more exciting was that my bowl supply was nearly reduced to half by late morning, and my new lidded and handled cooking vessels were almost gone. After the first morning wave, Elizabeth, who was assisting me, noticed my pieces were selling only after a few glances. So she went to get Jehoshaphat right away, and he encouraged me to double the prices.

"Clearly your work is admired among the crowd, Mary. Your pottery is selling faster than any of the other pieces here!" Jehoshaphat tipped his head back and let out a loud chuckle, rumbling from his large belly. "I knew it from the start, young Mary. God has blessed you. Oh, what fun this will be today! Go fetch Lazarus. He will need to handle your earnings from here on out. His salted fish can be moved over here." He pointed toward the side of my booth, between Deborah and me. He laughed again and continued, "Thanks be to God for you, Mary. Your work is drawing quite the favorable crowd! Take Deborah, once your brother is ready, and go enjoy the market! Find yourselves something to bring home, something for Deborah's father, and some figs and dates for Elizabeth and me. Get extra for me." He winked and handed me ten denarii. Jehoshaphat returned to his booth and smiled at me with the love of a proud father.

I ran down the road to the fish area of the market through crowds of playing children, bartering men, and chatting women.

"Lazarus!" I shouted. "Lazarus!" I waved my arms at him until he spotted me and excused himself from a sale in progress. "Jehoshaphat has asked you to come and handle my booth. My pieces are nearly gone, and he said I'll be bringing home more than three months' wages! He thinks it's best you carry on for me, to see that everything is done correctly and that I am not robbed!" Jumping up and down, I couldn't help but giggle. "Can you believe it, Lazarus?"

"Three months of wages! Oh, Mary, how incredible! Have you sold any of the garden herbs? Any flowers or bulbs?" Lazarus asked.

"Yes, I have sold all the lavender, half a barrel of sage, and one basket of mint leaves. People are gathering them with whatever vessels they choose. Oh! And Deborah has sold every single veil and women's tunic she brought with her—not that we're surprised! It's barely noon, Lazarus!" I was so thrilled that my heart was racing. "Jehoshaphat also gave me some money to go shopping around the market with Deborah. Can you please come now?"

"Let me finish with my sale, and I will close up. Did Jehoshaphat say what to do with my fish?" Laughing and wiping the sweat from his brow, Lazarus pointed at all his remaining bushels. No one got rich from salted sardines, but that didn't diminish the demand for them.

"He said it would be okay for you to set them up next to my wares. They may even sell faster with all the attention at the booth. One-stop shopping while people wait in line!"

Lazarus nodded and walked back over to his cart. The man there must have purchased about a pound of sardines. He walked off with quite a basketful. Lazarus covered everything and secured it. Then, lifting the end of the wagon, he pulled it down into the shaded grass behind him and took the back way up the road to our area.

Deborah and I walked arm in arm through the rows of vendors, gazing and gawking at the vast displays of food, clothing, wine, and jewelry. The merchant displayed such a verity, in style and value. Back home, one couldn't find as much fine jewelry for the wealthy to indulge in. We both spent time admiring the precious gems within the necklaces, earrings, and rings.

Deborah found a pair of earrings with red rubies the size of small beans and pointed them out to me. "How beautiful, Mary. Can you imagine the garment worn with these? Such extravagance!"

"I know! Maybe someday we will have a reason to wear such things! After all, Lavan works for the Romans. Maybe we will be called in at some time for a celebration dinner!" I said wistfully. Even though my family was among the wealthy in Bethany, our income did not compare with the wealth and opulence of the Romans. "Let's go gather the dates and figs for Elizabeth. We will surely be eating her pies this coming Sabbath." I waved toward the other side of the road as a suggestion of where to shop.

Gathering about a peck of figs and dates, half that many raisins, and another half of pistachios and almonds, I handed the price to the salesman and turned in joyous satisfaction. Deborah and I took out a fig and shared it. It was sticky and sweet, a yummy treat after an intense morning of sales. We were unable to contain our joy.

I purchased four jars of wild honey, four jars of Indian cinnamon sticks, and some black-and-white peppercorns for Martha. Deborah bought lengths of fine silks, ribbons of thread, two small jars of silver and gold rhinestones, and some new sewing needles. She also found an attachment for her loom she had wanted to replace, and bought that too. As we headed back to Jehoshaphat, Lazarus, and Elizabeth, I turned to take a last look at the booth full of nuts and beans...

Then I saw him.

Lavan.

My heart raced, and I nearly spilled the baskets and sacks from my arms.

Flashing back to that late afternoon, there in the potter's shed, I could feel again the weight of his body pressing down upon me, my arms pinned over my head by his large, strong hand. The cloudiness of my mind, the blurred visions of his dark hair across my face—it all came back to me.

Fear immediately stunned me in my tracks as the realization hit me that he was not where he'd said he would be. Only about a month had passed since that... visit. Questions flooded my mind as fear took over, just like my childhood encounter with the viper.

Deborah reached out and took my arm. To her surprise, I did not move.

"Mary? Is everything all right?" she asked. When I didn't respond, she stood next to me and turned her gaze, searching to find where mine was fixed. "Who is it, Mary? Mary? What is wrong? Are you okay?"

Grabbing Deborah's hand, I pointed at the red canopy hanging over the opening of a jeweler's booth.

"It's Lavan... It's Lavan," I repeated. Barely able to speak and trembling, I turned to Deborah as fear, shame, and tears instantly showed on my face.

We stood there watching him as he laughed and conversed with the jeweler. The owner of the booth held up a strand of white freshwater pearls that glimmered an iridescent glow in the sunshine. He lowered the strand of pearls around the neck of a beautiful, tall, and slender woman. She had locks of thick black hair spilling over her shoulders and wore a deep-ruby dress embroidered with gold-and-white stitching. Every inch of her was dripping with gold—golden earrings, bangle bracelets, rings, and even her hair was dressed with golden beads and dangling jewels. She looked to be a woman of great wealth. Someone... Roman. And that was how Lavan was dressed, in the full attire of a Roman guard. Clearly, he was no Jewish man, no tradesman working between our people and the Romans.

Liar! I screamed at him in my mind.

Lavan stepped closer to the woman and kissed her cheek, and two small boys suddenly ran out from behind them, laughing and chasing one another out of the tent.

Deborah looked at me, but I kept staring.

One of the boys tripped over the rope anchoring the right corner of the tent's opening and wailed in pain. Lavan turned from the jeweler and... that woman... and walked over to the boy. He lifted him from the dirt and quickly dusted off his tunic and legs. Running his hands through the boy's black curly hair, he kissed his forehead and lifted him into his large, strong arms. He was as bronze as the sun itself, a perfectly sculpted statue. As he turned, he saw me.

I almost lunged toward him, but Deborah caught my arm again.

"No, Mary. Stop. Look," she said.

The woman had left the tent as well, still wearing the necklace and walking the other boy by the hand. She approached Lavan and wiped the tears from the injured boy's dirt-streaked cheeks. Lavan placed the boy into her arms and wrapped his around her.

He stared into my eyes and sneered. Caressing the woman's arms, he mocked me. He lifted his chin as if I were a lowly servant who had just disgusted his master. Turning toward the woman, he kissed her passionately on the lips. Not even looking back at me, Lavan turned his family and reentered the booth, leaving me to wallow in my misery.

I ran.

Clenching the sacks and baskets in my hands, I ran.

I crossed the two main roads, crowded with people and booths.

I ran.

Down into the tall, shaded grass, past the spot where Lazarus's wagon once was, and into the thickening wild.

I ran.

Farther and farther into the wilderness.

I kept going until I reached the bank of a narrow river that passed under a small bridge. Finally hidden from the eyes of men, I stopped and tossed everything in my arms down against the stone wall of the bridge.

Falling and dragging my body into the streaming water, I vomited. I could feel the rocks cutting and scraping at my palms and the soft flesh of my knees. The cold water was seeping into the fabric of my tunic.

Over and over, my body attempted to purge itself of the overwhelming shame knotting my insides. Heaving and groaning in anguish, I pulled myself deeper and deeper into the current. As I moved farther and farther from shore, my feet slipped underneath me, and I gave into the water.

It flooded over my shoulders, pulling me even deeper into the current. I didn't care. Down I went, urging my body into the water's strong flow until it passed over my head. The light slowly faded as I allowed the river to pull me down into what I desired to be, a bottomless well. I could see his face—Lavan—laughing with me in the potter's shed. Sharing his special "bridegroom's" wine with me. I replayed his lies in my mind, and they engulfed my heart and soul with their poison.

A dark voice echoed in my head: *"You are worthless. You will die alone. How could you imagine a man like that loving you? Give up now. You are worthless."*

Over and over…

Chapter Nineteen

"No place to stand…"
Psalm 69:2, TPT

AN ARM REACHED DOWN, WRAPPING around my waist. I was thrust up out of the water and dragged to the shoreline. Choking and spitting up mouthfuls of water, I began drawing in gulps of air. I could see only gray shadows all around me and a blurry figure of a person bending over me. A cloudy voice repeated unrecognizable sounds in my ear. Slowly, as air filled my body, things slowly came back into focus. I felt sick and collapsed to the ground.

Deborah had saved me.

"Mary, oh, Mary, can you hear me?" She spoke urgently, tapping my cheeks. "Mary, Mary, come back to me!"

I could hear her, but I turned silently in shame and buried my face in the muddy grass.

"Mary," Deborah implored again. "Oh, Mary, you're alive! Oh, thank God!" She laid her body next to mine, holding me tightly, and wept there with me.

Shivers overtook my body, forcing me to respond to the reality of what had just happened. I sat up, numb and still. Deborah rose to her feet and quickly grabbed a piece of cotton cloth from her satchel. She walked to the edge of the water, dipped it in, and returned to me.

As I sat there trembling and shivering, Deborah wiped the mud off my face, neck, and arms. She returned to the water again and again until no trace of mud remained on me. She then lifted me off the ground and walked me over to a pile of stones under the cover of a large sycamore tree. She removed my hair veil and outer tunic, tossed them into the sun alongside a fallen tree trunk, then wrapped me in a clean blanket.

Just then, the voice of my brother came loudly from behind us.

"Deborah? Was that you and Mary I saw running through the market?" He came into sight and reached us in four long strides, leaping over the fallen tree trunk and down to the side of the bridge where we were sitting, trying to hide.

"What happened?" Lazarus demanded.

"It was nothing!" exclaimed Deborah. Not fully understanding what had happened herself, she did her best to thwart any further inquiries from my brother. "We were running through the market when Mary lost her footing. She stumbled into the water, and I was just helping her dry off."

Looking at Deborah and me and the discarded items on the ground, Lazarus was satisfied. "I'll take your things back up to our wagon, girls. Finish drying up, and make sure you both come back decent and presentable. Jehoshaphat wants to leave the market before the evening rush. All our supplies have been sold! We each have turned quite a profit. He doesn't want to remain in Jerusalem for the feast. The crowds are too cumbersome, and there is no longer a need. It will be much better to head home and enjoy the holiday with our family and friends."

"Sure, Lazarus," Deborah added. "We were just about to return with our purchases when this happened." She managed a grin.

"Never a dull moment with you two." Lazarus smiled at Deborah.

He then bent to gather our things, leaving only Deborah's satchel, and headed up the hill toward Jehoshaphat.

I sat, staring at my palms. A small trickle of blood ran down my right hand, slightly above my wrist. I just didn't care.

"It's just a scratch, Mary. Another rinse, and it should be fine. As for your knees? Let me see what I have in my bag. We will need to bandage them up."

She rummaged through her things and brought out a small jar of beeswax and some extra cotton fabric. She tore off two long strips and laid them to the side. After rinsing my wounds again, she smeared some beeswax on my tattered knees then wrapped each one with the strips. By that point, Deborah was ready for an explanation.

She sat back on her heels and asked me, "Mary, what in all Israel were you thinking? One minute, you're standing next to me in the market, and the next, you're running faster than a lioness. Do you realize you could have drowned, Mary? Speak to me, please. Tell me what is going on."

"It was Lavan," I managed.

"Yes, it was Lavan. I remember." She spoke a little more softly, realizing the pain and hurt that followed what we'd witnessed together. "He was with that other woman. This is the man who you have been raving about for months? The one who left you with the golden pot? The one who spoke of marriage?"

"Yes. It was him. Clearly married, clearly a Roman guard, not some Jewish liaison. Not some tradesman." I stuttered into a deep sob and buried my face into the shawl.

Deborah softly stroked my back. "It will be all right, Mary. It will. So he isn't the man for you. At least you know now. At least you didn't continue waiting." She attempted to draw my focus to the positive side.

What good...? I am ruined... I was haunted by every detail.

I had to tell her. She deserved to know, and I had already waited far too long.

"He... He..." I stammered. "He took me as his wife, Deborah," I confessed with a whimper.

I lifted my head to meet her eyes, waiting for her rebuke and disgust. I anticipated being left at the shoreline... to complete what I'd started.

Instead, she just sat there... quiet.

After almost half an hour had passed, Deborah didn't say a word but just took care of me. I had taken off the blanket and was nearly dry from the waist up when she stood. She walked over to her bag and held up her extra tunic, offering it to me. I rose slowly, took it, and wrapped it around myself quickly. I couldn't look her in the eyes anymore, so I walked over to the water's edge.

The sun and breeze had dried my hair, so I braided it as I stood there watching the horizon. Deborah then took out a plain cream-colored veil and walked over to me. She reached over and began wrapping my hair.

"No!" I said. "I'm a harlot now. I have no need for those!" I pulled away.

Then she finally spoke. "I was praying, Mary, waiting on what to say."

I nodded and waited for her.

"Tell me what happened before we return to the others. Tell me everything this time, Mary." As I stared at her in disbelief, she urged me to return to my seat next to her.

So I did. "It was that day he came to me in the potter's shed. Do you remember?"

She did.

"Well, there was more than what I told you. Lavan came inside, surprising me with a visit. He told me he was about to journey to Egypt with his group of men, in search of some rare white marble for the palace. He stayed for hours while I finished my work and helped me clean up. Then he surprised me with a nice meal, and we sat and shared it together. But before we left, after he asked for my hand in marriage…" I hesitated for a moment. "He brought out a special jug of wine. You know I had never tasted wine before, Deborah?" I said desperately, in my defense.

"I didn't know." She rested a hand upon mine and said softly, "go on."

"He had given me that small golden pot with the rare spikenard, the one I showed you, proclaiming it was his bride price, for me to give to Lazarus."

Because I was becoming frantic again, Deborah continued to reassure me that I was safe, and I stumbled on.

"You know I told him I could not bear children, so it seemed more than generous, the golden pot, the diamonds, and the pearls."

"And did you, Mary? Did you give it to your brother yet?" she asked.

"No, and I'll tell you why." Pausing to regain my strength, I continued. "He gave me the pot and then poured the wine. Lavan said, 'It will be months before my return, and I do not wish to leave you. Drink with me, Mary. Let us celebrate our union in private so I have these memories to take with me.' He was so persuasive, and I didn't want to dishonor the man who would marry me... So I obeyed his request. I can remember the first few tastes of the wine. They were much more bitter than I had anticipated. But before long, we had shared the entire jug—at least four cupfuls for me... or maybe more... I was beginning to stagger and slur my words, so Lavan helped me to a bale of hay in the back of the shed. I was so embarrassed, Deborah, I did not realize what was happening. The next thing I knew, he was upon me, lifting my tunic... shifting, grunting, and breathing heavily over me. He was so strong, so heavy, and he kept pressing down upon me... until he... He took me as a wife." I immediately burst out wailing.

Deborah quickly pulled me into her arms, trying to both soothe me and hush my cries.

"He took me, Deborah. He had me." I sobbed bitterly.

"Oh, Mary. My sweet and beautiful Mary." Deborah hugged me close with a hand upon my head and prayed with the sound of tears in her voice.

"Oh, God, have mercy on your daughter. She was deceived—she was robbed. Forgive her, Lord. This was not her choice. God, be near. God, be near. Like King David proclaimed, be near to the brokenhearted. She is innocent, Lord."

Deborah then grasped my shoulders and lifted me up.

"Mary," Deborah said. "Mary, you are no harlot. This was not a consummation. He robbed you of your virtue. You were defiled. There is a difference in the eyes of God. Oh, Mary, my sweet friend. God will deal with him justly. Have no fear."

She had said it, the word that haunted my dreams for weeks after it happened. *Defiled*. Time and time again, I buried that word down deep, convincing myself that love's great passion had caused his sin. I chanted to myself day and night that Lavan would soon be back for me, ready with a loud procession to claim me as his bride.

But I knew, deep down… I knew it was wrong. Why else would I have kept the golden pot hidden in my home from Lazarus and Martha, continually hesitating to tell them about the engagement?

I should have asked about where he had gotten that small honey pot because Jehoshaphat said a rich Roman woman bought them all. There were so many warning signs. I didn't know how I'd missed them.

Deep down, I knew. No great man of worth would ever take his woman outside of wedlock. I knew it when he kissed me goodbye at the beginning of the road leading to the cottage, leaving me to stumble home in the darkness. I knew it when I realized my hair was still tucked in its veil. I knew it when I awoke hours later, alone and dizzy. And I knew it that day when I saw his face in Jerusalem's market. He was a liar, and I had been used.

Chapter Twenty

"A sincere faith."
1 Timothy 1:5, TPT

I ARRIVED AT THE POTTERY SHOP extra early, every day, for months after the trip to Jerusalem. Jehoshaphat's work was slowing down as mine was increasing. I didn't care about the income or the attention. All I wanted was to keep hidden and make my family proud. Despite everything that had transpired in the past few months, I carried on. Deborah made every attempt to free me from my guilty mindset, but it only skimmed off the dross of impurity permeating my whole being.

I couldn't escape the trap in my mind and memories. My head and heart ached with what felt like swarms of bees, stinging and circling my emotions in a never ending attack. Sifting through the subtle voices reminding me of my filth and worthlessness became harder and harder. Mother's voice of encouragement and belief in my future was fading rapidly. All I could manage was to bury myself in my work and at least make Jehoshaphat and Elizabeth's life very comfortable.

Martha, who had sold her husband's home—he's now known as Simon the Leper—continued to live with Lazarus. Her husband's condition was worsening, and nobody had much hope for his improvement although he maintained trust in God. My brother traveled more often to the shores of the sea because Martha could tend to the needs of our estate. She worked in Mother's garden more often than I did in those days, allowing me more time to forget who I'd once dreamt I would be and accept who I was.

Rumors about me spread through our village. Those who'd seen Lavan and I visiting and conversing in the market surely noticed his sudden disappearance, which led to talk and gossip. I couldn't go anywhere without feeling the eyes and whispers of people upon me. Elizabeth, with all her sweetness and love, continued to reassure me that God wasn't finished with me. To my knowledge, no one knew what had happened, other than Deborah, but Elizabeth sensed the change in me. Even so, Jehoshaphat gifted me the cottage, and soon it became my home. I fired all my smaller pieces in the sandpits he'd created there and saved my large ones for his permanent kiln back in the village.

One day, my most prized piece was coming out of the cooling sandpit back at the main shop. Jehoshaphat had removed it from the kiln late the previous night and buried it in fine sand to cool. I could hardly wait to uncover it and see the finished piece. It was a very large jug embellished with roselike engravings that faded toward the mouth of the piece. I planned to paint the roses with Elizabeth after it was cooled and polished. The vessel was special, not only for its beautiful shape and decorative design, but because it was to be the first of its kind.

Jehoshaphat and I met with the village ironworker to create a unique fitting that would hold a lid in place. The mechanism was simple. It went around the mouth of the jug, with a hinge connected to the lid. When closing the lid for travel or preservation of the contents, you simply pressed the lever down, and it locked the top firmly into place. I believed it sealed the lid more efficiently than a cork and was much easier to use.

When I placed my palms on the fine sand, I could feel the remaining warmth from the fired piece buried beneath. After several hours of cooling, the time had come to dig it out for inspection. After I put on my gloves, I pushed the sand to the side, going deeper and deeper while paying attention to the level of heat. I could tell my jug had cooled completely since the sand closest to the piece was no longer hot. Slowly, I revealed the handles then lifted it up out of the sand.

It was beautiful, everything I had anticipated and more. The color was a deep tan, and the carved roses remained as defined and smooth as I had hoped. With a little polishing, painting, and glazing, it would truly be something to behold. I stood carefully, sweeping the side of my foot over the piled sand to level the surface. After dusting off myself and the piece, I went inside to inspect it further.

I took my jug over to the large water barrel inside the shop and slowly dipped it in. Lifting it in and out of the water, filling it up and pouring it out, I rinsed it thoroughly. Once all the sand was cleaned off, I performed the most important test.

Can it hold water?

Dipping the jug in deeply, I slowly pushed it farther down into the water. I watched with great anticipation as I lifted it out. Drip after drip of water rolled off the sides of the piece. I brought it over to the table and placed it on a few folded rags while I dried the outside of the jug, eager to celebrate.

A few minutes passed, and I couldn't see any obvious cracks or leaks. I was turning the rags to check for moisture when I saw it. Along the bottom decorative rim of the jug was a hairline crack running around the edge of the piece. The rags had moistened just underneath, where the water was discreetly seeping out.

I sat back in my chair, completely numb from the revelation of failure. I didn't know what to feel and wondered if I should dump it out and smash it outside with the other ruined pots. It was so beautiful, so visually flawless. All my pain, all my brokenness had sculpted this beautiful vessel. And for what? Only to symbolically expose my own cracks and brokenness hidden beneath a beautiful face. I picked up the jug and poured the water back into the barrel, dried it thoroughly, and set it back on the table. Pacing back and forth, contemplating what to do with it, I could feel the past flooding in like a mighty wave.

The voices in my head rang louder and louder as despair opened the door: ***"Nothing you will ever do will be good enough. You are*** *worthless, like this broken vessel. Give in. Give up. You're only good for pleasure. You are flawed. Cover it up."*

Cover it up? That's it! I'll fill it with wax, polish it, and paint it! No one will ever know the difference!

I took the piece off the table and quickly went to work on polishing. Once everything was smooth, I carefully laid the jug on its good side then dripped hot wax into the crack. After several coats, I set the jug on its bottom and repeated a similar process to the inside of the crack. When I was satisfied that the wax had dried in place, I filled the jug with water once again and waited to see if it had worked. *Success!* I saw no seepage whatsoever. I cleaned up the surface of the jug once more and set it on the shelf for painting.

Just then, the bell chimed, and Jehoshaphat's jovial singing filled the shop: "Through our God, we shall do valiantly, for He it is Who shall bring down our enemy! Good morning, young Mary!" he added.

"I see you have been hard at work, as usual. Have you unearthed your vessel?"

"Good morning, Jehoshaphat!" I greeted him with a hug then nodded. "Yes! It came out beautifully! I've been working on polishing it all morning."

The thought crossed my mind that I should explain my disappointing discovery, but I decided to wait and see if his trained eye could spot the flaw. He walked over to the shelf, still singing, and selected my jug. He brought it over to the side door and opened it, allowing the bright morning sun to light up the room. Lifting it up into the air, he oohed and aahed as he turned it slowly.

"Your work is exquisite! I have never seen anything so intricate come from a Hebrew potter's shop! You are a gifted woman, young Mary!" Jehoshaphat winked and smiled at me. "Just a minute now," he added inquisitively.

He turned the jug upside down and began to "hmm" to himself.

"I see," he said, in a surprisingly disappointed tone.

I watched quietly, tipping my head down.

He knew.

"Come have a seat here with me, young Mary. Let's take a closer look at your work, shall we?" he said very kindly yet sternly.

I made my way over to the table and sat down. He did the same.

"I see the piece is everything you said and more. Would you like to share in greater detail what you found during the testing routine?" He waited patiently.

He stood quietly from his chair, set my jug on the table, and walked to the front door. Jehoshaphat lifted a small sign from an old hook on the shop door then returned to his seat.

"Read this sign, young Mary." His bench creaked as he leaned forward on the table, watching me with the patience of a father.

"*Sine cera?*" I said, poorly attempting the Latin.

"Do you know what these words mean, young Mary?" Jehoshaphat asked.

"No, I am sorry, I do not."

"Ah, well, it is time you do, then, my young and gifted one. 'Sine cera' means 'without wax.' You see, young Mary, potters and artists all around the world hang signs just like this one in their shops to assure customers that their work is sincere. Many corrupt tradesmen will take their cracked vessels, fill them with wax, and sell them for a greater profit than they're worth. Take your new jug, for example. it's beautiful to the eye and also quite useful." Jehoshaphat ran a large calloused thumb around the bottom lip of my jug. "With a fine hairline crack like this, one could fill it with wax, paint and glaze the jug, then sell it as if it were whole. Unfortunately, the buyer would then bring the piece home and begin to use it. Over time, the wax, whether held over heat or containing warm liquid, would eventually wear out, revealing the flawed vessel. Then the buyer would feel betrayed, and the potter would be discredited for selling a piece that is 'untrue' or 'insincere.'"

"I see." A storm of shame and embarrassment welled up inside me. I hid my face in my hands and began to cry. "Forgive me, Jehoshaphat," was all I could manage.

"Come, come, my young one. Everything is all right. You will make many mistakes in life, Mary. You must not give up but instead press forward and try again and again until you succeed. This jug will still sell, and for quite a nice profit, I might add! It can be used to store grain or other dry ingredients. It is not a complete loss."

I continued to weep, secretly reflecting on how impossible hiding my own cracks would be, for the rest of my life. Jehoshaphat's words were touching me more deeply than he knew. *How can I ever fulfill Grandmother's words? How can I ever hold anything of value now?* I was a cracked vessel whose true purpose was lost. I was now 'insincere.' No matter what I portrayed outwardly, I would eventually be seen for what I was: barren, defiled, and unwanted.

Seeing me in such a morose state, Jehoshaphat paused before saying one more thing. It would stay with me for the rest of my life.

"Young Mary, the daughter Almighty God has entrusted to me, your value is not in your brokenness but in God's eyes. You, my dear one…" He lifted my chin and looked into my eyes. "You are not defined by your cracks either, child. God, the only potter that matters, is not done with you. Do not tell the potter what He is making. Do not assume you are ruined. Trust Him and be the yielding clay in His hands."

I leaped from my chair into his big open arms and cried some more. His words had unknowingly saved me from my hidden fears.

"I love you, Papa Jehoshaphat. Thank you," I whispered through my tears.

"Ha ha! I love you too, young Mary. God be praised!" His belly rumbled as he laughed with that unshakable joy and wisdom that strengthened him through life. He held me out in his arms, smiling down at me, then lifted the jug and placed it in my hands.

"Now, take this piece home, young Mary. I think you should keep it and remember our talk. Why don't you take the day off and head back down to the cottage? Maybe, you'll imagine some new ideas while you rest and think things over. I'll send Elizabeth down with an evening meal, and you two can share about today," he suggested kindly.

I wiped my tears and nodded in reply.

"I think I will, and thank you."

I took the jug into my arms, collected my things, and walked to the side door. Pausing for a moment, I looked back over my shoulder to see Jehoshaphat rehang the sign on the front door, then I left as he started singing once again. As I drifted down the field, reflecting on his words, I could feel joy and hope stirring within me… and for the first time in almost a year, I began to sing.

When I arrived home to my little cottage by the stream, I entered the house with renewed strength. I set the jug up on the windowsill and spotted my alabaster jar. Suddenly, I knew what I had to do.

I ran over to the storage cabinet and shuffled through some linens and pottery until I found a small burlap bag. I took it out and shut the doors. Sitting on the edge of my bed, I unwrapped the small golden pot from Lavan. I ran my fingers over the pearls and diamonds then shook my head.

"You do not define me!" I shouted at the pot then leapt to my feet.

I opened the alabaster jar and poured the expensive, perfumed oil into it. Having joined the tainted value of my past failures together, I then rewrapped the golden pot in the burlap bag and headed to Deborah's for the afternoon.

Chapter Twenty-One

"Even the barren…"
1 Samuel 2:2-5 NKJV

A S I WORKED IN THE soil, shifting rocks and mounds of dirt, a song welled within my heart. It was another one my father had taught me, from an ancient scroll used during the time of the prophet Samuel. I was blessed to have learned some reading, writing, and pieces of the Torah at home because women were never schooled in such things. Yeshiva was only for men. My father had been amazed by my memory, my ability to learn, and my hunger for God. So he would allow me to practice basics outside his study while he worked with Lazarus. I could even eavesdrop during his Torah readings as well—if my chores were done, of course.

The beautiful portions I memorized through writing were always rising within me when I needed them most. Lost in the lyrics the graceful Hannah had sung so many years before—and in the memories of my kind father—I felt comforted and not so alone.

"No one is holy like the Lord, for there is none beside You, nor is there any rock like our God… Those who stumble are girded with strength. Even the barren has born seven."

Over and over, I sang her words to the rhythm of my own broken heart while my teardrops watered the earth between my fingers. When

I closed my eyes, I could feel Mother beside me and hear her humming along sweetly with me. I missed her so much…

There I planted another new young lavender plant in her memory. Each one helped me to privately mourn both my mother and my lost dreams.

My mother's garden had changed so much since she left us. The areas once home to lush flower beds were housing simple, dense rows of sage, mint, thyme, and rosemary, and they grew abundantly. I sat back on my heels, amazed at how far and wide the garden had spread into the open field. My heart had also grown stronger over the past few years, and the garden was a very precious and accurate depiction of that.

Martha decreased her gardening time once I got back into my morning routine, but she still continued to help. I would leave my cottage at the break of day and arrive just in time to catch each sunrise in my usual rooftop spot. Martha and I would often share breakfast then work in the garden together before I went to the potter's shop.

Lazarus continued to upkeep the fencing and water troughs between his new rabbinical duties. Just like our parents, he tended to the sickly and needy. Lazarus was immensely proud of our little family. We worked together and helped each other through a long season of heartaches.

After I finished my work that morning, I planned on returning to my home to finish some new jugs I'd been working on. That little place really had become my home, sometimes more than my father's house. Maybe that was because the walls and sand knew me better than anyone else. That was where I worked and wept over piece after piece, talking to God, the birds, and the butterflies, feeling far away from the world. I didn't have to hide there. I didn't have to pretend to be someone I wasn't. My home loved me just the way I was, cracks and all.

That little workshop was tucked so perfectly in a wild glade of wheat and grass that I felt free from the rumors of others. The small stream running alongside the property was calming and tranquil. The choice to build there had been a wise one, and the workspace was proving to be very productive.

After gifting it to me, Jehoshaphat and Elizabeth rarely visited the shop without invitation, giving me my privacy. I still wonder if they somehow knew what had happened to me at the main shop, but they never said a word. They never stopped loving me, so it didn't matter even if they did. At twenty-five years old, I was finally feeling content once again.

Just as I rose from the ground, still humming aloud the song in my heart, a man came around the side of mother's garden.

"Hello, dear woman. I am sorry to intrude. Is the man of the house in?" he asked.

"Hello," I said and shyly bowed. "Lazarus, my brother, is just inside with our sister Martha. I will go fetch him for you."

"Thank you very much, and if I may, what a beautiful voice you have." The man removed his turban, revealing a charming wave of salty white-and-gray hair. He bowed back at me, and when he lifted his head, our eyes met. The most beautiful, bright-blue eyes twinkled back at me. I couldn't help but notice his wide, ear-to-ear smile. It sent an unexpected rush of blood to my cheeks. I quickly left him standing there, still smiling, at the opening of the garden gate.

What a charming man.

I glanced back over my shoulder then entered the house to get my brother.

"Good afternoon," Lazarus said kindly. "My name is Lazarus. I am the head of this house now, and this is my younger sister Mary. Martha, my other sister, is inside. She is preparing our afternoon meal in the kitchen. Please, come in and rest." He welcomed the man inside with a wave. My brother was still the kindest man I knew.

"Whatever you may need, we will be happy to help," he said as the man entered the garden.

"So very kind of you. Thank you. My name is Silas, Silas of…" He paused and laughed. "Well, I'm not from anywhere, really. I was born in the northern country of Caledonia." He bowed. "I am an itinerant traveler, trading in the finest herbs, spices, and oils from sea to sea.

I was told the house of Lazarus had the finest lavender garden west of the Sea of Galilee. I was hoping to see this garden and possibly purchase some of your plants and dried herbs."

"Ah, well, you have come to the right place. My sister, Mary, tends to this garden, and it is her blessed hands that have caused our herbs to flourish! We would be honored to share it with you. Mary can take you through the garden. But please, first come and join us for a meal." Lazarus led this strange yet charming traveling man inside our home and winked at me.

Oh, brother, why you... I crinkled my nose with embarrassment, mumbling little snickering remarks under my breath as I entered the house. *How could he possibly have seen or interpreted anything from that brief moment? Teasing me with a wink like he was reading my thoughts? I guess I'm staying a little longer,* I thought as I followed them.

After finishing our delicious afternoon meal, Martha went to work on cleaning inside the house, and Lazarus had me give Silas a tour of the garden. We started off at the back of the house, where mother's roses were still growing wonderfully. They were one of the few flowers I managed to sustain since her passing. Spring was ending, and summer was warming the earth, causing Martha's irises to bloom. I showed Silas the section of bright-blue bearded iris and the small cluster of the softer pinks.

As we drifted naturally down toward the back of the garden, his eyes widened. The earthy rows of velvet sage caught his attention. He reached out delicately, like Mother and I had, and touched the tips of the soft leaves as we passed along. He inhaled deeply as he bowed down into the rosemary, remarking with awe at the abundance. Then we paused.

That was where mother and I had removed the back gate. The lavender began there and spread neatly in rows, out into the back of the property.

"What splendor and design!" he said with a depth of appreciation.

"I love how this section takes you into the wild. It creates such an emotional transition, expressing how our human lives blend with creation." His observations nearly brought me to tears.

I managed to reply, "Thank you. After my mother passed away, I took over the garden's design, and I did just as you said. I wanted to remove the barrier completely and allow the lavender to run as far and wild as the soil would take it. I never imagined it would spread so beautifully. Sometimes, I imagine Mother sends the perfect rain, still gardening from above, while I work the soil below." I wiped a few tears and walked deeper into the field, leaving Silas to enjoy the view in silence.

I couldn't help but enjoy his company.

How can a man be so sensitive, so… observant of the depth and thought behind this place?

I watched him from a safe distance. This man, who'd appeared suddenly, was now so present, so interested in my dearest treasures.

He walked out into the fields, whispering words I could not hear. He knelt to the earth, taking a handful of soil and rubbing it through his fingers. Then he stayed in a low position and caught the perfect view, losing himself in the surrounding lavender.

I walked off into the tall grass and closed my eyes. Both the sun and breeze caressed my face, and for one moment, I just felt free—free of my past, free of my pain, free of fear.

———————

What I knew about God was probably more than most, yet my hunger grew for a deeper experience. Being around nature seemed to amplify my desire to be closer to God. He was everywhere I looked. I knew God was with me, but fear and doubt were never too far behind.

Around every corner of my life, pain, heartache, loss, and rejection lurked for me. I remember asking myself question after question: Could I be brave enough one more time? Did I even want to look his way and wonder what was happening? Was there something in this man that was catching my attention for a reason? Did I dare respond? I stood there, silently waiting for answers.

A quiet, gentle voice rose within my heart, sweet and warm: *"I am with you, Mary. I will never leave you nor forsake you. Come to me, drink, and never thirst again."*

I lifted my hands toward the heavens and asked God to give me strength one last time.

A gentle touch on my shoulder brought me back into time, back into reality. I turned to find Silas watching me with a look of awe.

"Your God meets with you in the fields?" he asked, this time with no smile but with burning curiosity.

"My God?" I said. "Are you not Jewish? Do you not serve the God of Abraham, Isaac, and Jacob?"

"Ah, well, my father was Jewish. He migrated to the region of Caledonia when he was a young man. He was the adventurous type, you know? The kind of person who just couldn't live in one place while he was young. He met my mother... later on in his years, in the town where I was born, and we never left. I suppose his faith faded through the years because he didn't speak of it. We did keep a few traditions from his childhood, like keeping the Sabbath day holy, but I'm afraid I don't know much detail about his faith." He bowed his head, almost looking ashamed.

I reached out my hand and placed it on his shoulder. "Well, you have come to the right place to find both herbs and God. My brother is a rabbi in training, and I don't think you can find a safer place or a person more delighted to share than Lazarus. He believes in reaching all mankind with the love of God, which is not common in our culture."

"Hmm. Well, it would be wonderful to learn more. My heart is open to all the new things around me." He paused, still smiling at me with a very boyish glow.

Something about that smile made me nervous and shy all at once. He was very handsome for an older man. He stood with strength and assurance, but his eyes held a gentleness I could not ignore.

"Mary. If you are ready? May I have your permission to gather from your mother's garden?" Silas asked me gently.

"Sure, that would be all right. Thank you for taking the time to appreciate it. I know my mother would have loved to share it with you."

I invited him back toward the house, where I kept some baskets and cutting tools.

As we walked together, Silas added, "I can teach you how to make some different oil mixtures if you are interested."

"Oh, really? I would enjoy that. I've been making my own lavender oil for some time now. I really enjoy the scent."

"So serene and calming, right?" Silas spoke, taking the words from my own lips.

"Yes, I was just going to say that!"

We laughed.

"My sister, Martha is the real cook in our family. She uses some herbs in her cooking, and I have tried to learn from her, but I'm not as skilled in that area. So I focus on the drying and storing of the herbs. I would love a lesson from someone who must know so much about them," I replied.

"Wonderful!" he exclaimed with such genuine enthusiasm.

"You have a great selection of mint leaves. More than one variety. Did you know that?" he asked with a smile as we walked past them.

"Not intentionally, I must confess." I shrugged, giggling a bit.

"They would make wonderful oils, and they each have a distinct taste for cooking. And... over here"—he pointed—"you have more than one kind of mustard. Can you see the difference in the bushes and colors?" he asked with excitement. "Your aloe vera..." He walked over and touched the large thick spiny leaves. "They can be used for medicinal purposes. I'll teach you what I can. Again..." He paused, shyly. "If you're interested." He looked up with his bright-blue eyes, which caught the light of the sun and shone even brighter.

"Yes, I am interested." I nodded with a youthful smirk, glancing shyly into his eyes then looking back at the ground.

"Wonderful," he said again, this time in a softer voice.

He then grabbed a large basket along with my gardening shears and began swiftly yet skillfully pruning and harvesting.

Lazarus came out into the garden to help Silas gather. He looked excited, and I couldn't figure out why, but for the first time in a long time, my brother smiled like a young man again. Losing our mother and father hadn't changed his joy or kindness but Lazarus did exhibit a heavier side thereafter. Not only did we suffer their loss at a rather young age, but my brother became my guardian and my protector. He carried the unspoken weight and concern for my future that our father and mother once bore. Then Martha's husband took ill with leprosy, and Lazarus so lovingly took her in and gave more of his time to Simon's leprosy camp. He was just like my father, and I was very proud of his big, loving heart. But he was growing tired, and I was subtly concerned.

However, under that bright afternoon sky, Lazarus's face looked relaxed with genuine enjoyment. The two of them laughed and shared with the ease of old friends. Maybe that was because Silas was older and displayed the experience and guidance of a fatherlike figure. Or Maybe it was Lazarus's passion for people and his desire to lead all men to God that drove his enthusiasm. Either way, if Lazarus liked Silas, then he must have been a good man. And maybe... it was okay to like his smile.

Seeing that they were content in their own company, I took the opportunity to slip away and head down to my cottage.

Chapter Twenty-Two

"Pleasant and easy to bear."
Matthew 11:28-30, TPT

S ILAS STAYED FOR A COUPLE of weeks after we first met. True and kind in nature, Lazarus took him in. He tried to supply all Silas's needs, but Silas was the one who ended up blessing us with bountiful meals and herbal wisdom. Before his departure, he insisted we invite Jehoshaphat, Elizabeth, Deborah, and her father to join us for a great time of fellowship and feasting. It was wonderful. He even took a wagon full of healing oils, bandaging supplies, and leftover food to Simon's camp outside Bethany before heading off on another adventure.

Something else happened that was surprising and long overdue. Lazarus and Deborah's father began to talk. After all my brother's years of focused studying and traveling, Lazarus was finally able to see Deborah as more than just his little sister's friend, which warmed my heart.

I knew she had the love and passion for God and His work that Lazarus was looking for, and she was an amazing cook. Their conversations were always very intense, and she kept up with his understanding of the Torah by practicing and memorizing any pieces she could get her hands on—not to mention the close connection we all made during the tragic loss of my parents. I was extremely pleased for my friend and my brother.

To our surprise and delight, Silas continued to visit Bethany throughout the year. We shared many meals together in the comfort and protection of my brother's home, and Silas was always willing to invest in the people in Bethany. Even Jehoshaphat and Elizabeth adored his stories from around the world. I often caught Elizabeth winking at me when Silas was in a monologue. She could see something there between us, a spark and many common passions and interests. Even I could see that, but I wondered if it was enough.

By the time of the following year's harvest, Silas expressed to my brother that he wanted to restore his faith. He began meeting with Lazarus and Rabbi Carmi at the synagogue and learning from the Torah. His desire was to officially walk the earth as a Jewish man and carry the religion of his forefathers. That made me incredibly happy, but I still wasn't sure what my role was in his life. A clear attraction and affection were developing, but I could not discern his intentions. Every time I thought he was interested in me romantically, he would set out again on a long journey, and I was then left rethinking everything and wondering if he would ever come back.

Just when I thought I could no longer wonder about the shifting tides of Silas and his signals, something changed pleasantly around the time of my twenty-sixth birthday. Silas surprised us with a sack of poppy flower seeds and, with that, the news that he wished to stay for several months. My brother agreed and enjoyed his company and support. The two of them worked together on the land and took to the local roads, visiting the sick.

On the days my work was firing in the kiln, Silas and I would work in the kitchen together. His love for interesting tastes and diverse cooking methods was uncommon but wonderful. He taught me many things, like how to make several unique types of bread from all over the world. Martha even joined us and enjoyed herself.

Silas was thrilled when he learned I could read and write. He wanted me to learn more words and taught me many. Some of his favorite recipes became my study work because they were made with many new ingredients.

We cooked stews, roasts, and even a few sweet treats. I showed him my mother's recipe for preserved lemons and baba ghanoush. Every time we worked together in the kitchen, I felt my cooking actually improved. Maybe his sweet helpful ways were what kept me engaged, or maybe I wanted to impress him and make him proud. Either way, I was getting better and better, and we were having great fun together.

For the first time in a long time, I was enjoying life.

My pottery work was taking a new turn, and I was producing more plates and platters. My cooking vessels remained the popular items, but my attention was on my service pieces. When Silas was in Bethany, he often would surprise me at the pottery shop with unique finds from around the world, which was inspiring. They helped me to create new ideas for my own work that made my pieces stand out from the ordinary.

I continued to stay at my little cottage down by the stream, and after our relationship began to blossom, he would stop by with unique oil samples for me to try. I couldn't deny that I was looking forward to his visits. I even started keeping a small list of things he could do when he came. He was always so helpful.

Along the side kitchen wall, Silas helped me hang strings of dried lavender and peppermint. It looked beautiful and made my home smell of their sweet fragrance. It meant so much to me that Silas understood my love for herbs and that he genuinely shared it with me.

One evening, during Silas's final week with us before a long trip to the Asian countries, a storm blew through Bethany and impacted our village dramatically. The skies were gray, and dark clouds billowed through the heavens all day long. Wind blew in great gusts, sending leaves and dust whirling through the streets. Most people took shelter, for the fear of lightning out in the farming fields was a serious concern. We gathered around the kitchen table and watched through the stony gray windowsills as nature unleashed its power. The cool temperature encouraged us to keep the kitchen fire burning throughout the day, and we shared stories and teachings during the downtime.

Lazarus spoke in great detail about his time with Jesus in Nazareth. Silas was captivated by his stories and filled with questions. As always, watching and listening was a pleasure.

A loud rumble of thunder crashed mightily over the big house, causing Deborah and I to scream and huddle close together. Martha rolled her eyes and continued working on a batch of bread without the slightest flinch.

"Oh, girls," she said in a motherly tone.

"Take a look at this!" Silas called out as he ran to the back door, waving at us to join him.

"Oh, wow!" Lazarus gasped.

"The whole left side of the garden fence was destroyed by a large branch! It must have come down during that last gust of wind. Martha, some of your irises may be lost," he said sadly. "Don't worry, my friends, I will help you repair everything before I leave, and we can plant the poppies, Mary!" Silas lifted our disappointment with his enthusiasm and loving ways.

He was so sweet, with not a corrupt bone in his… lovely body.

Sure enough, the storm passed, and we all took a walk around the property to assess the damage. The garden was torn up badly, but most of the plants and herbs could recover. We did lose a patch of yellow roses and one of Martha's blue iris plants, but that was nothing a little time and care couldn't replace. Fortunately, Martha knew how to split the remaining plants and could start new ones when the right time came the next year.

In the sections left bare, Silas and I planted the poppies. He assured me that in just one warm season, we would see them grow waist high and that the petals would be quite large. He also had hopes that they would be a bright burnt-orange color, much like the intense sunsets over the west valley. That was something new to look forward to, and we were all happy.

While we were working alone, Silas leaned in closer to me, allowing our arms to brush one another's, and the most exciting feeling of timidity and pleasure ran down my spine. I could smell him from a safe distance—he smelled of warm spices and pine, which was becoming a new favorite of mine, and a hunger for him to stay burst right through the closed doors of my heart. I couldn't deny it anymore—I was falling in love with Silas.

He would be gone for several months on his trip, and I badly wanted to ask him to stay. But if I did, he might think I wanted to clip his wings and keep him in town. No, he would have to stay because he wanted to. If we were going to have a future, I would have to prepare my heart to leave Bethany and follow his dreams beside him.

I knew I had earned enough to make Jehoshaphat and Elizabeth ready for their retirement whenever they might decide the time was right. I took care of adding to Martha's dowry and my own, and Lazarus had faithfully protected our estate for generations to come. The future was bright and full of possibilities. If he would only ask me...

The following morning, Silas was ready for his trip with a full wagon of goods and food. I was saddened by seeing him standing there, prepared to leave. But Martha made sure he would not grow hungry, and Lazarus was sending him with material for studying. If he was going to go, I was glad he had all that he could need.

My gift was a letter:

Silas,

Come home to me.

Mary

I tied it with a lavender sprig, just like my mother had done for me, and slipped it into the satchel he kept over his shoulder—when he wasn't looking.

Expressing something so boldly was a risk, but I needed him to understand I had stronger feelings within. Marriage was something I was beginning to hope for once again. I hoped he would open it when he was far away and remember me.

I watched him ride down the street, said my goodbyes to Lazarus and Martha, then ran home to my cottage. Tears were coming, and I didn't want anyone to see.

When I opened my door, the scent of Silas filled the air. He must have stopped by sometime in the early morning, after I left for the sunrise, because my house was filled with his lingering fragrance.

I noticed a small cooking vessel, out of place, upon my kitchen table. I walked over to it and lifted the lid.

Cinnamon, anise, cardamom, and a delicate hint of pine wafted into the air, and I was sure he had been there. He'd come to my home in secret... and made a batch of his personal perfumed oil.

Why would he? Why did he?

I stood there breathing in his scent, and tears slid down my cheeks as little pricks of loss pained my weary heart.

"What if he never comes back?" I said aloud.

Silas's deep, gentle voice responded. "Oh, I'll be back, my Lavender."

I turned quickly to find him standing at the door, smiling.

"My Lavender?" My heart raced with longing at the sound of that meaningful name.

"Silas! What are you doing here?" I ran over and without thinking wrapped my arms around him tightly, secretly drying a few tears on his cloak.

"Ah, well... I had hoped for a moment alone with you, Mary. If that is all right?" he asked shyly.

"Yes, of course." I replied. *This is it. He's going to ask.*

"When I return, Mary, I'd like your permission to come and see you here, at your cottage. You see, I have grown quite fond of you, and I think you are fond of me. Am I correct?" he asked.

"Well..." I thought for a moment. "As long as you have honest in-tentions, then yes, that would be all right... and yes, I am," I answered shyly with a smile, my cheeks flushing pink.

"How wonderful! Then I will be back, my Lavender, to see you again and again…" He leaned in closer and kissed my cheek. On his way out, he reached up and untied a lavender bundle from the hanging strings and waved it under his nose.

"You have my scent, and now I have yours." His beautiful blue eyes melted me, and he ran a hand through his salty gray-and-white hair, making me want to touch him.

"Goodbye, Silas. I'll… be waiting for you…" I bowed slowly, making sure to catch his eyes through my eyelashes one last time before he turned to leave…

Then he went… and I knew I was in love.

Chapter Twenty-Three

"All is exposed…"
Proverbs 15:11, TPT

T O MY DELIGHT, JUST A few months later, I heard a charming whistle from someone strolling up the pathway to my cottage. I peeked through the window and saw Silas. His arms and back were full of satchels and sacks, and I quickly set down my paintbrush to meet him at the front door.

"You're here!" I giggled with sweet delight and relief.

"I am! I have returned!" Silas flashed his dashing smile, and my heart fluttered once again, in the way only he could make it.

"I am so glad you're here! And you look so well!" I blushed a little. "Look at all these bags! Setting up shop, are we?" I giggled again, welcoming him to the table.

"I have come with many surprises, my dear, my Lavender!"

"Before I go, I plan to teach you several new herbal healing mixtures I picked up from the eastern Asian countries!" He smiled at me and continued talking while he unpacked a large satchel.

"And how is your writing practice going? Have you been copying the ingredient lists I left you? With everything I've brought with me this time, you will have plenty to practice with for weeks!"

"Oh… Yes, I have finished everything you suggested already, and I have been doing some writing for Jehoshaphat as well. Thank you, Silas." But my joy had quickly diminished the moment he said, "before I go."

"What is it, Mary?" Silas asked. "I know you. Something is on your mind. Here, help me carry my bags inside, and we can sit and talk. I have left my cart down the hill in the heavy thickets and tied up the mule in the village stable on the way in. No one turned an eye at this old goat passing through." He smiled so beautifully as he spoke, eyes all aglow as he teased.

That had become a new and enjoyable habit for Silas on his last few trips, to come to visit me in secret before heading to my brother's house. He was always respectful during our time alone, and at my age, no one paid attention to my affairs unless, of course, to continue the gossip that I had gone the way of a harlot yet to be caught.

"And I have some beautiful new teas to try, all the way from India. One is called 'chai'! You brew it in a pot with hot goat's milk, add some of the dusted cinnamon I purchased for you, then finish it with a touch of honey! It is truly something of a treat!" Silas was so full of conversation whenever he first arrived.

Once we got inside, we laid the bags down and removed our sandals. He took me into his strong arms and embraced me. Being held by Silas felt like being wrapped in the warmest blanket of comfort. He always smelled of warm spice and nature.

"Wow, you have brought quite a load this time. There must be five sacks of herbs and spices alone!" I exclaimed.

Silas smiled and replied, "There is more!"

"What is the occasion? Have you been asked to prepare for a wedding celebration or a rich man's burial?"

"No," Silas replied. "Just overcome by your beauty once again, my dear Lavender." He took one of my hands between his and squeezed it tightly. "I wanted to leave you with your worth in treasures this time, my lovely."

"Oh," I said again, pausing to hide my disappointment. *"Leave you with?"* I sharply repeated his words in my mind.

"There is that sigh again, Mary. Come, sit with me. Tell me what's on your mind."

"It's just that… We have been courting for over two years now, Silas. I'm twenty-seven years old… and you keep coming such a long distance to be with me… I suppose I had hoped that you would be ready to stay here with me in Bethany for good this time." I waited for a response, but Silas just listened patiently. So I continued, "We can be married, allowing us to stop visiting in secret, and you know Lazarus will give you his blessing. And Silas… Look! You have brought such a large collection with you this time. Surely, you have enough to set up a shop and trade here in the village."

The room echoed with the final sounds of my voice, and stillness followed. I felt all my words crashing to the floor with undesired passion. For some reason, the dreams in my heart seemed so silly and childlike, having been spoken aloud.

Silas sat at the table to think in silence. Panic began to take over, and all I could think about was that horrible day when I saw Lavan's face in the market, sneering at me with derision in his eyes. He knew I'd seen him. He knew I could do nothing about it. No woman could run out into the village market, screaming, "Stop him! This man, Lavan, he's persuaded me into his chambers and stolen my purity with lies and false promises of love and marriage!"

I would have been the one scorned and shamed. Even more horrifying, I could have been taken and stoned. Lavan would only have needed to deny the claim and to move on with his life. My stomach lurched at the memories, and my heart began racing.

Hush now, I whispered to myself. *Give him time to think. This is Silas, not Lavan nor Eli. Remember what Grandmother Lillian always said: "You are like this alabaster jar, designed to contain the greatest of love, Mary. He will come and never leave you nor forsake you."* I had to keep believing.

Surely, Silas was that great love Grandmother had spoken about. The way he looked into my soul with those sparkling blue eyes… The way he held me as I rested upon his chest… We shared a wonderment at the world around us, for nature and all its beauty. Our hearts and bodies seemed to be joined in perfect harmony and comfort.

Suddenly, another thought seeped into my mind, sending a chill down my spine, as if it were my own voice: ***"You'll never be good*** *enough. He only uses you for your beauty. You have nothing else to offer any man. You are worthless, Mary, and he will leave you. They will all leave you!"*

"No!" I almost shouted aloud.

I quickly covered my mouth in embarrassment and turned toward the window to regain my peace. I had endured the pain of the past, and it brought me there, to Silas. Looking at all the bags and treasures across the floor, I reassured myself that he had come all this way to stay. We had talked about a permanent future—Silas just hadn't ever answered me about it.

"I know you want to marry me, Mary. I have given it a great deal of thought. I even tried one of those prayers your brother taught me. But, Mary, we are so different. I am not from here, not accustomed to your way of life. What we have is a beautiful gift. I'm not sure... I can offer you any more—"

"Oh, Silas, stop now, darling. Come and rest. You know I would love to travel with you and enjoy the changing scenery. We are not different in any real way... I would never ask you to stay here and give up what you love."

"Mary"—he called me Mary again; he rarely called me Mary— "Listen, dear, I am nearly twice your age and cannot offer you what you deserve. A husband... maybe, but a father for your children? I now see I can no longer mislead you and allow you to believe I can give you those things."

Did I hear him correctly? It's children he wishes to avoid. Could this be my prayer, my answer? Could this be my chance to live free of being barren? He must be the one I have been waiting for! I must tell him! But do I dare? Oh, Mary, don't you do it. Remember Eli? I battled with myself in my mind.

Just then, a voice entered my heart, a gentle, still small voice whispering inside of me: *"Mary, trust in me, I love you and will never forsake you."*

Tears were brimming in my eyes. I felt afraid to receive the voice I was hearing, so afraid of the hope that had been reborn within me.

Fixing my eyes on Silas, I slowly walked toward him, words coming out of my mouth before I had more time to think.

"I am not like other women, Silas. Those dreams were once mine but are no longer."

"What do you mean, you are 'not like other women,' Mary? Of course you're not. You are the most beautiful creative soul I have ever met! You are a precious flower that brings sweet fragrance everywhere you go. I am unworthy. You are so young and will make such a beautiful mother someday."

I paused then continued, "Silas, in regards to mothering children, I am different… I cannot."

He stood from his chair, even more confused, waiting patiently for me to continue. His eyes were the softest, sweetest blue, like winter pools of water. Staring into them made me even more afraid to tell him the truth. I had allowed myself to love again, and I was at his mercy.

"I do not know how to explain it, Silas… I… I have never experienced the normal flow of blood that most women experience—not once." I couldn't believe I'd said it.

Silas and I were always incredibly comfortable together, and I didn't know why was I so afraid. Before I could even begin to talk myself into some kind of fleeting comfort, my head was spinning, and all I could think of was the unread letter left by Eli, hidden in a small box next to Mother's.

Why haven't I read them? I thought briefly.

He stared at me, bleak and expressionless. "Mary, you're… you're barren?" he asked.

That sickening thought crept through my mind a second time: ***"You are not worthy."***

Silas suddenly shook me gently, and reality came into focus.

"Are you all right, Mary?" he asked, with great concern and love in his voice.

I nearly melted with the seedling of hope that he just might understand. "Yes," I said, "It's just… I haven't spoken of it since… since…" Clearing my voice and breathing in deeply, I walked across the kitchen again and leaned on the small stone hearth. "Silas, there is more… I was defiled a few years after my arranged husband left me."

I waited in silence, squeezing my eyes tightly closed and waiting for Silas to give me any indication he could still want me, let alone love me. After all, Eli had taken but a matter of minutes to break apart our betrothal, shatter our bond of love and loyalty, and flee from me entirely. Or maybe he would be like Lavan, learning of my barrenness and scheming to use me. My thoughts were clouded, and staying calm took all that I had.

Then he spoke. "Mary, I… I do not know what to say. I had no knowledge of these things." He paused. "Surely, there must be something you can do, something that can be done about your womb?" He stood, determined to hear my response.

"No, Silas. It has been this way since my coming of age. Father and Mother spared no expense with physicians and treatments through my younger years. They only left me more broken and deeper in shame. I will never bear children. I will never be 'new' again." My breath felt cold as I uttered those condemning truths.

"This is why you have never married, Mary?" Silas asked. "The real reason? You truly can have no children?" He waited.

"It matters so greatly to God's people to be clean, to be fruitful and multiply. And yes, it is why I have never wed. I was once betrothed, many years ago, and he left when he found out I could not bear children. After that, I was to be married again, but that man was filled with deceit and sought only my body. I closed myself up inside, content to be alone for the rest of my life, until I met you."

There I was, exposed once again and ready for the fire to char my skin yet again. I could hide no longer. My shame and brokenness had been exposed to Silas, and I melted to the floor and wept uncontrollably.

Looking overwhelmed, Silas ran his hands through his salty hair and stared long and hard at me. After a few seconds of thinking, he walked over to me, reached down to caress my cheek, then quietly walked outside.

Oh, it is happening again. He will leave me! I'm worthless to all men. Why won't this ground open up and swallow me and my shame? Who would create a woman that can hold no life, unworthy of love! I cried out to God from within as my heart beat as rapidly as the wings of a hummingbird. I felt like I was disappearing into dust… again.

150

I must have lain on the ground for some time. The sun was high, but I still saw no sign of Silas.

Pull yourself together, Mary. Get up off the floor and remind him of your worth! I told myself, willing the broken woman to lift her head and carry on.

I will give him time. I remembered the times Mother left Father to roam outdoors after aggravating conversations.

Father always returned. Silas will return.

I gasped.

But Eli did not.

Chapter Twenty-Four

"The bride belongs to him."
John 3:29, TPT

URING THOSE WAITING HOURS, I lost myself in dinner preparations, chopping up onions and carrots and adding them to a simmering chicken stew. I prepared fresh *dosa* with the garlic and used some of the green onions Silas had brought. I poured out freshly pressed olive oil and took out a jug of his wine. Little by little, my heart was resting and renewing strength in the belief that all would be well. The anticipation of his return grew intensely as I finished all the preparations.

I loved to cook for Silas. I studied Martha's instructions carefully, remembering her loving taunt, "If you can follow my directions, anyone who eats this meal will be confident that you are a suitable woman."

Do not mess this up, Mary, I told myself.

I did have some skill in the kitchen by then. After all, Silas always came with fresh herbs and spices from his travels, and he loved to teach me about them, showing me how to cook with certain kinds and recognize the unique scents and flavors. He even showed me some simple medicinal uses, like how mint can soothe indigestion and freshen breath when chewed.

So I went to work, adding fresh rosemary and thyme to the pot and felt very pleased with the results.

"Take that, Martha!" I shouted into the pot.

The table was set, the mats were brushed, and every pillow Silas loved was fluffed and ready for comfort. My tiny cottage was filling deliciously with the savory and tasty aromas of a well-cooked meal.

The sun was fading in the sky, with still no sign of Silas. I decided to bathe quickly, adding some dried lavender to the water. I still couldn't bring myself to use the oils stored in the alabaster jar, despite their extravagant fragrance and value. They only reminded me of the shame and pain of my past. I slipped into a new dress Mother had given me a long time ago, which I'd kept tucked away for a special occasion.

It was a deeper lavender color and sewn by Deborah. I'd never had a chance to wear it for my mother—she died so suddenly. Wearing it… made me feel close to her, and it felt so luxurious. It was a perfect fit.

Deborah has such a gift, I thought to myself as I turned and felt the smooth material.

After I was dressed, I noticed a small wrapped package that had dropped to the floor.

It must have been inside the dress all this time. I was amazed that I'd never noticed.

A sprig of lavender was twisted in the package's twine, and I knew it must be something special. It was a brand-new shawl, a lighter lavender color made from fine silk, which was hard to justify wearing on any normal day, and my heart warmed as I felt the cool material. It had delicate swirls of gold stitching along the edges, reminding me of sunrise clouds sweeping through bright rays of sunlight. On each end were perfectly embroidered bundles of lavender.

"Oh, Mother!" I gasped, placing the shawl close to my heart and holding back tears. She was there with me, and that was just the sign I needed. Surely, Silas was my rising sunshine, the one for Mother's little Lavender.

When I wrapped it around me, I twirled, feeling like royalty. Deborah was the greatest seamstress of all, and that was, by far, one of the most beautiful things she had ever made me.

What a friend.

Deborah was the only person who knew me, who truly knew me. She had stood by my side despite the shame of my past and supported me like a sister. Like my mother, she never stopped believing in me and reminding me of God's good plans for my future.

I contemplated taking my hair down but refrained. Even if Silas would agree to stay, the last thing I wanted was to appear to be wooing him into my bedchamber. Surely, he would be pleased enough to see the meal and my glowing love... He would enter my home and see once more why he should stay.

Not long after I finished dressing, Silas walked calmly through the door. He looked at peace, but his face was not giving me any indication of his feelings.

"I went for a long walk, Mary, with much to think about. I see you have prepared a meal. May I sit?"

"Yes, Silas. Come sit and rest." My eyes were glued to him, watching his every move. *He came back.* "I've prepared all of this for you to enjoy. Can you smell that? I added the herbs just like you showed me, in both the stew and in the dosa you love so much. You know... the recipe from India! I have also tended to your bags, clothing, cleaned your shoes and..." I smoothed my dress and looked down shyly. "And bathed." I stood there on display. "There is nothing left for you to do but sit and enjoy this wonderful evening. Let's take our time tonight. We need not speak unless you are ready."

Silas smiled at me and quietly removed his shoes then came and sat at the small table. He smelled the steam rising from the different dishes then licked his lips. "It smells wonderful, Mary." But then he sat back in his chair with a more serious look on his face. "I do have something to say, my dearest Lavender," he said softly.

"I have thought long and hard for some time now. Your being such a young woman had begun to weigh heavily on my heart. Our time together has been so wonderful to me yet so unfair to you. I came to say goodbye, Mary."

He paused for a moment, and I could feel my fears closing in on me.

"But, Mary, your news both saddens me and brings me great relief equally. I would like nothing more than to spend all my remaining days with you. However, I have misled you. As you and your brother have shared with me about your God, I realize I have never respected Him,—or you—according to your traditions. You have given of your private time to me in a way that is displeasing for your family and faith, and I will not dishonor you as the one before me has done. Therefore, I have two conditions." He paused again, repositioning himself as he sat on the edge of his seat. I listened as tears flowed down my face in disbelief.

"I will take you to your brother tonight and make my intentions known to him, that I will marry you. I will come under your Jewish faith and your brother's blessing… If I am to marry you, we must do it right. I wish to honor you, your father and mother, and your God." Finally, he chuckled as he took my hands into his, pulling them up to his mouth for a kiss… just like mother had always done.

"You must agree to travel with me, which I know will be absolutely awful for a woman with such a lack of adventure." He broke out into teasing laughter, sweeping me up off the floor as he rose and twirled me in his arms. "We must go to Egypt so I can show you where I purchased these wonderful oils! And to India, the land of many spices! If we can travel together to those two wonderful places, my life will be full, and we can retire here in Bethany, near your family." He buried his charming nose into my neck then rested me back on the floor to look for my reaction.

I had no words, only tears streaming down my face. My body quivered with the new and breathtaking feeling of being wanted and loved. I was finally safe. I was finally good enough, just the way I was…

"Yes, my darling Silas. Yes, I agree to your terms!" I whispered through my tears.

"I am a blessed man. The most blessed in all the world! Now, my dear Lavender, let us eat this wonderful meal you have prepared and then head to the house of Lazarus to share our news. We should not delay!"

Silas and I sat close to one another on one bench, inseparable, while we enjoyed what I thought was the best meal of my life.

We reached my brother's house before nightfall and found that Lazarus had just finished cleaning up with Martha.

"To what do we owe this fine surprise?" Lazarus greeted us at the back door.

Taking me completely by surprise, Silas shouted, "I have come to ask the hand of your younger sister, Mary, in marriage!"

"What did he say?" screamed Martha, as she came billowing out the back door behind Lazarus. "What did you say?" she asked again with happy disbelief.

"You heard him right, Martha. Silas has finally decided to make it official! We are delighted for you both. Praise God, Who is rich in mercy and provision!" Lazarus answered loudly. He stepped off the porch and embraced Silas with great joy and passion.

He released Silas and took hold of his shoulders, saying, "What took you so long, my good friend?"

Laughter arose between Martha and Lazarus, but Silas and I only laughed in jest.

"Please come inside, and let's hear all about this wonderful news! I'll fix us some mint tea and treats!" Martha volunteered while taking me by the hand to pull me inside before the men could catch up.

"Does Deborah know, Mary?" Martha asked.

I giggled pleasantly at my sister's excitement for me. "No, not yet."

"Silas wants to officially convert and make things right with Lazarus before anything else happens," I responded.

"Yes. Well, that's good. I know he and Lazarus have had many talks about his lack of Jewish upbringing. I am so relieved he desires to do things the right way. But really, Mary, I'm the first to know? I would have thought I would be second to Deborah when this day came."

"You are my sister. It matters to me that I have your blessing as well as Lazarus's. Besides, you live here now. Silas and I came looking for the two of you on purpose! I'll send word to Deborah tomorrow morning. I'm sure she will want to be here during all the fun." I tried to speak into my sister's heart and reassure her of my love.

"So you plan to wed soon?" Martha replied.

"That will be up to Lazarus. Silas has faithfully seen me now for well over two years. It's possible once a mohar is discussed that we will be permitted to marry, especially with my circumstances."

Martha nodded silently then responded, "We will leave that to the men to discuss. It's not our place to figure all of that out."

"Thank you, Martha, for being so happy for me. I never thought I would have a future in marriage, and then Silas just walked into our garden... the garden, Martha." I began to tear up.

She quickly got to work fixing the water for tea. "God is too much for me to understand, Mary, but I do believe He loves His people. We must do our part in the home and make our men comfortable, for that is the purpose God has given to us. Well...to you now." I could tell Martha was thinking of her husband, lost to the leprosy camp. "Simon may never make it home." Her voice became short and direct, and the brief expression of joy and emotion was already gone, lost to the kitchen work.

"Don't lose hope, Martha. Don't lose hope." I placed a hand on her shoulder, smiling, but she never looked up at me.

Lazarus and I walked Silas down to my cottage after a few hours of celebration and planning. We had his blessing, and to me, that was all that mattered.

Slightly behind me, Lazarus walked with Silas, discussing a few more things about marriage conditions. "You can prepare a place for my sister at the potter's cottage, and Mary can remain with us in our father's house until everything is finalized. I'm sure a man with your knowledge and experience can turn it into something a bit more appropriate for the two of you. I cannot say that I have been comfortable with Mary living there all this time—alone. But with her independent spirit and focused work ethic, it has suited her simple needs." He placed a hand on Silas's back.

"Oh, and I will, brother! She deserves the world!" Silas glanced at me and winked.

"We will be there not long after sunrise to walk you to the synagogue. Once there, Rabbi Carmi can perform the official Jewish conversion. Then you'll need to see a local physician about the more difficult task... as we privately discussed." Lazarus cleared his throat. "But I will be with you and take care of you during the healing process." He quickly changed the subject. "Afterward, we will meet with Jehoshaphat and discuss purchasing or building you a shop of your own for medicinal herbs."

At that point in the conversation, I slipped inside my house for just a moment. I took my little box from the cupboard with my unopened letters, some garments, and my mother's shawl.

Once I came outside, Silas took my hand and spoke softly to me.

"Good night, my lovely Lavender. Tomorrow, we will start this journey together. We will be right before God and one another." He gazed into my eyes with such depth that I lost myself for a moment, once again, in the pools of blue.

After he embraced me, I felt him slip a twig of lavender up under my hair and behind my ear. Then he brushed my cheek with the back of his beautiful hand, slipped my lavender scarf from my shoulder, and bowed his head.

My brother and Silas embraced once more before we turned to head back.

Chapter Twenty-Five

"Now we lay..."
Psalm 44:25-26 TPT

MORNING CAME, AND I DRESSED early before anyone else began to stir. My father's house, Lazarus's house, was still and quiet in those early hours, just like I remembered. I pulled on Mother's shawl, remembering how Silas had taken my lavender scarf a few precious hours before, and I smiled. I walked out into the garden in my bare feet and stood at the end, looking out into the open field. After just a few relaxing moments, the birds began to awaken, and their songs and calls filled the morning air.

Closing my eyes, I lifted my hands up toward the heavens, and the wind took my heart's prayer up to the Lord. When the sun finally peeked through, it sparkled the most brilliant golden yellow. I turned to see the light touching mother's white roses, and I quickly hurried up to the roof to see more.

Being up there felt quite strange. Many years had gone by since I first climbed that old tree to seek out the morning light. Life was getting better, and I still couldn't believe someone knew everything about me and still wanted me. Silas was different. He didn't compare with any other Jewish man in Bethany. He didn't want things, he didn't want riches, and he didn't want a simple, repetitive life. He longed to be outside, traveling and experiencing all the beauty of our world. The conversations he had with my brother about the connections between the spiritual and the natural were breathtaking. The man wanted me more than any other, which left me speechless.

Once the sunrise was over, I simply climbed down, washed my feet, and headed to Deborah's. The time had come for her to hear the news. Besides, my brother wanted to arrive at the cottage early to collect Silas, and I knew Deborah would want to come along.

When I reached Deborah's corner of the road, I could see her father instructing the new young farmers in the back field. I was pleased her father had taken Lazarus's advice about hiring help to maintain the land. Even though the idea had been Deborah's, he respected hearing it from my brother.

I stepped up my walk to a gallop. After two knocks, my lovely friend opened the door and welcomed me inside.

"Good morning, Mary! Has it been ten years already since we last saw each other?" she asked with a wry smile then squeezed me… almost too tightly.

"Good morning, Deborah, and yes, I'd say nearly that long," I teased right back.

"With all the pottery you've been making, I'm surprised you could find the time to come see me. So what brings you here this—"

"Silas has asked for my hand." I covered my ears.

She shrieked in pure excitement. "I knew it! I just knew it! I told your brother! How many times did I tell your brother? Thousands! There has always been something so warm and wonderful about him, Mary, and I just knew he was the one!" She exclaimed all that in one long breath.

I uncovered my ears halfway through her expression of joy to jump up and down with her, holding her hands.

"So he's here? In Bethany?" Deborah asked.

"Yes, Lazarus had Silas move his things into the cottage while I stay with him and Martha until we marry. We are going down to the cottage to meet him this morning and then to visit Rabbi Carmi!"

"Oh, what joy! What wonderful joy, Mary! Have you told Elizabeth and Jehoshaphat yet?" she asked.

"No, not yet. Just you! After Martha and Lazarus, of course, because they were there!"

We giggled.

"Well, I finished all my orders last night, and I happen to be a free woman today. Any chance I can join you?" Deborah was already tying up her sandals.

"Yes! That is why I came, silly. As if you didn't know." I gave her a sly little smirk and opened the front door for her.

Lazarus was waiting outside with Martha as Deborah and I hurried up to the house.

"Good morning, Deborah." He bowed.

"Good morning to the bride." He bowed once again, in my direction.

I looked at Deborah, winking at her predictable thought of her future marriage. Martha and Deborah greeted each other, then my sister told us she wouldn't be joining us that morning.

"I'll see to the preparations for tonight's dinner. It's a lot of work, and someone has to do it!" Martha tried to laugh like her comment was a joke, but we all knew she was serious.

"Thank you, Martha. It won't be too big of a dinner, right, Lazarus?" I turned to my brother.

"Ah, well, when I saw you had gone to Deborah's this morning, I took the liberty of informing Jehoshaphat and his wife about the news! They will be joining us as well this evening." My brother's voice was as warm and loving as my father's, which led me into his arms for a hug.

"Thank you, brother! How thoughtful of you." I smiled up at my hero sibling, feeling his support.

"Martha!" I hollered just before she entered the front door.

"Deborah and I will come straight home to assist you after we drop the men off at the synagogue. Do you need anything from the market?" I asked her.

"That will be of some help, yes. And no, thank you, I've already been." She disappeared into the house.

"Well, now that everything is settled, let's go get your bridegroom." Lazarus laughed at the irony of the reversed roles.

Lazarus had Deborah and me stay outside for a bit as he entered the front door.

"I can't have my sister seeing her husband in any unfit condition!" He shook his hand in the air and called out, "Silas, oh Silas, your bride has come!" He laughed like a young man.

Deborah and I watched him disappear inside and we whispered back and forth about the previous night while we waited.

A few minutes went by, and I noticed Silas had never lit the fire pit just outside the cottage. I walked over to it, looking around the corner at the pile of undisturbed wood by the house.

"Lazarus, is everything all right in there?" I started to wonder why Silas would have spent the night with no fire. He always told me that was the best way to protect myself from the cold, being out in the valley as I was.

I walked over to the front door, but just as I began to push it open, my brother appeared.

"No, Mary. You cannot go in!" he nearly shouted at me.

"Why? What's wrong?" I asked with increasing concern. "Silas! Come outside, please," I called past my brother.

Lazarus gripped me more tightly, and I couldn't help but feel scared.

"Lazarus! Let go of me. What are you doing? Where is Silas?" I pushed past him and nearly stumbled through the doorway, falling onto my knees inside.

"Silas!" I shouted in disbelief.

Deborah came bursting through the door behind me and gasped.

She covered her face and turned to Lazarus, who had entered behind me.

Silas's body was sprawled out on the floor, still and cold... My beloved was dead.

"Silas! Silas!" I screamed as I crawled toward him and grasped at his cloak, shaking his body in denial.

Lazarus took hold of my waist and lifted me as I kicked and screamed at him to let me go.

"No, Mary. You can't. You shouldn't. Oh, Mary, let him go!" he insisted in a voice choked with tears.

I continued to kick and scream his name until I could no longer see clearly and collapsed to the floor.

Deborah came to my side, crying and pleading with me to go out into the yard. Both she and Lazarus took one of my arms and lifted me to my feet then pulled me to the door. Right before I passed the threshold, my eyes cleared, and I could see Silas's hand wrapped in my lavender scarf. I began to scream through my tears once again.

"Mary, Mary!" Lazarus held me in his arms as he waved for Deborah to close the door. "Mary, I am so deeply sorry, Mary. He is gone. You cannot touch the body. Please, Mary, please." He begged through his own tears for me to stay calm.

I gasped for air, choking and crawling in the sand, searching for something to hold, something to grasp, until I reached the hem of Deborah's tunic and pulled her down to me.

She lifted my face to meet hers, and before she could say a word, she turned her face to release her own cries. She, more than anyone else, knew the utter death I felt inside, and I could see it in her eyes. She knew.

"Lazarus!" I cried out.

He came over in an instant. "Yes, Mary. I'm here."

"Lazarus, are you sure? Are you sure he's gone?" I pleaded.

"Yes, Mary... I don't want to explain..." He hesitated.

"Just tell me, Lazarus..." I whispered as the numbing truth seeped its way into the broken pieces of my heart.

"He's... he's... quite cold, Mary. He's been gone for several hours. It seems whatever happened to him happened just after he arrived. His sandals are still on his feet, and there were no lamps burned... That's all I can say, Mary." He took my hand and waited for me.

"Thank you, Lazarus... I know how hard this is for you too... Please," I said, looking at the two of them. "Please, let me go."

I stood to my feet and backed away from them, stepping farther and farther before I turned and ran. I heard Deborah calling briefly, then my brother called after her, telling her to let me go.

I ran through the valley, deeper and deeper into the bushes and thickets. Thorns and branches scraped my legs as I passed without hesitation. I leaped over large rocks and fallen tree limbs, taking flight up into the glade that led to the back of my father's house. I could see the glow of purple growing larger and larger as the wild lavender came into view.

My feet landed in the soil newly tilled from my most recent planting, and I knelt down right into the plants. Mother said I could clean a field, and that's what I planned to do.

I took hold of every lavender plant I could find and tore it up by the roots. One after the other, throwing them up over my shoulder, I tore violently without end. I made my way into the garden and kept pulling one after another, screaming at each one and crying myself blind. Mother's trimming shears were in a basket near the garden pathway, and I took them up and began chopping up the herbs, the flowers, and everything in sight.

Martha burst through the back door, calling my name desperately, begging me to stop. But I ignored her.

I made my way down the garden bed, through the irises and the poppies, and came to mother's roses, and... stopped. I lifted the shears towards them, staring at their luxurious white petals, and began to shake.

"Mary... what have you done?" Martha cried out.

I turned toward my sister and dropped the shears into the rosebush as reality began to sink in. I gazed in horror at the total destruction of my mother's garden then looked back at my sister. She stood there silently with tears streaming down her face.

My hands and my legs were bloodied, streaks of mud ran down my arms and tunic, and I stood there panting. I was completely disconnected from the damage I had caused, drowning in a wild sea of devastation.

A laughing voice crept into my mind: *"Mary... Oh, Mary. Why are you surprised? You are worthless. You are nothing. You have no one, and you never will. Run off, out into the wilderness, and never look back. Save your family from your shame. You are a filthy used woman who will never be loved."*

The voice was right—I was finished.

I walked right past my sister, through the shredded garden, and down into the valley. I could feel the shards of my heart turning to dust, and I didn't care anymore. Mary was gone, and she wasn't coming back.

Chapter Twenty-Six

"When it looked hopeless…"
Romans 4:18, TPT

MY HEART CONTINUED TO DARKEN throughout the next few years of my life. I drifted further and further from those who loved me, those who tried to help me find new hope. The garden lay in sorrowful disarray. It was scarred and neglected, with little love or attention. Martha and Lazarus finished the work I had started and removed every lavender plant that grew on our side of the field. No one planted anything new. They only mended what was left.

Grief worked its way through me and my family. Lazarus could no longer lift my heart with his kindness, so he set out for the Sea of Galilee once again about a year later. He was gone for months at a time, only returning to bring provisions for Martha and Simon the leper then returning to the sea.

My sister and I barely spoke. When I did see her, disapproval stared back at me. I no longer felt a desire to meet her expectations, and our relationship suffered.

Elizabeth often came to my cottage with Deborah, trying to bring me back to life, but I grew cold and shunned them. I couldn't bear to leave the last place I had shared with my beloved Silas. I worked from home, creating only the simplest pieces of pottery. Gone were the days of design and inspiration.

In their old age, Jehoshaphat and his wife closed down the potter's shop and only sold from their traveling cart. Twice a month, he would come to the cottage and pick up my pieces to sell across Israel. After so many failed attempts to help me, even they decided that leaving me be would be best.

When I reached thirty years of age, further darkness came knocking at my door late one evening. When I opened it, I was surprised to see it wasn't Deborah. It was Simon the Pharisee, a man most Bethany villagers tried to avoid. He was an outsider, a man sent from the temple in Jerusalem to take our beloved Simon's place when he took ill with leprosy. This man was cold and dark, unlike Martha's husband. He walked through town upholding the "unwritten" Torah and profiting from whatever he could get away with.

"Hello," I said in a dry, defensive tone, looking into his mischievous eyes.

"Woman, won't you invite me in, to wash my feet?" he insisted.

"I'm sorry, I am not accustomed to allowing any man into my home, thank you."

I attempted to close the door, but his hand forced it to remain open.

"Do not be rude, woman. I have things to discuss with you. I was merely suggesting that you allow me inside so I can present you my offer."

"Any and all sales of my work are done through the house of Jehoshaphat. I make no sales on my own. Thank you for your interest, but I believe you are here mistakenly," I snapped back quickly.

"Ha, foolish woman—as if I am interested in your pottery work." He laughed in mockery at my attempt to stand my ground. "Are you not Mary of Bethany, of the house of Samuel and Lazarus?" he asked me intensely.

"I am she. My brother is away at the Sea of Galilee, and you have no business here, Simon the Pharisee."

"Ah, so you do know who I am. It's not an easy job teaching you peasant Jewish people what is right and wrong," he said with obvious scorn.

"If you are Mary, then I have come to the right place, and I strongly urge you to let me in. We would not want rumors to begin spreading of a harlot caught in the act, would we?" Simon stared me down.

My heart sank deep within myself. I slowly stepped away from the doorway, and he huffed as he closed the door behind himself and brushed past me. I quickly lit a few lamps around my kitchen and sitting area and pulled the curtains closed over the windows.

"What is your business here, Simon? I am not a harlot, and your accusations are incorrect!" I stood, hugging my mother's shawl tightly around myself while he poked around my shelves and cabinets, carelessly knocking things over and smirking at the simplicity of my cottage.

"It has come to my attention that you are unmarried, Mary. And blessed are you on this day, for I am in search of a wife," he said with a pompous smile, eyes tracing the lines of my body and licking his lips with repulsive desire.

"I am sorry. You have been misled. I am not looking for a husband. I was betrothed, and my husband passed away in this very house where you stand." I pointed toward the door again.

He turned, ignoring me. "So I have heard. You are the most unfortunate woman in this village, Mary. Some say you have been seen with many men over the years. No one quite knows what to believe." He paused and walked closer. The scent of him was an overpowering smell of burnt cloves and sweat. I had to turn and face my kitchen hearth to escape its pungency.

"Misfortune or not, I am in no need of a husband and cannot bear children, so I am unsuitable for any man." I wielded my weapon of defense at him with total abandonment. Not one man had ever spoken another word to me after those words were declared, and I waited for him to take his leave.

"Yes, I am aware of your... condition," Simon said with disturbing confidence.

"Then you should be on your way, sir." I bowed and made my way to the door, only to be seized by the arm and forcefully turned around.

"Look here, woman! I am Simon the Pharisee of Jerusalem and, now, Bethany. I have the authority to pay your cleansing price, make you my bride, and salvage your worthless life. Do not turn from me. You will allow me to take you as my wife, and there will be not another word against it. If you refuse, I will leave here and report straight to your precious Rabbi Carmi to proclaim your harlotry. You and your brother will be ruined, and I will be sure you are punished to the fullest extent of the Jewish law!" His eyes were small and dark, and he held my arm tightly, yanking harder with every expression and demand.

I pulled free from him and gave my best attempt to deny his proposal, but his threats continued and I succumbed. *Who was I to anyone?*

A burden.

A disappointment.

If I didn't meet his demands, my family's name would be ruined. I would most likely be stoned in front of those who loved me and believed in me. *What choice did I have? And why would I care?* At the very least, I would give what was left of me, for the benefit of my family.

Intruding on my devastation, Simon continued with his demands. His voice was fading and his image blurred as I sat back in my chair, engulfed by the horrid understanding that what little life I had would soon be gone.

He finished yelling, and all I could hear was "Three days, Mary. You have three days!"

Then the door slammed, and I ran to it. Shrinking to the floor, I cried out to God, desperately asking for a miracle.

For the next two nights, I hid, staying with Deborah then with Jehoshaphat and Elizabeth. Everywhere I went, I was haunted by his voice, his demands, and his scent.

During those nights, I sat brushing my hair and thinking of Mother. That was the only time I could still feel close to her. For a woman, her hair is her glory or most beautiful treasure, only to be enjoyed by a husband... I knew Simon the Pharisee did not intend to become my husband. After all the pain and torment I'd experienced through my adult life, my hair was the last petal yet to fall... I would fight for it.

On the third day, I was with Deborah in the marketplace for an afternoon meal when Simon the Pharisee's scent arose. I could do nothing but duck inside a tent until he passed. I was so afraid to be identified by him in public, for even though I was no harlot when he first crept inside my door, he would surely accuse me if it suited him.

Deborah was sharing her wonderful news with me, how Lazarus had finally asked for her hand in marriage in his last letter. Unfortunately, I couldn't give her my full attention. I was too busy watching out for Simon.

A few of the guards who followed him stopped just outside the tent I was in, and I listened carefully to their conversation, hoping to glean something useful. They went on and on about a young woman named Miryam. I recognized that name, for my mother had spoken to me often about a young girl orphaned at a young age from an outlying city.

I wonder if it's her?

The guards continued sharing how they had taken turns with her in unspeakable ways and that she was up for grabs because Simon had a "fresh offering" starting that night.

My heart sank into my stomach.

"Mary? Are you all right?" Deborah called my attention back to her. I nodded that everything was fine, but I couldn't get that name out of my mind.

Miryam. Poor Miryam. Mother knew you. She tried to help you. I mourned her plight.

Simon made no attempt to interact with anyone in my life those three days, but the final night was drawing near. I wondered what to do.

The thought of a life of harlotry was like a heavy stone tied to my ankle, slowly dragging behind me. *How was I ever to be free? How was I supposed to find the hope Deborah and Lazarus tried to lead me toward?*

Even though I kept my head down and worked faithfully, trouble and pain always found me. *Where was the little girl, Mary... the one full of vibrant dreams?* I'd always planned to be a lovely woman of God, bringing honor to my family... *But now what?*

Those three days of my life were terrifying. When the night came, I locked myself within the darkness of my cottage, huddled against the overturned table and chairs, begging God to save me.

Then...

Lazarus came home...

Chapter Twenty-Seven

"Into the fire..."
Acts 28:3-5, TPT

"MARY! OH, MARY!" LAZARUS BURST through my door and swung me in his arms, dancing and laughing with more joy than Papa Jehoshaphat could ever have expressed.

"Lazarus!" I actually laughed and pushed him away.

"What is all this about?" I asked him with blushing embarrassment.

"Oh, Mary!" he shouted. "It's Jesus. It's really Jesus! He's the Messiah!" Lazarus yelled aloud with hands raised toward the roof.

"What?" I asked in surprise with a budding glow of hope.

"Jesus? Our Jesus? You mean... What? How?" I exclaimed.

"Mary, I was down fishing at the shoreline. There was a man there named Simon. Jesus came with his followers and called Simon to follow him. He wasn't the same as I remembered him from my last trip to Nazareth. He was... different. I asked around, and people told me he was baptized by a man named John and that God himself spoke from the heavens, saying that Jesus was His dearly loved son!" Lazarus began laughing and jumping. "That's not all, Mary! There have been miracles!" He paused this time, looking into my eyes.

"Miracles?" I asked.

"Yes. A woman..." He paused again. "A woman was found to be an adulteress. She was dragged out to the street to be stoned." He paused again.

I turned away then, walking toward the open door, and stepped outside, hugging myself... He followed me and took my hand, turning me slowly.

"Jesus was there... and he spoke boldly to the crowd, asking for anyone without sin to cast the first stone... Not one person threw a stone! He then bent down to the woman and forgave her sins! Mary? Did you hear? He forgave her sins, and she went free." His eyes filled with tears, but no sadness came from his lips... only joy.

"I don't understand, Lazarus." I paced, feeling the familiar glimmer of hope warming through me.

"Mary, you do know... We have always known... It's really Him. He is the Messiah... And he says that those who come to Him will have life, abundant life. He comes for the sick, Mary. He heals them with his prayers..." Lazarus continued.

"The miracles! Oh, the miracles, Mary!" My brother then began to cough violently and nearly lost his breath.

I took his hand and led him inside to sit at the kitchen table.

"No, dear sister. I must go tell Deborah and bring word to Martha. I just came from Simon's leprosy camp... I stayed for three days, untouched by fear of sickness, and told them about Jesus. He's going to come here, Mary. He will heal us all!" Lazarus reached out for my shoulders and said one last thing before he left: "Believe, Mary. He is the answer..."

Then my brother turned and ran up the hill, back toward the village, laughing and singing the praise songs of King David.

"Jesus," I said aloud while sitting alone in my cottage.

I had forgotten all about Jesus. All the things he'd spoken about in the synagogue flooded my heart once again, like fresh fire.

"The bread of life," I said aloud. *I do remember... But what does this all mean? I have to go back to my brother's house this evening. I have to know more.*

But what about Simon the Pharisee? He will come looking for me after dark. What will he do? Will he go to my brother's house, looking for me? Will he call me out in the streets tomorrow? I frantically questioned myself.

Suddenly, another loud knock came at the door, then it was thrust open.

It was Simon.

"Simon! What are you doing here? You cannot be here! Go!" I thrust him back out the door with all my might.

He slapped me across the face, and I dropped to the sand.

"Silence, woman. You have no right to speak to me in such a way!" he scolded me. "Where were you?" he demanded

"Lazarus is home," I managed to whimper.

"What's that? Ha ha ha! Oh, so the holy brother has returned, has he? Has he come after his harlot, Deborah?" he continued, laughing.

"He's been with the Messiah!" I shouted up at him then covered my mouth.

"The Messiah!" He laughed harder then bent down toward me. "What do you know about the Messiah, you foolish woman?" He spat on the ground near my hands.

"Jesus," I said boldly.

"Oh, great. Jesus, you say? So the blasphemy has reached the ears of Bethany. Jesus, you say? Are you aware that he is parading himself around Israel, gathering followers? The man is a hypocrite, claiming to be the son of God. He is no Messiah!" Simon continued laughing.

"You will come to my house this night! Whether your brother is in town or *not*! I will leave the back door ajar after nightfall. Wait until the lights are out on the bottom floor of the servant's hall and all the guards are relaxed for the evening. Then follow the far wall towards the stairwell. Be silent and unseen, woman, or I will deny you and publicly declare your sin." He turned from me, kicking sand in my face as he walked away without another word.

I remained kneeling in the sand until I could see him no longer.

How was I to see Lazarus that evening if Simon was demanding that I come to him?

"O God," I prayed, "have you heard me, truly, all these years… I'm a foolish woman… I am worthy of less than this sand that I sit upon. Have mercy, O God. Have mercy on me. If Jesus is your son, please show me." I sat there and cried for a few more minutes, completely filled with guilt and fear for what was to come.

But Lazarus said he freed the harlot… He let her go and forgave her sins… Why did he tell me that? Does he know?

Oh, what do I do? How could I have grown so dark inside? How will I ever be good enough for Jesus now?

My thoughts began to race… Fear… Guilt… Shame… Worthlessness…

What will I do? What will I do?

That night, I followed Simon's instructions carefully. I waited for several hours after nightfall before leaving my house dressed in a dark robe with a veil pulled over my face. I crept through the village in silence, keeping to the shadows. A cool wind was blowing through the darkened sky, and the eerie sounds of the night came to life.

Once I reached Simon's home, I waited quietly in a back alley, making sure nobody was moving inside. The back door was ajar, just like he'd explained, and I entered into the servants' kitchen. The house was dark, the only light coming from embers glowing in the kitchen hearth. I continued to the back wall and slipped up the stairs one at a time. I tried to prepare a plan of escape if I was seen… but there was little hope of that. Unfortunately, nothing interrupted me, and I arrived at Simon's bedroom door and opened it.

Nobody greeted me, no one was in the room, and my heart raced as thoughts of capture and accusation flooded my mind. Trying to calm myself, I quietly walked around the room, looking for any sign Simon might have left for me… but nothing was there.

Do I leave?

No, if you leave, Simon will— I stopped my own thoughts, and my attention was suddenly drawn to the ledge of his windowsill. On it was a small familiar clay pot.

I went back and checked the doorway once again for Simon but saw no one. Lifting up a small, dim lantern, I took it closer to the window and set it down upon an old wooden table.

I was right!

When I lifted the small clay pot, I noticed it was one of my own.

"Now, how did you get here?" I whispered to the clay.

Remembering Lavan and his Roman position in Jerusalem, I pondered the possibility that Simon had somehow heard all about me from Lavan. After all, he was sent here from Jerusalem to replace our beloved Simon.

Maybe he knew. How else would he have assumed so much about me and my life? How would he have this pot?

Lifting out the swollen cork, I took a deep sniff of the contents. It was Simon's scent, burnt clove… and… aster honey. Immediately, I recognized the foul, pungent smell. It was his personal body oil.

If I take this, then I can prove to anyone that Simon invited me into his chambers. I can prove he lay with me… Well… I can at least try to defend my honor and explain his false proposal. No one who knows Simon could deny this oil mixture is his.

I considered the risk of stealing something that could in some way either convict me or possibly protect me.

A noise came from the stairwell, and the time to consider was over. I quickly tucked the small pot into the inner pocket of my robe, rolled it into a ball, and tossed it on the floor by the door.

It will be safe there on the floor. I'll keep him busy then go once he is asleep. My mind was made up.

The sweat of fear trickled down my neck as I stood waiting for him to enter. Flashing back, I remembered being caught in the viper's grip. But this time, the snake was Simon, and he was slowly winding up the stairs to devour me.

Chapter Twenty-Eight

"A way of escape…"
1 Corinthians 10:13, TPT

THE DOOR SLOWLY OPENED, AND a figure in a dark cloak entered. To my surprise, a woman lifted her hood and hurried close to me.

"Mary? Are you Mary of Bethany?" The woman asked with haste.

"Uh, yes. Yes, that is me. Who are you?" I asked.

"My name is Miryam. I've come to help you," she whispered quickly as she undressed.

"There isn't much time, Mary. Quickly, give me your clothes… He will be here soon," she pleaded with me.

"What? Why?"

"Look, Simon is just outside of town. I encouraged him to drink an entire jug of wine. He will be a confused sluggard by the time he reaches this room! I wish to help you, Mary! Please change into my cloak and leave this place before he arrives! He will not know the difference!" She dimmed the lanterns and began removing my clothes.

As I complied, I turned to the broken woman, asking her why she would do such a thing.

She replied, "I know of you, Mary, of your good name, your beautiful mother… I had heard the men talking about some new 'offering' coming tonight, so I began to listen closely. The more they drank, the easier it was for me to find this woman's identity. When I heard your name, I knew I had to help you for your mother's sake. I couldn't let him do this to you. He's evil, he's a liar, and no woman can stand against his power. Please, Mary. My life is already lost, and I will not let him defile you! Your mother, your precious mother, she tried to save me time and time again from this fate of mine, but I failed. You will not!" She swiftly put on all my garments, including my rolled cloak from the floor, then helped me finish dressing.

"Oh, Miryam! Miryam! Won't he know?" I asked her.

"No, Mary. Like I said, I led the men into heavy drink tonight, and with your fine clothes and scent, Simon won't bother to look upon my face. I will meet his needs and depart before he wakes. Now, go! There is no more time." She cupped my face and lifted her hood, covering me.

"Wait!" I turned to face her once more.

"In that inner pocket, you will find Simon's oil. I took it and was going to keep it for proof that he forced me into his bedchambers. You keep it, but keep it hidden. You may need it."

She nodded while patting the cloak to feel its presence.

I peered back one last time to see Miryam standing in my place, dimming the lanterns and kneeling on the floor near the bedside. Tears streamed down my face as I ran.

Hours went by, and I hid behind the town stables. I had to make sure Miryam was all right, so I waited. I waited for the men to stumble in through the gates and disperse throughout the house.

I prayed and prayed for the Lord to spare Miryam from any harm.

"Please, O Lord, do not lay punishment upon her shoulders. Please, do not let them recognize her. Please, O Lord, deliver this woman from the hands of her enemies."

The prayers came from within me as I prayed unlike I ever had before.

Sure enough, the hours passed, and the dawn was nearing when I saw Miryam slip out of the shadows just long enough for me to catch a glimpse.

She's alive! She did it.

I turned and sat back against the barn wall and stared at the fading starlight.

What do I do now? I let one more prayer leave my lips with a final breath and sat still, mourning the loss this poor woman just suffered for my honor.

I walked slowly through what was left of the night, feeling guilty and ashamed.

"How did I get here?" I asked the dark, empty sky. *Was it the loss of my dreams? My parents?*

At one time, I'd thought I could never forget who I was or where I came from. Life seemed full of dreams and wondrous uncharted adventure. But my steps kept leading me further into darkness, further into the unknown wilderness of a lonely life, and further from whom my parents raised me to be.

Was I really going to cower in fear and fade away? Was I really going to let this man destroy what was left of my life?

I felt power and strength welling within my belly.

Then, in the stillness of the night, a warming, gentle voice soothed me. The words of my beloved grandmother came back to me.

"Mary... Mary.... Are you listening?"

I turned from side to side, looking for the source of this voice. When I realized I was still alone, a great sense of awe came over me.

"God?" I wondered aloud.

The voice was as gentle as a breeze, yet it drew me in reverence.

"I'm listening." I spoke aloud, if only for the trees to hear me. "I'm listening…"

"Mary, do not worry. Do not lose hope."

And as simply as it came, the voice left.

"Oh, God. If you can hear me, please deliver us! I don't know how, I don't know when, but please, Lord, make a way. Give me strength one last time. Help me to have hope and rid me of this fear!"

The warmth of my breath upon the cool night air rose in whispering clouds above me. I stared into the sky, searching for something. No response came, but my heart filled with belief... belief that God was listening.

The time had come to let my loved ones in—the time to rise again. For far too long, I had let my pain define me. For far too long, I had left my faith behind. Though I could not know what the next day would bring, I decided that night that the time had come to stand.

I'll go to Jehoshaphat and Elizabeth. I'll go to Lazarus and Deborah. They'll know what to do. And Miryam... We have to fight for Miryam. I will take her under my wing. I will teach her everything I know, and we will leave this place. If need be, we will start a new life wherever God leads us. Lazarus will know what to do.

As I neared my cottage, determination sparked within me. Everything would be okay.

Chapter Twenty-Nine

"To see who I am…"
John 11:15-44 TPT

"**W**HERE HAVE YOU BEEN, MARY?" Martha scolded me the moment I opened my front door and stepped across the threshold.

"What are you doing here, Martha? You nearly scared me to death!" I almost fell backward at her unexpected presence.

"What am I doing here? Where have you been, Mary? Scared *you* to death?" she replied sharply. "Surprising you is the least of my concerns, Mary. You are out doing who knows what in the middle of the night, while we are broken and suffering!" she went on in desperate anger.

"Martha, never mind where I was. What is wrong? What do you mean 'broken and suffering'?" I tried to calm her down and brought her back to the chair she'd been sitting in. Lighting a few more lamps helped to brighten the room, and I could see Martha's face more clearly. She looked as though she'd been weeping for hours.

"Is Simon all right, Martha?" I asked with concern.

"Simon? Simon? Mary, Lazarus is dead… and where were you?" She exploded my heart with just a few words.

"Lazarus, is… dead? Martha, what are you talking about? I just saw him yesterday… He was here!" I replied.

"Yes, he returned early yesterday morning from the lepers' camp. That is true… But later in the evening, we were sitting at the table, talking about Jesus… Deborah, Lazarus, and me. He had so much to tell us, and we stayed up well into the night… He kept saying surely you would come, and we should wait." She took a deep, trembling breath then continued.

"He wasn't looking well, but he wouldn't let Deborah and I tend to him. He kept pressing on about Jesus and how He was coming here. He then began violently choking and coughing for air… The color left his lips… Something took his breath, Mary, and he… he…" Martha's voice lost all its strength, and she broke with a sob, crying and sinking her face into her palms.

"What? No! Martha, what do you mean… Martha, explain!" I desperately tried to pull a better report from her, but she gave no reply. She only sat and wept before me.

"Martha… I…" I had no words. There was nothing I could say.

While I was out dealing with Simon the Pharisee, hiding while another woman bore my shame, my precious and most beloved brother… died.

Abruptly, Martha stood, pushing her chair out as she rose.

"You were not here." She stared into my eyes, and I shrank back.

"Go to the house, Mary. Bring what you have left from Silas's collection of herbs and oils. The physicians are preparing the body, and you will help. It's the least you can do… and be ready because Deborah is there." Martha collected her things and pushed past me into the waking morning.

————— ❦ —————

I approached my brother's body with quiet reverence.

Deborah had met me at the back door, and after a few minutes with her outside, she cleared the room and allowed me time alone with Lazarus.

He was laid out on the table, white linen sheets under and around him. The physicians and the rabbis had nearly finished dressing and preparing him for burial.

Gently, I sat down at the table near my brother's right side and checked the room once more for any prying eyes. Then, against tradition, I slid my fingers down his arm and found his cold hand. I couldn't say goodbye to my hero brother without touching him one last time. Tears flowed from my eyes for the first time since the news came to me. He was gone... He was really gone.

Whatever had happened was real... and my heart couldn't bear it. I reached into my satchel and pulled out the jar of lavender I had left for my mother the night she passed away.

After taking the sprigs of lavender out from the oil, I placed one in each of his hands. Then I stood and anointed his head.

His hair was still a dark, rich brown, with streaks of white coming through around his ears. He was so young, so beautiful, so perfectly holy and kind...

I ran my fingers through his hair, smoothing the fragrant oil over every strand. Down his neck and over his shoulders... If there was a specific way to anoint a body, I was not aware of it. But I continued while my tears dropped down upon him. Finally, I cleansed his feet and poured more oil upon them as well.

On the table lay a small selection of mother's white roses that someone had recently clipped. I took the flowers off the stems and placed them down his chest, over his heart, and down to his waist. Then I sat back down and prayed.

After only a few words, both Deborah and Martha entered the kitchen and stood behind me. Our voices flooded the room with the uncommon sound of women's voices praying.

Martha's voice was calm and direct. "God, welcome our brother into your heavenly dwelling place. He is... was a holy man who lived his life according to your commandments." She finished.

Then Deborah spoke. Her voice was filled with sincerity as she reached out a hand, placed it upon my shoulder, then whispered, "Lazarus, you were my dearest friend, the one whom I hoped to love all my life. Mighty God, please... Jesus... The one you know and love has died... Please come, Jesus." Her voice faded into crying.

I picked up where she left off. "Yes, Almighty God, Lord, let it be as Lazarus has said. Send the Messiah, show us your son, and forgive us of our sins."

Elizabeth and Jehoshaphat arrived back in Bethany on the same morning of Lazarus's death and came sorrowfully to our side. We shared with them about Jesus and everything Lazarus had told us, honoring what we knew he would want most. Jehoshaphat then arose, took his mule, and left for Jerusalem, for that is where Lazarus had told us Jesus would be. He was determined to find the Jesus our Lazarus believed in and bring him back.

For three days, we waited in mourning and in hope. The morning of the fourth day came, and the crowds had grown significantly as people from all over Israel traveled to show their respect for the life of Lazarus. Even the lepers came and camped just outside the village limits, near the burial grounds.

A young servant from Deborah's father's farm suddenly came running toward the house, calling, "Hello! Hello, is anyone within from the family of Lazarus?" His voice caused the crowds to chatter as he was led into our home to where we were sitting around the table.

Martha rose, leaving us in the kitchen and greeted the young man. We could hear her explaining that she was his sister.

"Jehoshaphat walks alongside Jesus. They are just outside of the village now. Come quickly and see for yourself!" The boy flew out the door without another word.

Without returning to us, Martha ran out the front door, following the boy toward the edge of Bethany. Deborah and I didn't know what to think.

Martha explained afterword, how she grieved to him, saying…

"My Lord, if only you had come sooner, my brother wouldn't have died. But I know that if you were to ask God for anything, He would do it for you."

Jesus told her, "Your brother will rise and live."

"Yes, I know he will rise with everyone else on resurrection day," she replied.

"Martha," Jesus said, "you don't have to wait until then. I am the Resurrection, and I am Life Eternal. Anyone who clings to me in faith, even though he dies, will live forever. And the one who lives by believing in me will never die. Do you believe this?" He waited patiently.

"Yes, Lord, I do! I've always believed that you are the Anointed One, the Son of God who has come into the world for us!"

When Martha hurried back to gather Deborah and me, she kept rehearsing every word spoken between her and Jesus. My heart leapt with hope, and all hesitation began to leave.

It really was Jesus...

The servant returned once again, this time lingering with his message. "The Master is now here, and he's asking for all of you."

Here?

When Deborah and I heard this, we quickly joined Martha and went to Him, for Jesus was lingering outside our home.

I fell at his feet in tears, crying...

"Lord, if only you had been here, my brother would not have died," I said desperately.

Jesus looked down at me then at Deborah and all those who had followed. He spoke with great emotion and tears of his own. "Where did you bury him?" He asked gently.

"Lord, come with us, and we'll show you," Deborah responded.

Then tears streamed down Jesus's face.

Seeing Jesus weep caused many of the mourners to say, "Look how much he loved Lazarus."

Yet others said, "Isn't this the one who opens blind eyes? Why didn't he do something to keep Lazarus from dying?"

When Jesus arrived at the tomb, a cave with a stone placed over its entrance, Jesus called to the crowd, "Roll away the stone."

"But Lord, it's been four days since he died. By now, his body is already decomposing!" Martha called out in grief, not understanding.

Jesus looked at her and said, "Didn't I tell you that if you will believe in me, you will see God unveil his power?"

"Yes, my Lord." Martha looked at me while nodding in agreement.

So they rolled away the heavy stone.

Jesus gazed into heaven and said, "Father, thank you that you have heard my prayer, for you listen to every word I speak. Now, so that these who stand here with me will believe that you have sent me to the earth as your messenger, I will use the power you have given me."

Then with a loud voice, Jesus shouted with authority, "Lazarus! Come out of the tomb!"

Then, in front of everyone, Lazarus, who had died four days earlier, slowly hobbled out. He still had grave clothes tightly wrapped around his hands and feet and covering his face.

Jesus told them, "Unwrap him and let him loose."

The crowds broke out in shouts of praise and awe, while Martha, Deborah, and I ran toward Lazarus and tore the wrapped cloths from his body.

He stood in a daze but smiled with the whitest teeth I'd ever seen. "Jesus. He has come!" he sang out in praise, looking toward Jesus, who stood at a distance.

I couldn't understand what was happening. It was too much to absorb. Jesus, our Jesus, stood there surrounded by his disciples in a loving glow, and my brother was suddenly alive and well. I couldn't hold back my tears, they flowed with such force, yet joy filled my heart.

As the people came and circled Lazarus—reaching out to touch him and see that he was, in fact, alive—voices called from a distance, and the crowd dispersed, creating an opening.

It was Simon, our Simon.

"Lord, Lord! I am healed. I am healed. We are all healed!" he shouted.

Martha rose from the ground to greet her husband and recognized immediately that his face and body had been completely restored.

"It is Simon! He has been healed as well! Glory, glory to God!" she sang out as she embraced her husband for the first time in years.

"My brother, Lazarus!" Simon yelled as he made his way through the crowd.

"Lazarus, we have been made whole!" Simon continued with shouts of joy.

"Go, and be seen by your physicians. All of you. Go and be well," Jesus instructed.

Lazarus's laughter was contagious, and soon all were weeping and rejoicing together in a worshipful harmony.

"Join us, Jesus. Tonight, we will feast in celebration of the Lord's return to Bethany. Simon and I welcome you into our home!" Lazarus held his hands open wide, and Jesus came with tear-filled eyes and embraced his dear friend with acceptance.

I noticed that a few men were speaking behind the mighty crowd and overheard one say they were going to tell Simon the Pharisee, and my heart shuddered at the sound of his name.

I stood at a distance, watching in awe of the miracles unfolding before me, but the miracle I just witnessed was too much for my shamed heart to bare. Slowly, I faded back through the crowds and down into the wild wheat valley, disappearing from everyone's sight.

Once I felt free from the eyes of men, I began to run home.

That was the only thing I knew to do when the sorrow and pain became too unbearable.

I ran all the way to my little cottage and went inside immediately, closing the doors and windows tightly and lighting a few oil lamps. I climbed up on my bed, wrapped myself in mother's shawl, and cried.

Simon will come, he will expose me, he will hurt my family, they will find out. Miryam... What about Miryam? What will they do to her? I cannot go. I cried and cried.

Hopelessness entered my thoughts, and I laid my head down under a pillow, trying to drown out the torment.

"You foolish woman. You are unworthy of Jesus. Do not go to the feast. You will be called out and stoned by the crowds. You will bring further shame upon your family. You have no worth, and you will not be welcome there. What you have done is detestable, and there is no future for you..."

Chapter Thirty

"Faith, then, is birthed…"
Romans 10:13-17, TPT

I AWOKE HOURS LATER, AND THE sun was falling behind the distant mountains.

"Jesus?" I called aloud.

Nobody answered.

"It was Jesus!" I crawled to my knees and began replaying a dream I'd just had over and over again in my mind so that I wouldn't forget.

"There was a man…" I continued to speak aloud, scrambling for paper to write down my thoughts. "There was a man. It was Jesus. I saw him in the synagogue, just as if I was still a little girl. I was watching him through the cracked door again. I could hear him talking about how he was the bread of life and that Immanuel would give his life as an atonement for sin. The dream flashed suddenly to a beaten man walking up a dirt road, carrying a cross upon his shoulders. The man was so badly wounded that I could barely recognize his face, but I could see he was wearing a crown. It was glowing. Though it was made of great thorns, it was glowing. His eyes… They looked right into me… just like Jesus did when I was facing the viper and just like when Jesus looked at me through the cracked synagogue door. It was him!"

I finished writing and sat back upon my bed, pondering what I had seen. The power of that dream was unmistakable… but I didn't know what it all meant.

Pacing, I unwrapped my hair and let it flow free. I prayed aloud again, asking God for answers.

"I know! I'll work! I always find peace of mind when my hands are busy."

I went around to the back side of my cottage and down into the ditch and picked up a raw piece of clay and placed it upon a clean wheel. For some time, I began to work with it, dipping my hands into a basin of water, then placing them on the lump of clay. Over and over, I lifted and pressed the clay with gentle repetition. I pressed my fingers deep into the center. After several trips from the basin to the clay, it softened and took shape, and my mind began to quiet.

I drew the clay out farther and farther until it opened and spread out into a shallow bowl. As I worked in silence, my thoughts wandered.

When I was younger, my future had seemed bright and full of purpose. I was going to be something special for my family—a "pearl," my mother would call me. Yet there I sat, working with soil and water, alone in a dimly lit cottage, feeling like nothing more than a broken clay pot, destroyed by tragedy. There had to be more…

Everyone around me was beaming with light. Jesus was here, and miracles were happening…

"For those who deserve them," a sly voice whispered in my head.

"No!" I shouted in reply. "There must be more! What are you saying, God?"

At that moment, I remembered Mother's letter. I stood from my place, abandoned my work, and washed my hands.

After opening the small cupboard, I took out the little wooden box that held the precious letter from my mother and the goodbye from Eli.

I'm not waiting anymore! I had made my choice. I was going to open the letters.

I placed Eli's letter on the table and took my mother's over to my bed.

Slowly, I unwrapped the twine, snapped the white wax seal, and set the dried lavender sprig upon my pillow. When I opened the outer cover, two letters dropped to the floor. As I lifted them in my hand, I could see one was written in my mother's handwriting and the other… in my grandmother's. I began to read.

My darling little Lavender,

I write to you today on our journey back from the sea. For whatever reason, I have become ill, and I know not how long I shall live. My little precious one, there are things I must tell you before I go.

Ever since you were a young girl, your eyes have looked to the skies. The captivating awe on your face lifted the hearts of your father and me. Through our service to God's people, our hearts were often heavy and burdened though we did not share that. It was you, my little Lavender, who led us through every difficult season. Your joy and love for life kept us going. It was as if the very love of God was within you from your birth, and you could see Him in the world.

I know you carry the weight of your condition and the fear of being unworthy, but my dear one, let it go. Let it go up into the wind and off into the hands of our faithful God. There is no pain nor tragedy too great for the light inside you to overcome. You were given to this world for a purpose. Arise, and be radiant, like the beautiful sunrise that you are. Let your light shine before all…

I am with you always,

Feel my love when the sun shines upon your cheek and when you are gardening with the birds and the butterflies.

Your loving Mother

I wept as I held mother's gardening shawl closely around me.

"Mother... Oh, Mother!" I cried out, desperately hoping to hear her reply.

She doesn't know what's happened to me, the mistakes I have made, what I have become...

I placed her letter on the bed and lifted the one in my grandmother's handwriting.

Mary,

Remember these words. Are you listening?

Almighty God has an important plan for your life. You will hold a great and valuable story of unending love. You, my dear one, will come to be loved by the greatest love ever known, one who will never leave nor forsake you. And your story will be told throughout the ages.

Do not worry. Do not lose hope. Pour your life out at his feet and fulfill your destiny, my child.

Grandmother Lillian

Suddenly, I looked at the alabaster jar on my windowsill, and revelation awakened my heart. I leapt from my bed and ran to the sill eagerly, to lift the jar into the air. I thrust open the window, and a fresh, cooling breeze blew in. The fading sunlight beamed through the white alabaster. It was nearly full of all the oils I had collected from my failed loves... I never thought I would find a purpose for them, until now...

The love grandmother and mother spoke of… it was Jesus. All that time, it was Jesus. I had been searching all these years for a man to fill a void within me that no man was meant to. I was to be poured out at His feet…

Will he love me… as I am? It hurt to wonder. *If I come to Jesus, humbly bowing at his feet… surely he will receive this valuable oil as an acceptable offering, one worthy of the Messiah.* I saw myself pouring out the contents, asking for mercy and forgiveness.

A warm, gentle voice spoke deep within. It flowed out from my belly and brought me peace: *"Remember what Lazarus said to you."*

"He forgave her sins," I whispered aloud in response.

I replayed my brother's passionate words to me.

Hope budded and blossomed within my heart.

My next tears were those of relief, and I knew deep inside what I must do. I grabbed my mother's shawl, wrapped it around myself, then picked up the sprig of lavender from my pillow. Silas had taught me that lavender was used for cleansing during burial or for anything that may be unclean. So I took what I had and dropped it into the alabaster jar, then I resealed it as tightly as I could. With the jar in one hand and Eli's letter in the other, I was ready to leave.

Once outside the door, I set the jar down on a small stool and held Eli's letter out over the cold fire pit. I unhooked the hanging oil lamp by the front door and lit the bottom corner of the letter, allowing it to burn. When it was nearly ash, I placed what was left in the cool fire pit to finish. I then picked up the alabaster jar and ran home.

For the first time in years, I was running to something, not from. My feet moved swiftly, and I flew over the ground like an ibex leaping upon mountain cliffs. My heart was beating fiercely inside my chest. The lover of my soul had come for me, and I'd nearly missed Him. Revelation struck me once again, and the enemy's lies were exposed. I had been robbed. The adversary of my soul had plagued me with his darkness, but I could feel the sunlight of truth piercing the horizon.

My Lord is here! Surely, He will restore me.

I saw the viper flash before me, and I saw Jesus. I saw the enemy's snakelike grip, slowly wrapping itself around me, hiding under the cloak of pain, loss, and tragedy. *No longer! No longer was I prey!*

———— *❧ ʙᴇᴇᴛʟᴇ* ———

The house was glowing with lanterns and torches, and people were crowding around every corner, down both sides of the house, and out in the back garden. I walked slowly toward the front door and paused to look through the window. Jesus was sitting on a chair facing the front entrance of the house, still and quiet. Others around him were speaking and laughing within a beautiful atmosphere of joy and peace, but Jesus sat still. Then, knowingly, he lifted his gaze to the window where I stood just outside.

This is it, my only chance…

I took a deep breath and opened the door.

The voices lowered, and all eyes were suddenly upon me as I entered my brother's house. I saw Lazarus, Simon the leper, and Jesus's disciples gathered around the table, but I looked only at Jesus.

Slowly I walked toward him and lowered myself to the floor.

I removed his sandals and wiped the sand from his feet. Then I reached up to the table for a large bowl and brought it down. As I lifted His feet, I was overwhelmed by His holy presence and began to weep. This precious man had always been a friend to our family, but on that day, I bowed before my Messiah. I carefully unwrapped my hair and let it down. It was the last pure part of me left untainted, and no one was more worthy than Jesus. As I opened the alabaster jar, the purest fragrance of lavender nard filled the house. I was amazed at how all the other scents, like those horrible memories, had simply faded away.

As I continued anointing, weeping, and cleansing Jesus's feet, secret prayers poured out from deep within my heart.

Oh, Lord. My precious Lord… I remember you. You are the bread of life, and I believe. Please, Jesus, cleanse me of my shame, of my guilt, and of my pain. I am a barren, worthless woman in the eyes of men, but I believe I am more in your sight. I realize now that your love is all I need. Forgive me.

Jesus leaned forward and gently reached down and touched my head. "Go and be healed, my child. You are valuable to me, you are loved, and you are forgiven." His gentle voice spoke with authority within me, and I looked up into his all-knowing, loving eyes and felt immediate peace wash over me.

Every tormenting thought that had haunted my mind now fled as I came to understand that Jesus's words within my heart were the only truth. His truth replaced every lie I had struggled with, and I knew I was forever changed.

A voice loudly interrupted our internal conversation. It was a man named Judas. He said, "What a waste! We could have sold this perfume for a fortune and given the money to the poor."

Jesus sat back in his chair, looking up at the man, and replied, "Leave her alone! She has saved it for the time of my burial. You will always have the poor with you, but you won't always have me."

He then looked upon me once again with the warmest smile and began to teach the gathered crowd.

I remained on the floor by his side the entire evening, listening and soaking in every truth and revelation he shared.

Toward the end of the evening, Martha came and tapped me on the shoulder, urging me with exasperation to come and assist her in the kitchen, but I could not bear to leave the feet of Jesus.

Unexpectedly, Martha stood to her feet and interrupted Jesus's teaching. "Lord, don't you think it's unfair that my sister left me to do all the work by myself? You should tell her to get up and help me."

The Lord answered her, "Martha, my beloved Martha. Why are you upset and troubled, pulled away by all these many distractions? Are they really that important? Mary has discovered the most important thing by choosing to sit at my feet. She is undistracted, and I won't take this privilege from her."

Taken aback with embarrassment and shock, Martha turned slowly and hid within the walls of the kitchen, and my heart broke for her.

"Mary… is right?" I could hear her whispering to Deborah. She broke into a quiet cry and I leaned over trying to catch a glimpse of my dear sister. Down she went, falling upon her knees to pray.

I had never seen Martha pray, other than that morning beside Lazarus's sleeping body. I knew the revelation had pierced her heart as well, and she could now see the old religion was being renewed through Jesus.

After all the people dispersed to their homes, Lazarus, Martha, Deborah, and I cleaned the house together, reflecting on the holy presence that lingered in our home. Our whole village was changed because of the gospel of Jesus Christ, and we felt inspired to work alongside his disciples, whatever the cost.

Lazarus and I walked Deborah home, and we spoke mostly of what the future might look like. They still planned to marry, and soon, and they both decided to walk in the footsteps of Jesus for the rest of their lives.

As we were walking through the market square, three men came out of a dark alley and swiftly moved in front of us, blocking our path. Lazarus leapt forward, demanding that the men cease in the name of the Lord.

One of the men barreled toward my brother in aggressive accusation. "Blasphemers! Who are you to command me?" Simon the Pharisee stepped into the light, revealing himself alongside two others.

My heart raced. *Oh, no! The time has come. Simon will falsely accuse me! I could be stoned!*

Though I was panicking, a sweet voice came up from my belly and spoke to me: *"Peace. Be still, for I am the Lord your God, and I will never leave you nor forsake you."*

"We have no trouble with you, Simon. Be blessed and know Jesus is the true Messiah! May my very life be the proof you need to believe!" Lazarus spoke in a commanding voice. He was so sure of himself, so sure that Jesus was forever with us that the faith he exuded radiated around him like a glow.

"Ha! You have fooled many, Lazarus, but you have not fooled me! I will be sure to expose this 'Jesus.' He will be dining with me tomorrow night. Then we will see who your loyalty lies with." He remained at a distance as if he was too afraid to be touched by my brother, alive again.

Lazarus noticed that and took a step forward—Simon shrank back again.

"Do not be afraid," Lazarus said. "We are all sinners in need of the Messiah, Brother Simon. May God show you His mercy and righteousness tomorrow evening." He lifted his hands and prayed this over the doubting men.

"You and that… that… that sister of yours! You will see!" Without another word, he turned and left with his men and disappeared back into the darkness.

Chapter Thirty-One

"Your faith has healed you."
Matthew 9:22, TPT

L AZARUS OFFERED TO STAY AND keep watch throughout the
night, but I knew I was safe, safer than I had ever been. So I
sent him on his way with a warm embrace.

"I love you, dear sister. I am so pleased for you." Lazarus held my
shoulders, and I saw my father, for a moment, smiling back.

"Thank you, Lazarus. I'm so glad you are okay... So glad Jesus
came, just like you said he would. I know I have made many mistakes,
that I have caused you all grief because of my own suffering... Please
forgive me, brother." I reached up to touch his hand.

"Ah, you are forgiven, dear sister, and you are a blessed woman.
Rest and join us in the morning at our father's house." With one more
tap on my shoulder, he released me and closed the door.

I took a few moments to ready my bed for the night and light a small
fire in the kitchen hearth for warmth. I felt a little... uncomfortable...

*It must be from all the walking and intense emotions throughout
the day.* I was very tired and ready for sleep.

Under my bed I kept a small trunk, one Silas had given me a few
years before. Inside I kept a few of his things that my brother had saved
for me after Silas's death. His cloak and tunic were folded neatly on

top, covering one small pot. Inside it was the last portion of his special perfumed spikenard oil. I took it out, along with his cloak, and climbed into bed.

Once I was tucked warmly under the blankets, I took his cloak and formed a pillow to rest my arm upon. I ran my thumb across the coarse clay of the pot and traced the small lavender imprint. It had been his idea to press a fresh lavender sprig down into the wet clay, and it worked. Slowly, I opened the pot, and his scent filled my senses, bringing tears to my eyes.

Out of all the expensive oils I had received throughout my past, this was the only one I cherished—true and pure Indian spikenard, scented with cardamom, anise, cinnamon, and a slight hint of pine. The scent brought memories flooding back into my heart, and I realized I needed to leave one last thing at the feet of Jesus—Silas.

"My God, my Father in Heaven, thank you for today. Thank you for everything. I praise you for your loving mercy. I praise you for the bees and the butterflies. Thank you for the gift of Jesus, for forgiving me. Lord, you are all that I want. Please give me the strength to walk in your footsteps. Show me what I am to do."

I blew out the light and drifted into a deep sleep.

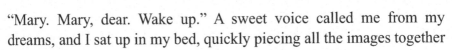

"Mary. Mary, dear. Wake up." A sweet voice called me from my dreams, and I sat up in my bed, quickly piecing all the images together once again.

"Deborah? Good morning! What are you doing here?" I smiled and pulled off my covers.

"Well… I'm not sure, really. I woke up this morning and felt like I needed to come here. And… well… I now see why." She smiled at me, blushing, and put her hands down upon my bed.

I looked down and saw the markings of blood underneath me.

"Oh my!" I jumped from the bed, embarrassed and scared all at once. I kept pulling the blankets up toward me to cover up, but it was nearly impossible.

"Don't be afraid, Mary. I believe it's a sign that Jesus healed you.

All of you." She stood still, covering her heart with her hands. "Come out to the stream, and I will help you clean up. We will know for sure in a few days. How do you feel?" She bundled up the blankets.

"I... I... I feel.. okay, I guess. How am I supposed to feel?" I asked shyly.

"Umm... well, sometimes unwell, but 'okay' is a good sign." She took my hand, and we walked out the door and quickly went down to the stream.

The water was a rush of coolness, but I welcomed it. I waded out to the deepest spot in the stream, just above my knees, and sat down in the water. Deborah stayed by the shoreline, washing out my blankets, and I managed my best, privately. She was right. It must have been a sign that I was healed, for I had never bled before.

Once I was all cleaned up and dressed properly, I sat Deborah down at the table and shared with her.

"Deborah, there is something else I want to share with you, but I know it will sound quite troublesome." I waited for her nod then continued. "I had a dream the other day before I came to Jesus. I have kept a lot from you over this last year, and I am very sorry. I'm sorry for my darkness, for my lack of faith, for any pain I have caused you... But I must tell you about the dream. It's why I came to the feet of Jesus."

"Oh, Mary, all is well. Do tell," she said with beaming eyes of love.

"It was... It was about Jesus. I saw him in the synagogue when we were just little girls. I could hear him talking about how he was the bread of life and that Immanuel would give his life as an atonement for sin." I looked into Deborah's curious eyes then continued. "Then the dream flashed to a beaten man walking up a dirt road carrying a cross upon his shoulders. The man was so badly wounded that I could barely recognize his face, but I could see he was wearing a crown. It was glowing. Though it was made of great thorns, it was glowing. His eyes, Deborah... They looked right into me. Just like with Jesus and the viper, just like when Jesus looked at me through the cracked synagogue door, and just like he did last night. It was him, Deborah. What Jesus said is true. He will give His life for our sins, and it will be soon. I'm not sure what will happen to Him, but I know He knows what's coming." I finished speaking and sat back in my chair, breathing deeply.

"Wow, Mary. That is… I do not know what to say… It's heart-breaking," she replied quietly.

"Then I read Mother's letter. Did I tell you there were two letters? One was from Grandmother. When I read them, I just suddenly understood I needed to run to Jesus. He was the love Grandmother spoke of, the one who would heal my broken heart and restore my soul!" I shared with renewed excitement.

"I understand!" she replied to my joy.

"But, Deborah, last night, as I slept, I had the same dream. When I woke this time, to your presence in the room, I had an inner feeling that I am to pass this dream and the revelation of who Jesus is… to someone else," I said.

"Well… what do you think you should do?" Deborah sat back also, and we both let our thoughts wander for a while, in silence.

"I think I need to go to Miryam," I said cautiously.

"Miryam…? Do you mean Miryam the… the harlot?" Deborah asked delicately.

I stood from my seat and picked up the lavender pot from my bed. Handing it to Deborah, I encouraged her to open it. Once she did, she looked right up at me.

"Wherever did you get this, Mary? This is Silas's, is it not?" She stood to hand it back.

"Yes. You'd better sit back down. I have much more to tell you." I placed the pot on the table and told Deborah everything. I shared how Simon the Pharisee came to my door and how he trapped me with threats. I told her all about the night Lazarus died and how I met Miryam.

"Oh, Mary! You shouldn't go to her. Please, if Simon sees you, he may accuse you! Do you have his oil too? Where is it?" She asked desperately.

I told her I'd given it to Miryam for her protection. Even if Simon the Pharisee had noticed the small pot was missing, nothing had come of it… yet.

Then we both agreed that forgiveness and healing needed to come to Miryam as well.

Deborah still urged me to stay away from Simon the Pharisee's home that evening, but I asked her to try to understand how I could not. Our paths had crossed for a reason, and if I held the key to her forgiveness... I had to go. I had to encourage her to go to Jesus. I had to stand alongside Miryam. She would be terrified, and I needed to help walk her into freedom. This had to be why God shared this dream with me, twice. It was not meant to be solely for myself...

"Then I'll go with you, even if only to wait outside the door with you," she offered. "But let her go in alone, Mary. Please, it is her journey as well..."

"We can share all of this with Lazarus before I do anything. I don't want to keep any more from him," I said in partial agreement.

"I'm certain Lazarus will want to go as well." With that, she nodded and encouraged me to get ready. "Now, before we go to your brother's house and discuss all this with him, we need to visit Elizabeth. She will be so overjoyed with the news of your healing, and she will know if everything is all right with your body." Deborah remade my bed and spread out new, clean blankets in an attempt to hurry me along.

I picked up a few things to bring with me for the day's needs and wrapped Silas's cloak around myself. Once all the lanterns were out and the fire was quenched, Deborah and I walked to Elizabeth's house.

"I am interested to hear what your brother thinks of the dream, Mary. I know it will be difficult to tell him about Simon the Pharisee's threats, but remember God made a way out for you. He is the one who has saved you. Lazarus will see that." Her words encouraged me.

"Yes, I agree." I took hold of Deborah's arm, and we rejoiced together once again.

"You have been healed, Mary! You were healed!" Deborah chanted. *I was healed...*

I meditated on those incredible words along our journey to the house of Jehoshaphat as the image of Miryam remained in my heart.

Chapter Thirty-Two

"Eyes of your own understanding"
Ephesians 1:18 KJV

W E SAT AT THE TABLE quietly while Lazarus reclined with his eyes closed, reflecting on the dream. Then, suddenly, his eyes opened and he leaped to his feet.

"I understand!" He shouted!

We all sat with wide eyes, watching and waiting for him to say more.

"Mary, remember that moment when Jesus approached my grave and called me forth? I was dead and now I am alive!" He paused.

Paying no attention to the details I expressed about my encounter with Simon the Pharisee, Lazarus flew in the spirit of revelation, about Jesus.

We all agreed, cheering once again.

"Now you can see that my very life is a testimony, authenticating the power of Jesus, the Messiah, the Son of God! Jesus said, 'I Am the resurrection and the life.' So, if He is the resurrection and the life, then He too must die and then be resurrected by the power of God, thus fulfilling the law's requirement of a perfect blood sacrifice! With His resurrection, He can then offer forgiveness of all sin and give eternal life to all who will believe that He is the Lamb of God! Mary! Jesus is going to die, just like you dreamt, but He is going to live again! That's why Jesus taught about Jonah and the great fish! Jonah was within the belly of the fish for three days and then released! You watch!" He said, erupting in laughter and praise.

"Jesus will rise from the grave in THREE DAYS!"

We all stood to our feet, cheering and rejoicing in the power of Jesus Christ, our Lord. Our little family here in Bethany was part of the most beautiful love story ever told.

"The final blood sacrifice...forever forgiven..." I whispered out loud.

"Mary, you need not be afraid. God has delivered you from the serpent time and time again! You must go! Go! Find the woman and do what God has placed within your heart. Deborah and I will come along and see to your safety. But, what can mere man do to those who move in the name of the Lord Jesus Christ of Nazareth! Simon the Pharisee's threats no longer hold any power over you!" Lazarus continued on, connecting the dots aloud while I withdrew to my room to pray.

"Lord, I praise you. Thank you for saving me, again and again. Thank you for my brothers love and wisdom. Please, prepare Miryam for me. I will go and search for her. Let it be as you have shown me."

It didn't take very long to locate Miryam in the shadow of the market place. She was in the corner of an alley, asleep.

"Miryam, come with me. Quickly!" I spoke swiftly, to wake her and flee before wondering eyes could identify me.

Without hesitation she took my hand and I lead her out of the town and down the road to my cottage. Once inside, we removed our cloaks.

"Please sit, Miryam." I pointed to a chair then began to close the window coverings and light the oil lamp.

"First, I must ask you. Are you alright?" I waited patiently.

"Yes, Mary, I am alright. Why have you come to me? Do not risk being seen with me." She said in simple speech.

"Miryam, I have much to tell you. Please, listen closely. Have you heard of Jesus?" I paused again.

"Yes. Jesus, the one from Nazareth who claims to be God? Simon cannot keep from shouting on about him. He will be dining in his house on this very night." She paused and waited for me to go on.

"Good, that is what we have heard as well. Miryam, I want you to go to Him." I said very simply.

"Go to him?" She laughed.

"To tend to this god's needs, you mean?" She said scornfully.

"No! Miryam, go to Him… For forgiveness… For cleansing." I replied.

"Forgiveness? There is no forgiveness for me…" She looked to the floor.

"I am hopeless."

"Miryam. You are not hopeless. God has made a way for you. I believe it is His will that we met. It was His will you knew my mother in your childhood. And now, it is my turn to help you."

I began to share my story. Painfully, I opened up the sealed wounds of my heart to Miryam, so she could see that she was not alone. I told her everything. Eli… Lavan…about the sudden death of my parents… and finally, about Silas.

I watched as tears dripped down her dusty cheeks as she began to see the real me. I reiterated Simon's threats and could see the reflections of my words, my feelings, and the evil ones lies, in her eyes. She understood my pain and it was clear that she too had heard the tormenting thoughts herself.

I told her about how I had the dream of the broken and battered man, carrying a cross and wearing a crown of thorns. And how I ran to the feet of Jesus to find only grace, love and healing.

She froze.

"I… I… I had the same dream. Mary, I have seen what you have seen!" Miryam surprised me with her comment.

"But, I knew not the meaning." She began to rock in her chair, trembling.

Fear. It was fear trying to surround her.

"Miryam!" I called her back to me.

"You need not be afraid. God will be with you. It is His will that you are redeemed. You are not too far gone. Those thoughts in your head are lies! There IS hope for you! A new life of freedom is waiting for you at the feet of Jesus."

Breath began flow freely once again from her lungs, and I could see the relief rising in her eyes.

"Do you still have Simon the Pharisee's oil? The one we took from his room?" I waited hopefully.

"Yes, yes I do." She reached into her cloak, pulled it out and set it upon the table.

"Good, Miryam, take it with you. This will keep Simon from accusing you. He will not reveal you, for if he does, they all will be exposed of their guilt. Set it on the table and fall to the feet of Jesus. Take all that you have and break it before the Lord, anointing Jesus's feet."

I paused for a moment, then reached into my cupboard, took Silas' spikenard, and handed it to Miryam.

"Please, Miryam, take this precious spikenard that I give to you, and anoint Jesus's head for burial."

"I can't Mary, I simply cannot! How can I approach the Savior? I am a sinner." She cried desperately.

"But you can. We are all sinners, Miryam."

I paused for a few moments then shared. "Miryam, I went to Jesus. When He came to my brothers house, I went. I brought the oils I had collected through my years. Miryam, they represented more than their monetary value. To me, they represented my past. I wanted to give all that I had, all that I was, the truth of all that I had been through…to Jesus. Miryam, He looked down upon me with grace and mercy. He set me free, and He healed me. He accepted me. He… He loves me."

Her face was blushed from crying but she sat still now. Something inside of her changed and I could see it in her eyes.

"You can, Miryam. He has come to give us life, to atone for sin, once and forever. He is the son of God, Miryam; the Messiah. The dream we had reveals to us that He is the final sacrifice. No more goats, pigeons, lambs… He is the perfect spotless lamb. Once He gives His life for us, God will never remember our sin again!" I urged her to be strong and have faith.

She nodded.

"And this?" She held out Silas' spikenard.

"This is the last offering I have for Jesus. I didn't bring it with me when I went to Him. But now that I know and understand Jesus will give His life for our sins, I want Him to have it. Please use it to anoint His head, Miryam. Please."

A few tears slid down my cheek and I waited, still, for her to rise. When she did, we rose together and I knew she was ready.

"Come to the house of Lazarus, just before dusk, at the dinner hour, and we will go with you. I have shared everything with my brother Lazarus and he agrees, you need to go to Jesus. You will see Miryam, your life will forever be changed. Have faith and take courage."

While she stood there considering everything we had discussed, I silently prayed, 'God, Oh, God, thank you! You have lead Miryam to me, and I have done all that I can. Please, give her strength in her weakness. Let her be free, as you have set me free. Thank you, for you have heard my prayers once again. Praise you Lord.'

She twisted her braid nervously in her fingers for a few minutes then rose quickly. Miryam gathered the two pots of oil, safely placing them within her cloak and timidly agreed to meet me at my brother's house.

"Mary? Why are you doing his for me?" Miryam asked.

"For my mother... For you... For Jesus. We are sisters in Christ, dear Miryam, and you are worthy."

Chapter Thirty-Three

"That she hath done"
Mark 14:9 KJV

S IMON THE PHARISEE'S HOME WAS in front of us and we
could see another crowd gathering outside to listen through the
windows. I squeezed Deborah's hand, nodded to Miryam and
encouraged her to enter the house boldly.

I stood just outside the windowsill and could see the rage in Simon's eyes as she walked through the door effortlessly, and uninvited.
The guards began to chatter and point in her direction making snickering remarks. Simon began to break out into a sweat as he saw Miryam
pull the small pot of oil out of her cloak. He rose abruptly from his seat
in fear, making the connection that it was Miryam who had lain with
him that night, and it was her who was in possession of his unmistakable oil. He pulled on his beard and paced back and forth nervously. I
could see the fear in his eyes. The fear that if Miryam remained when
Jesus arrived, his sin would become known.

Surprisingly, the love of God filled my heart toward Simon as I
waited there watching, and I felt mercy instead of anger. Jesus had
removed every thorn his threats once pricked upon my heart. He was
just another broken man needing his Messiah.

Miryam, simply placed his small worn pot upon the table and
waited. No one spoke a word.

Only a few moments went by before Jesus passed through a crowd
and entered Simon's home. Jesus greeted Simon and his guards, as

they hurried him past Miryam, to a seat. I could hear many questions being thrown in His direction but Jesus remained silent.

Immediately, Miryam ran through the crowd of men and fell to the ground. She began to kiss His feet, asking for mercy. Her small delicate hands reached for a large box within her cloak and she broke it open revealing a collection of expensive spikenard perfume. Miryam was trembling and weeping but she managed to pour out the oil upon his feet. She took the ends of her hair and wiped them clean leaving only her tears behind.

When Simon saw what was happening, he mumbled under his breath, "This man cannot be a true prophet. If he were really a prophet, he would know what kind of sinful woman is touching him."

I know how he knows... I glared at him through squinted eyes.

Simon the Pharisee dragged broken women, like Miryam, into his den of deception and sin. His guilt was plain to see and he scrambled to misdirect the attention back on Miryam's past.

Jesus suddenly said aloud, "Simon, I have a word for you."

Surprised by his address he replied, "Go ahead, teacher. I want to hear it." Simon replied.

"It's a story about two men who were deeply in debt. One owed the bank one hundred thousand dollars, and the other only owed ten thousand dollars. When it was obvious that neither of them would be able to repay their debts, the kind banker graciously wrote off the debts and forgave them all that they owed. Tell me, Simon, which of the two debtors would be the most thankful? Which one would love the banker most?"

Simon answered, "I suppose it would be the one with the greatest debt forgiven."

"You're right," Jesus agreed.

I took Deborah's hand and pulled her closer to the window, to hear.

As Jesus continued to speak, Miryam returned to her cloak and pulled out my Silas's pot of Indian nard. The worry she once wore had left her face and Miryam looked to be more at peace. She quietly walked behind Jesus and carefully poured it over his hair, smoothing it through her fingers. For just one moment, Jesus closed his eyes and deeply breathed in the loving fragrance of my dearest love. He then turned to Simon and continued to speak to him about Miryam.

"Don't you see this woman? She is doing for me what you didn't bother to do. When I entered your home as your guest, you didn't think about offering me water to wash the dust off my feet."

"You didn't even welcome me into your home with the customary kiss of greeting. But, from the moment I came in, she has not stopped kissing my feet. You didn't take the time to anoint my head with fragrant oil, but she has anointed my head and feet with the finest perfume. She has been forgiven of all her many sins. This is why she has shown me such extravagant love. But those who assume they have very little to be forgiven will love me very little."

He looked into Miryam's eyes and said, "All your sins are forgiven."

All the dinner guests began to speak among themselves saying, "Who is the one who can even forgive sins?"

Then Jesus continued speaking to Miryam, once more,

"Your faith in me has given you life. Now you may leave and walk in the ways of peace."

She collected her things and walked out the door to meet Lazarus, Deborah and I, as we waited patiently.

"Your part is finished, dear sister. Now we shall gather together in our home, with those we love most... and wait." Lazarus took hold of Deborah's arm and walked her across the street, to give me time to speak with Miryam alone.

When Miryam came out, her face was radiating with peace and freedom. I took her hands in mine and embraced her warmly. She smiled sweetly and uttered three simple words.

"I am free." She beamed.

Just then, before I could say another word, one of the disciples who traveled with Jesus approached us. It was a man named James.

"Excuse me, dear woman. We would like to welcome you to follow us back to Jerusalem." The man looked into Miryam's eyes with kindness and love.

"There is a woman there named, Mary Magdalene. I know she can can be of assistance to you and help you on your new journey as a believer in Jesus Christ, the Messiah." He stood patiently waiting and Miryam looked at me with birthing hope.

"Go." I said softly.

"Go, Miryam, and start a new life. Forget your past, it doesn't matter anymore. Who you were, what you may have done, no longer defines you. Follow Jesus and be well."

Miryam embraced me once more and made the arrangements to meet Jesus's group for departure at dawn.

As we parted ways and I rejoined Lazarus and Deborah, I couldn't help but feel my mothers love in the warm setting sun. I knew now that she tried to help Miryam so many times and God had brought us together. Miryam gave so much to help me and now she was finally free. Jesus had set her free...

Lazarus took our arms and we walked home, quietly reflecting on the majesty unfolding before us.

That night my beautiful family and I sat fellowshipping and rehearsing the teachings of Jesus. Jehoshaphat declared how he would continue to spread Jesus's message all throughout Bethany and that his door would be forever open to all those who wished to come in and hear the gospel.

Simon, our Simon, the now healed leper, and my dear sister, Martha, agreed to stay here in my father's home, making it another pillar in Bethany for people to come and hear the messages of Jesus, our Lord. They spoke of filling the rooms with children and carrying on the ministry for ages to come.

Lazarus and Deborah were going to arrange a small wedding over the next few days with Rabbi Carmi, who was present during the resurrection of Lazarus and could not deny the truth of Jesus the Messiah.

When it came time for me to share, I stood and declared that I would join Lazarus and Deborah on their journey once it was time. Many cheers erupted and Deborah embraced me with love and joy! We sat together on that evening, knowing something of what was to come for Jesus, and began to pray the prayer Jesus taught at the mountain.

"Our Father, dwelling in the heavenly realms, may the glory of your name be the center on which our lives turn. Manifest your kingdom realm and cause your every purpose to be fulfilled on earth, just as it is fulfilled in heaven. We acknowledge you as our Provider of all we need each day. Forgive us the wrongs we have done as we release forgiveness to those who have wronged us. Rescue us every time we face tribulation and set us free from evil. For you are the King who rules with power and glory forever. Amen."

Sweet rest fell upon our household, and everyone slept soundly beyond the rising of the sun.

But not me.

I rose early, stepping out into the garden with my toes in freshly tilled soil, ready for whatever the new day would bring. I lifted a lavender plant from a small pot. Martha had selected it from the wild ones still growing just outside the garden limits and brought it indoors the evening of my healing. I carefully dug an appropriate size hole and buried it in the earth with a prayer for life and prosperity. It looked beautiful, sitting there in the soil, awaiting it's chance to blossom and bloom. I closed my eyes and remembered mother, dropping a few small tears upon the small purple buds. This time they were tears of freedom, love, new life and perfect peace.

Dusting off my knees, I rose slowly and walked back toward the side of the house. I reached up for the trusty, sturdy branch of that old white sycamore tree and pulled myself up onto the roof. Making my way eagerly, I hurried to my spot and stood with arms raised toward heaven and welcomed the sun.

When I looked out into the open sky, my spirit swelled within me. I worshipped the Lord with a unique song that flowed effortlessly in melodious rhythm.

"Arise, Arise Oh Lord. Go into the city and carry out the will of our Father. I will sing your praises, I will believe, I will trust in you and you alone. Arise, Arise Oh Lord."

As I lowered my arms, I caught a glimpse of a small crowd leaving Bethany. It was Jesus, his disciples… and Miryam, heading for Jerusalem. I sat quietly, watching the sun rise upon the day of our Lord, Jesus Christ, of Nazareth.

Scripture References

Chapter One

Luke 10:19 KJV- "Behold, I give unto you power to tread on serpents and scorpions, and over all the power of the enemy: and nothing shall by any means hurt you."

Chapter Two

Proverbs 8:17 NKJV- "I love them that love me; and those that seek me early shall find me."

Chapter Three

John 6:32-35 TPT- "The truth is," Jesus said, "Moses didn't give you the bread of heaven. It's my Father who offers bread that comes as a dramatic sign from heaven. The bread of God is the One who came out of heaven to give his life to feed the world." "Then please, sir, give us this bread every day," they replied. Jesus said to them, "I am the Bread of Life. Come every day to me and you will never be hungry. Believe in me and you will never be thirsty."

Chapter Four

Luke 22:20 TPT- "After supper was over, he lifted the cup again and said, "This cup is my blood of the new covenant I make with you, and it will be poured out soon for all of you."

Chapter Five

Hebrews 13:5-6 KJV- "Let your conversation be without covetousness; and be content with such things as ye have: for he hath said, I will never leave thee, nor forsake thee. So that we may boldly say, The Lord is my helper, and I will not fear what man shall do unto me.

Let us go forth therefore unto him without the camp, bearing his reproach."

Chapter Six

Proverbs 16:9 TPT- "Within your heart you can make plans for your future, but the Lord chooses the steps you take to get there."

Chapter Seven

Ecclesiastes 3:20 KJV- "All go unto one place; all are of the dust, and all turn to dust again."

Chapter Eight

Jeremiah 18: 2-6 AMP- "Arise and go down to the potter's house, and there I will make you hear My words." Then I went down to the potter's house, and saw that he was working at the wheel. But the vessel that he was making from clay was spoiled by the potter's hand; so he made it over, reworking it and making it into another pot that seemed good to him. Then the word of the LORD came to me: "O house of Israel, can I not do with you as this potter does?" says the LORD. "Look carefully, as the clay is in the potter's hand, so are you in My hand, O house of Israel."

Chapter Nine

Psalm 141:2,8 KJV- "Let my prayer be set forth before thee as incense; and the lifting up of my hands as the evening sacrifice.

But mine eyes are unto thee, O God the Lord: in thee is my trust; leave not my soul destitute."

Chapter Ten

Ecclesiastes 3:1-2 KJV- "To every thing there is a season, and a time to every purpose under the heaven: A time to be born, and a time to die; a time to plant, and a time to pluck up that which is planted;"

Chapter Eleven

Psalm 42:8 KJV- "Yet the Lord will command his lovingkindness in the daytime, and in the night his song shall be with me, and my prayer unto the God of my life."

Chapter Twelve

Psalm 51:8 TPT- "Satisfy me in your sweetness, and my song of joy will return. The places within me you have crushed will rejoice in your healing touch."

Chapter Thirteen

1Peter 5:6 NLT- "So humble yourselves under the mighty power of God, and at the right time he will lift you up in honor. Give all your worries and cares to God, for he cares about you."

Chapter Fourteen

Proverbs 4:23 TPT- "So above all, guard the affections of your heart, for they affect all that you are. Pay attention to the welfare of your innermost being, for from there flows the wellspring of life."

Chapter Fifteen

Psalm 71:10-17 TPT- "For all my enemies whisper behind my

back. They're waiting for me to fall so they can finish me off. They're convinced you've left me and that you'll never come to my rescue. They're saying, 'Let's get him now! He has no savior!'

O God, stay close to me! Don't just watch from a distance! Hurry to help me, my God! Cover these accusers of mine with shame and failure! Destroy them all, for they only want to kill me! No matter what, I'll trust in you to help me. Nothing will stop me from praising you to magnify your glory! I couldn't begin to count the times you've been there for me. With the skill of a poet I'll never run out of things to say of how you faithfully kept me from danger."

Chapter Sixteen

Micah 5:2-4 KJV- "But thou, Beth–lehem Ephratah, though thou be little among the thousands of Judah, yet out of thee shall he come forth unto me that is to be ruler in Israel; whose goings forth have been from of old, from everlasting. Therefore will he give them up, until the time that she which travaileth hath brought forth: then the remnant of his brethren shall return unto the children of Israel. And he shall stand and feed in the strength of the Lord, in the majesty of the name of the Lord his God; and they shall abide: for now shall he be great unto the ends of the earth."

Chapter Seventeen

Jeremiah 29:11 KJV- "For I know the thoughts that I think toward you, saith the Lord, thoughts of peace, and not of evil, to give you an expected end."

Chapter Eighteen

1 Corinthians 13:9-10 TPT- "Our present knowledge and our

prophecies are but partial, but when love's perfection arrives, the partial will fade away."

Chapter Nineteen

(The whole chapter)

Psalm 69 TPT- "God, my God, come and save me! These floods of trouble have risen higher and higher. The water is up to my neck! I'm sinking into the mud with no place to stand, and I'm about to drown in this storm."

Chapter Twenty

1 Timothy 1:5 TPT- "For we reach the goal of fulfilling all the commandments when we love others deeply with a pure heart, a clean conscience, and sincere faith."

Chapter Twenty-One

1 Samuel 2:2-5 NKJV- "No one is holy like the LORD, For there is none besides You, Nor is there any rock like our God. "Talk no more so very proudly; Let no arrogance come from your mouth, For the LORD is the God of knowledge; And by Him actions are weighed. "The bows of the mighty men are broken, And those who stumbled are girded with strength. Those who were full have hired themselves out for bread, And the hungry have ceased to hunger. Even the barren has borne seven, And she who has many children has become feeble."

Chapter Twenty-Two

Mathew 11:28-30 TPT- "Are you weary, carrying a heavy burden? Then come to me. I will refresh your life, for I am your oasis. Simply join your life with mine. Learn my ways and you'll discover that I'm gentle, humble, easy to please. You will find refreshment and rest in me. For all that I require of you will be pleasant and easy to bear."

Chapter Twenty-Three

Proverbs 15:11 TPT- "Even hell itself holds no secrets from the Lord God, for all is exposed before his eyes, and so much more the heart of every human being."

Chapter Twenty-Four

John 3:29 TPT- "He is the Bridegroom, and the bride belongs to him. I am the friend of the Bridegroom who stands nearby and listens with great joy to the Bridegroom's voice. And because of his words my joy is complete and overflows!"

Chapter Twenty-Five

Psalm 44:25-26 TPT- "Now we lay facedown, sinking into the dust of death, the quicksand of the grave. Arise, awake, and come to help us, O Lord. Let your unfailing love save us from this sorrow!"

Chapter Twenty-Six

Romans 4:18 TPT- "Against all odds, when it looked hopeless, Abraham believed the promise and expected God to fulfill it. He took God at his word, and as a result he became the father of many nations. God's declaration over him came to pass: "Your descendants will be so many that they will be impossible to count!"

Chapter Twenty-Seven

Acts 28:3-6 TPT- "When Paul had gathered an armful of brushwood and was setting it on the fire, a venomous snake was driven out by the heat and latched onto Paul's hand with its fangs. When the islanders saw the snake dangling from Paul's hand, they said to one another, 'No doubt about it, this guy is a murderer. Even though he escaped death at sea, Justice has now caught up with him!'

But Paul shook the snake off, flung it into the fire, and suffered no harm at all."

Chapter Twenty-Eight

1 Corinthians 10:13 TPT- "We all experience times of testing, which is normal for every human being. But God will be faithful to you. He will screen and filter the severity, nature, and timing of every test or trial you face so that you can bear it. And each test is an opportunity to trust him more, for along with every trial God has provided for you a way of escape that will bring you out of it victoriously."

Chapter Twenty-Nine

John 11:15 (1-44) TPT- "And for your sake, I'm glad I wasn't there, because now you have another opportunity to see who I am so that you will learn to trust in me. Come, let's go and see him."

Chapter Thirty

Romans 10:13,17 TPT- "And it's true: "Everyone who calls on the name of the Lord will be rescued and experience new life."

"Faith, then, is birthed in a heart that responds to God's anointed utterance of the Anointed One."

Notes

Dream Interpretation:

A Beginner's Manual and Dictionary
Understanding The Divine Messages Within Your Dreams
By Gary Fishman

Gary Fishman is a Jewish believer in Jesus who ministers with a heart for seeing a restoration of true New Testament Christianity. Gary's primary teaching emphasis is on understanding the Jewish roots of our faith as well as equipping the body of Christ in the prophetic gifts through classes, seminars, workshops and conferences. Gary is currently the Associate Pastor of Sanctuary Fellowship in the Bronx, NY and is the author of two books: Distorted Images of God's Heart and Dream Interpretation: a Beginners Manual and Dictionary. He is also a co-founder of the Dreams Network (dreamsnetwork.tv) and teaches at The Kingdom Training Institute (kingdomti.com) as well as at IM-PAKT which is a monthly mentoring program.

"It's impossible to read the Bible and not notice that God speaks through dreams. Throughout Scripture, the Lord used these "visions of the night" to communicate to us. The purpose of this manual is to equip you in the area of dream interpretation so God's messages to you (and your loved ones) will not fall by the wayside. All God's children can develop basic dream interpretation skills in partnership with the Holy Spirit. The more we practice and persevere, the more adept we become. If you are a seeker of truth, this manual and the accompanying dictionary are for you. I pray that the Lord will help you as you learn the unlock the door of understanding and revelation." —From Introduction.

Made in USA - Kendallville, IN
1232987_9781736187807
02.15.2021 1214